# Praise for Lynn Cahoon and Her Irresistible Cozy Mysteries

## THREE TAINTED TEAS

"A kitchen witch reluctantly takes over as planner for a cursed wedding... This witchy tale is a hoot."
—*Kirkus Reviews*

## ONE POISON PIE

"*One Poison Pie* deliciously blends charm and magic with a dash of mystery and a sprinkle of romance. Mia Malone is a zesty protagonist who relies on her wits to solve the crime, and the enchanting cast of characters that populate Magic Springs are a delight."
—**Daryl Wood Gerber**, Agatha winner and nationally best-selling author of the *Cookbook Nook Mysteries* and *Fairy Garden Mysteries*

"A witchy cooking cozy for fans of the supernatural and good eating."
—*Kirkus Reviews*

## A FIELD GUIDE TO HOMICIDE

"The best entry in this character-driven series mixes a well-plotted mystery with a romance that rings true to life."
—*Kirkus Reviews*

"Informative as well as entertaining, *A Field Guide to Homicide* is the perfect book for cozy mystery lovers who entertain thoughts of writing novels themselves... This is, without a doubt, one of the best Cat Latimer novels to date."
—*Criminal Element*

"Cat is a great heroine with a lot of spirit that readers will enjoy solving the mystery (with)."
—*Parkersburg News & Sentinel*

## SCONED TO DEATH

"The most intriguing aspect of this story is the writers' retreat itself. Although the writers themselves are not suspect, they add freshness and new relationships to the series. Fans of Lucy Arlington's 'Novel Idea' mysteries may want to enter the writing world from another angle."
—*Library Journal*

## OF MURDER AND MEN
"A Colorado widow discovers that everything she knew about her husband's death is wrong... Interesting plot and quirky characters."
—*Kirkus Reviews*

## A STORY TO KILL
"Well-crafted... Cat and crew prove to be engaging characters and Cahoon does a stellar job of keeping them—and the reader—guessing."
—*Mystery Scene*

"Lynn Cahoon has hit the golden trifecta—Murder, intrigue, and a really hot handyman. Better get your flashlight handy, *A Story to Kill* will keep you reading all night."
—**Laura Bradford**, author of the Amish Mysteries

## TOURIST TRAP MYSTERIES
"Lynn Cahoon's popular Tourist Trap series is set all around the charming coastal town of South Cove, California, but the heroine Jill Gardner owns a delightful bookstore/coffee shop so a lot of the scenes take place there. This is one of my go-to cozy mystery series, bookish or not, and I'm always eager to get my hands on the next book!"
—*Hope By the Book*

"Murder, dirty politics, pirate lore, and a hot police detective: *Guidebook to Murder* has it all! A cozy lover's dream come true."
—**Susan McBride**, author of the *Debutante Dropout Mysteries*

"This was a good read and I love the author's style, which was warm and friendly... I can't wait to read the next book in this wonderfully appealing series."

# Books by Lynn Cahoon

### The Tourist Trap Mystery Series
Guidebook to Murder * Mission to Murder * If the Shoe Kills * Dressed to Kill * Killer Run * Murder on Wheels * Tea Cups and Carnage * Hospitality and Homicide * Killer Party * Memories and Murder * Murder in Waiting * Picture Perfect Frame * Wedding Bell Blues * A Vacation to Die For * Songs of Wine and Murder * Olive You to Death * Vows of Murder

### Novellas
Rockets' Dead Glare * A Deadly Brew * Santa Puppy * Corned Beef and Casualties * Mother's Day Mayhem * A Very Mummy Holiday * Murder in a Tourist Town

### The Kitchen Witch Mystery Series
One Poison Pie * Two Wicked Desserts * Three Tainted Teas * Four Charming Spells * Five Furry Familiars * Six Stunning Sirens

### Novellas
Chili Cauldron Curse * Murder 101 * Have a Holly, Haunted Holiday * Two Christmas Mittens

### The Cat Latimer Mystery Series
A Story to Kill * Fatality by Firelight * Of Murder and Men * Slay in Character * Sconed to Death * A Field Guide to Homicide

### The Farm-to-Fork Mystery Series
Who Moved My Goat Cheese? * Killer Green Tomatoes * One Potato, Two Potato, Dead * Deep Fried Revenge * Killer Comfort Food * A Fatal Family Feast

### Novellas

Have a Deadly New Year * Penned In * A Pumpkin Spice Killing * A Basketful of Murder

**The Survivors' Book Club Mystery Series**
Tuesday Night Survivors' Club* Secrets in the Stacks * Death in the Romance Aisle * Reading Between the Lies

# Reading Between the Lies

*A Survivors' Book Club Mystery*

## Lynn Cahoon

**LYRICAL PRESS**
Kensington Publishing Corp.
www.kensingtonbooks.com

LYRICAL PRESS BOOKS are published by

Kensington Publishing Corp.
119 West 40th Street
New York, NY 10018

All Kensington titles, imprints, and distributed lines are available at special quantity discounts for bulk purchases for sales promotion, premiums, fund-raising, educational, or institutional use.

Special book excerpts or customized printings can also be created to fit specific needs. For details, write or phone the office of the Kensington Sales Manager: Kensington Publishing Corp., 119 West 40th Street, New York, NY 10018. Attn. Sales Department. Phone: 1-800-221-2647.

Lyrical Press and Lyrical Press logo Reg. U.S. Pat. & TM Off.

First Electronic Edition: August 2024
ISBN: 978-1-5161-1168-8 (ebook)

First Print Edition: August 2024
ISBN: 978-1-5161-1169-5 (Print)

Printed in the United States of America

*To Jessi Schoenewies—Thanks for being the kind of friend to me in real life that Rarity has in her fictional world.*

# Chapter 1

Rarity Cole loved date nights. Or at least she did now. Back in St. Louis, date nights meant having wings and beer at a sports bar while Kevin, the ex-fiancé, watched some game on the many monitors. Or a rerun of a game. Or a bunch of guys talking about a game either just played or coming soon. Rarity should have known after the first few weeks of those date nights that Kevin wasn't the one. Long before he walked out on her because, during chemo treatments, she wasn't fun.

Now, cancer-free with a new house, new business, and a new life in Sedona, Arizona, thanks to the urging of her best friend, Sam Aarons, she also had a new appreciation of date night. And the guy she was hanging out with, Archer Ender.

Tonight, he'd taken her to see Sedona's newest art gallery, Moments. Archer took a couple of flutes off the tray of a passing waiter and handed one to Rarity. "The dad of Jackson Sanders, our newest resident, works for the New York Metropolitan Gallery. His mom does charity events."

Rarity sipped her champagne and studied Archer. "You're not usually a subject matter expert in art galleries and their owners. Is this guy a new client?"

"Kind of. He's hired me for a private hike this weekend. We knew each other a long time ago." He pointed to a tall, thin man walking toward him. "Jackson's on his way over to greet us. Be nice."

"I'm always nice." Rarity stared at Archer, but he ignored her unasked question. Basically, what the heck? She put on a fake smile and waited for Jackson to arrive.

"Archer, I'm so glad you could make it." Jackson shook Archer's hand. Then he turned to Rarity. "And this must be Rarity. You didn't tell me how beautiful she is, Archer."

"I didn't want you getting any ideas," Archer joked.

Jackson reached out for her hand, then covered it with his other hand. "I'm so honored you took the time to welcome me to this lovely community. I hope you and Archer come back for the open house. I'll have many more artists on display then. This was just kind of a low-key event to break in the new place as well as let the Red Rock community find kindred spirits."

"It's a beautiful building and setting." Rarity wasn't sure what Jackson was talking about with Red Rock. From what she knew of the area, the gallery was just outside the Sedona city boundaries. She glanced toward the bank of windows that looked out over the town of Sedona and the hills surrounding it. The sun was just beginning to set, and the sky bathed the area in bright amber and orange. "I'm not sure I'd get any work done here. I'd be staring out the windows all the time."

"When you grow up in a seaside cottage in New England, you learn to block out beautiful scenery in order to work." He smiled, clearly amused by Rarity's awe of the setting. "Or you figure out a way, like our friend Archer here, to make your cubical an outdoor one, where you get to enjoy this beauty every day. I envy his choice of work-life balance."

"Honestly, I agree with Rarity. Your view here is spectacular." Archer met Rarity's gaze and smiled. "Although you're right. Running my own hiking business is a life goal achievement. What's that quote? It's a hard job, but someone has to do it."

"You're being modest," a woman's voice interrupted.

Rarity turned to see Calliope Todd, Archer's former assistant, joining the group. Calliope had gone all out for the little get-together. She wore a skin-tight little black dress that highlighted her toned body and ample curves. The short length of the dress also showed off her shapely legs. Rarity noticed most of the men in the room were watching the red-headed beauty. Including Archer and Jackson.

"Calliope, I'm so glad you could make it." Jackson leaned in and gave her a kiss on the cheek. "I think you all know each other?"

Rarity nodded and smiled. "How have you been, Calliope?"

"Fine. I was just telling Archer the other day at lunch that since I moved to Flagstaff, I never see you anymore. I hope everything's going all right with your little bookstore?"

Rarity hoped the jolt of learning that Calliope had had lunch with Archer didn't show on her face. Or the fact that Archer hadn't mentioned it to her. Calliope had thrown that piece of information into the conversation to jar her. That was obvious. Now she just needed to get through this face-to-face without looking like a jealous girlfriend. "The bookstore is doing great, thanks for asking. We're sponsoring a back-to-school stuffed-backpack drive. Stop by the store and get a shopping list if you're going to be in town. You know we're always looking for donations to keep our kids happy and learning in the classroom."

"Well, isn't that socially altruistic of you and the town?" Jackson pulled out his wallet and counted out five hundred-dollar bills. "Here's my donation. I don't have time to go school shopping, but maybe this will help?"

Rarity swallowed, and after a long pause, it was Archer who reached out and took the money. "That's very generous of you. I'm sure the school district can put this to good use."

"Well, I want to help where I can. Who knows, maybe one of those kindergartners' finger paintings will turn into the next big thing in art." Jackson waved at another couple. "Calliope, that's the Simpsons. Let me introduce you. I'm sure Rarity and Archer would like some alone time."

As they walked away, Calliope glanced over her shoulder. She didn't look happy to be giving Archer and Rarity any space at all.

Rarity drank down the champagne in her glass and traded it for a full one. "Well, Jackson's a force of nature."

"He's a big personality, that's for sure." Archer put his hand on her arm and moved her to the next painting in the gallery. "Look, I didn't tell you about having lunch with Calliope last week because it was business. She had a client for me. And I know how you feel about her."

"I don't care who you have lunch with, Archer. I just don't like surprises or to be lied to." Rarity stared at the geometric mess in front of her. "I guess I'm more of a fan of Renaissance or Impressionist style. The paintings where you can tell if there's a person in the painting?"

Archer chuckled and they moved to the next painting. "Like this one?"

The painting was old, Rarity could tell that by the cracking in the paint, but it had the rich colors she loved. There were three children in the painting, sitting outside in front of a lake. And a tree was to their left. Something was odd about the tree. She leaned closer, reaching her hand toward the canvas to brush away a cobweb, but someone grabbed her hand before she could get closer.

"Sorry, we don't allow people to touch the paintings." A woman in a black dress dropped Rarity's hand by her side. "This painting in particular is very rare. It's from before the Civil War and was found in Georgia at an estate sale. We don't know who the children are in the painting, but it's very realistic, isn't it?"

Rarity stepped back from the painting. "Sorry, I thought there was a shadow or a bit of dust on it. I don't know what I was thinking. I'm Rarity Cole, owner of The Next Chapter and usually a much better gallery visitor."

The woman laughed and reached out her hand. "I'm sure you are. I'm Eleanor Blanchet. I'm the gallery manager."

"Archer Ender." As he introduced himself, he looked at Rarity. "Sorry, I'll be right back."

Rarity watched as he headed to the corner of the room. In the opposite direction from Calliope. Okay, maybe she was a jealous girlfriend. She shook the thought out of her head and focused on Eleanor. "Are you new to the area?"

"Definitely. New York City is my home. I'm afraid I let Jackson lure me away with the promise of managing this gallery and a huge salary. And it doesn't hurt that my condo here in Red Rock is almost ten times the size of my New York apartment." She glanced over at Jackson and a softness changed her face. "He's very persuasive."

"You should visit my bookstore soon. I'm not sure I'll have exactly what you like to read, but I can order anything." Rarity sipped her champagne. "Jackson mentioned Red Rock too. Is that a nearby town? I'm kind of new to the area, but I haven't heard of it."

Eleanor laughed. "You'd think it was a town the way Jackson describes it. Honestly, I don't even know if the area has a real name. I've just taken to calling our neighborhood by that name because Jackson does. All of our employees who moved from another area live there. I think Jackson's family owns the street. Anyway, I guess I shouldn't keep saying it like it is a town or anything. We do have barbeques on the last Saturday of the month for everyone. I'm so domesticated now that my black-wearing New York friends wouldn't even recognize me. I need to get into your bookstore and grab some culture back before I buy a cowboy hat or something worse."

"You're welcome anytime. Except I'm closed on Sundays. You can help me order some art books. I think with your new gallery, people are going to be wanting to learn more about art in general. We're like that around here." Rarity had noticed that about the local community. They liked to know about the shops and stores they were supporting. And she could talk to Eleanor about the bookmark exchange she'd started with other local companies. Like Ender's Adventures, Archer's hiking tour company. She sold a lot of books on trails as well as hiking memoirs and how-to books for beginners. She glanced around the room to see if she could find Archer. He wasn't in sight.

"I'll try to stop by this week." Eleanor nodded to another customer. "Sorry, I need to mingle. Thank you for coming tonight."

After Eleanor left, Rarity moved to the next painting, sipping her drink. When Archer came back a few minutes later, they walked through the rest of the paintings. Some were new, some old, but all of them had a hefty price tag. Rarity saw a landscape she loved, but when she saw the cost, she sighed. "That's a lot of books to sell."

"Maybe we should go to Art in the Park in Flagstaff next weekend. They have booths by local artists with prices for the rest of us." He scanned the room. "Are you ready to get out of here?"

"Please. I feel poor and uneducated. I told Eleanor I'd order some art history books if she came in and helped me pick out some. I need a mini art history class myself." Rarity took his arm. "Do you want to learn with me?"

He shook his head. "Not on your life. Unless it's part of local history that I can use in my hiking tours, I don't have room in my head for useless facts. Let's go get some dinner at the Garnet. I'm starving."

"I need to go freshen up." Rarity nodded to the restrooms. "I'll meet you at the door?"

"Sounds good." He kissed her on the cheek and left to go stand by the front door.

Rarity had just stepped out of the restroom when she heard angry voices. They were coming from the back room. She glanced out toward where the party was happening, but apparently no one could hear the shouting that far away. She stepped over to the door that was cracked open and saw it was an office. Jackson was talking to a larger man. Jackson's face was beet red.

"You owe me. Don't try to back out now just because you're concerned you might look bad," Jackson said as he looked toward the door. Rarity stepped out of sight. Just before he slammed shut the door, she heard him say, "No one threatens me or my business. I know people."

Rarity hurried out of the hallway and toward the entrance. She quickly scanned the room to find Archer. When she did, she was just in time to watch Calliope plant a kiss on his cheek. It had been aimed at his mouth, but Rarity and Archer had just locked gazes and he'd moved just in time.

When she got within chatting range, Rarity was livid. "I'm ready to go."

Archer nodded. "Calliope, thank you for the introduction to Matthew. Rarity and I have a reservation."

"Here? In this small town? If I didn't know better, I'd think you were giving me the brush-off." Calliope turned and saw Rarity. "Oh, I didn't realize you were standing there."

There were so many responses Rarity wanted to throw out, but she took a deep breath and kept her cool. She was starving and didn't want to ruin dinner because Calliope was playing games.

"I guess not. Sorry, we're on our way out. It was nice to see you again." Rarity took Archer's arm in her own and they stepped outside.

"I didn't kiss her," Archer said before she could say anything.

She met his gaze and shrugged. "I don't want to talk about Calliope. Why is your friend Jackson arguing with someone about threatening the gallery?"

"He was doing what?" Archer unlocked his Jeep and then helped Rarity inside.

She told him about the conversation as they drove to dinner. Her head was pounding, probably a mix of the champagne and seeing Calliope. Dinner didn't help. She tried to keep up her end of the conversation, but she knew she was failing.

When they got back to the house, he turned off the engine.

"Do you want me to come in?" He took her hand in his.

The headache was worse. "Honestly, no. I just want to crash. Tomorrow's a long day with the book club and Amy and Staci are coming over to ask the group for help with the book drive."

"You're sure it's not about Calliope and what she did?"

Rarity met his gaze directly. "It's definitely not about Calliope."

Rarity climbed out of the Jeep and pulled her keys out of her clutch. The problem between them wasn't Archer's ex-assistant. The problem was why Calliope felt comfortable enough with him to kiss him, even when she knew Rarity was around. What she'd done was rude and cruel. Rarity didn't want to play games with Calliope or anyone else.

Even if that meant she and Archer weren't together anymore. She'd talk to him when she didn't want to scream or hit something or both. She decided it was time to go for a swim. All by herself.

# Chapter 2

Rarity usually enjoyed her book club nights. Especially since she was the founder of her brainchild get-together, the Tuesday Night Survivors' Club. Tonight, the energy was tense. Things were touchy with her and Archer. He'd arrived exactly at seven, bringing along Sam's boyfriend, Drew Anderson. Drew was also a member of Sedona's finest, so he was representing the police department for this community outreach. Maybe it had been a mistake to open tonight's club meeting to community members committed to The Next Chapter's back-to-school drive. Sam hadn't spoken a word since Drew and Archer walked through the door.

Archer hadn't smiled or made eye contact with her all night. Rarity understood why Drew and Sam weren't talking, since Sam's brother had almost been convicted of a murder he didn't commit. Drew had been the lead detective on the case. But she and Archer had had one little fight. Okay, maybe a big fight about his ex-employee, Calliope, who'd showed up last week with a huge client for Archer's hiking business. And then last night, she tried to kiss him. Rarity wasn't the jealous type, but everyone knew Calliope had a crush on Archer. Archer had tried to explain why Calliope had tried to kiss him during a phone call last night after he'd dropped her off. He'd been concerned about her headache and wanted to clarify how they ended the evening. He'd told her that Calliope's feelings for him didn't matter. He was in love with Rarity and she needed to trust him. That had been the last time they'd talked.

It had been a long day. Rarity tried to focus on the discussion in the meeting.

"Amy and I had a meeting with Miss Christy, the high school counselor, last week," Staci Patterson, a Sedona high school freshman who also wrote reviews for Rarity's bookstore, reported to the group.

Before she could continue, Amy Martin interrupted by holding her hand up in the air as she jumped to be seen. Amy was in middle school, and after Rarity had found out she hung out at the restaurant where her mom worked most afternoons, Rarity had invited her to hang around the bookstore instead. Amy was the one who'd brought the idea of the back-to-school backpack and supply drive to Rarity.

Staci rolled her eyes. "Yes, Amy?"

"Miss Christy took us out for ice cream and gave us a gift card for the bookstore." Amy stepped forward to speak, then stepped back, seeing the people watching her.

"Going for ice cream *was* fun. But I need to tell everyone that Miss Christy said if we get more than the fifty stuffed backpacks that the Sedona schools need, she'll send the rest to Flagstaff. So please keep promoting the school drive until next Friday. We'll put everything together here at the bookstore on Saturday and deliver them to the school on Monday when the teachers come back from summer vacation." Staci stood in front of the group, oblivious to the tension in the room. Then she turned back to Rarity. "I think that covers it, right, Miss Cole?"

"You and Amy did a great job of managing this project." Rarity stood and stepped between the two girls, looking around the circle. "Before I let you go enjoy your last few days of summer, I wanted to ask if anyone had questions for our budding charity fundraisers?"

Shirley Prescott, one of the club regulars, stood and smiled at the girls. "You two are doing a wonderful job with this. My church has gathered backpacks and will be bringing them over on Saturday to fill."

"And the Garnet is collecting money from their customers," Malia Overstreet, another Tuesday night regular, added. "Holly and I are going shopping on Friday night at Target."

"I've got a fund from my hikers for any additional supplies, so once you see what's missing on Saturday, I can fill in the rest. And Rarity and I got a donation last night from Jackson Sanders of five hundred dollars." Archer stood and tossed the paper-clipped bills to Amy.

Amy's eyes widened as she looked at the cash. She held it up and met Archer's gaze. "This is five hundred dollars? It's so small."

"It's five one-hundred-dollar bills, dork." Staci plucked the money from Amy's hand and handed it to Rarity. "Miss Cole will hold on to this so we have money for extra supplies."

"Maybe someone would come shopping with me on Sunday." Archer leaned back in his chair, his gaze on Rarity.

Rarity's lips twitched. It was as good of an olive branch as she was going to get. "That could be fun."

Drew checked his watch, then stood. "Let's give these girls a round of applause, then Archer and I need to get them delivered back to their parents. Joni's shift at Carole's just ended and Amy's dinner will be getting cold."

After the kids left with Drew and Archer, the tension eased a bit. Okay, maybe a lot. Rarity held up a copy of *The Midnight Library*, the book they'd chosen to read last week. "So shall we talk about our book since we still have some time?"

Shirley shook her head. "I didn't get it. How did she find this library? Did she really die? The book never explained why it happened."

"That wasn't the point. The point of the story was that you make the best decision you can and you go on. No regrets." Malia sighed as she rubbed the book's cover. She'd suggested the book, and although Rarity had known it wouldn't be everyone's cup of tea, Malia had loved it with a capital L.

Shirley frowned at the book. "Oh. I didn't understand that. So why didn't she pick a life that would turn out differently? Give herself a better outcome? If you know the decisions you make will cause you heartache later, why not change your life?"

"Would you? If you had known how things would happen in your life, would you go back and make different decisions?" Malia challenged her. "I know I would have with a few."

"No. Of course not. Your life is your life. You make the decisions you make as best you can. No reading ahead to the end of the book. You miss the life in between." Shirley tossed the book on the coffee table. "I think since I'm the oldest in the group, I can tell you that a life can't be judged based on where you are standing at one moment."

"I actually agree with Shirley, but I think that's what the book was trying to say. You do the best you can and go on. And if you don't like something, you have to change it." Holly Harper, another original club member, went on to explain how she viewed the book and its theme. Shirley sat back in her chair, crocheting a baby blanket for one of the expectant mothers at her church.

When the discussion ended, the store quickly cleared out except for Sam, Shirley, and Rarity. It was usually the three of them putting the area back together after the meeting. Shirley worked part-time at the bookstore, and Sam, well, she was a really good friend.

Sam grabbed two cookies and wrapped them in a napkin. "Do you mind if I take off? Marcus is calling me from Paris in a few minutes. He's there on a job so we FaceTime while he's walking. Now I want to go to Paris."

"Paris sounds fun. Maybe next year I'll go with you." Rarity folded the last chair and put it on the storage carrier. Rarity knew Sam enjoyed spending time with her brother, even if it was virtual. They'd only started to reconnect a few months ago. "First, I need to refill my emergency fund after replacing the air conditioner in this monstrosity."

"Malia's book said you should live life now," Sam retorted as she headed to the doorway.

Rarity called after her. "Not if you don't have the money to fly or eat. I think panhandling is frowned upon as a vacation strategy."

With a laugh and a wave, Sam disappeared out the door.

Shirley was clearing off the treat table. After Sam left, she turned toward Rarity. "Do you think the book was right? That we should make the most of every day?"

"Of course. Paris will be there when I can afford it. And I needed the air conditioner. Why are you asking?" Rarity pushed the rolling chair storage into the closet on the other side of the room. Then she returned to help Shirley finish cleaning up the discussion area around the fireplace.

"The book really hit me. Would I have still married George if I knew what was going to happen to him? If I'd had a clue how our golden years were going to play out?" Shirley sank onto a chair. "We had a lot of great years together."

"You can't go back. Besides, you wouldn't have thrown those years away. You love George, even if he's not the same now." Shirley's husband was in a memory care facility and from the gossip around town, he was getting worse. He didn't even recognize Shirley during most visits. "The book just reminds us to live a full life, that's all. And we all have had that lesson in our pasts."

"I'm being silly. That's what happens when you're alone too much. I need a hobby where I'm out and around people. Like working for you." Shirley patted Rarity's hand, then stood and finished filling the cart with the empty cups and pitchers of lemonade and water. "The ramblings of an old woman. Soon I'll be in the facility in the room next to George."

"That will never happen. You're in your prime. Sixty is the new forty, they say." Rarity gave her friend a quick hug. "Let's get out of here. Do you want to stop at the Garnet for a coffee or a dessert before we head home?"

Shirley declined her invitation. "You need to get home to Killer. He's probably already worried about you. I swear, when we had dogs, they could tell time. Especially when it was dinnertime. They always went into the kitchen and checked out their bowls as soon as it got close."

Rarity finished cleaning up and grabbed her keys and tote. She was about to ask Shirley if she wanted to go to her house for a coffee instead, but then Shirley spoke.

"I'll see you tomorrow for Mommy and Me. We're doing a small craft after reading the book. Everyone's excited." Shirley put on her sweater and grabbed her purse and her tote that held her books and yarn and hook. "I might even finish this baby blanket this week. I've got two more to complete before the mommies have their showers at the end of the month. I swear, everyone is having a baby this month."

Locking the door, Rarity headed home. Archer usually walked with her but even with the olive branch he'd thrown out tonight, their relationship was strained. She wished she could take back what she had said, but she knew if they talked today about Calliope, they'd have the same fight. Maybe they just weren't compatible.

And if that was true, Calliope would win.

\* \* \* \*

Rarity swam in her in-ground backyard pool as soon as she woke up on Wednesday morning. It was the perfect way to get in exercise as well as wash away the Negative Nelly who had taken up residence in Rarity's head. Typically, she could ignore the negative thoughts, especially when she was busy, but since the fight with Archer, she'd been revisiting a lot of their conversations trying to see where she went wrong. It was like watching the same episode on repeat, but not going on to the next show. And she was tired of it.

The swim washed away the unhelpful thoughts. When she moved to Sedona, she'd purchased the small house mostly because of the backyard pool. Rarity loved swimming and she'd put it off too many times before because of work. In St. Louis, she'd be too busy to go to the gym in the morning, and then when she was finally done working, the pool at her

*Lynn Cahoon*

gym would be closed. Having her own pool in Arizona made it possible to swim on her time frame. Like this morning. And last night before she had gone to bed. Okay, maybe she was addicted.

Now, with a cup of coffee, Rarity opened her planner to make sure she had the back-to-school supply drive schedule on her calendar correctly. Staci had told her the dates a few weeks ago when this project started, but she hadn't put the deadlines in her planner.

The day they were stuffing the backpacks was also the day that the high school book club was having an end-of-summer party. She groaned as she realized the two events would both be going on at the store at the same time. Katie Dickenson, Rarity's newest hire, had put the dates on the bookstore's online calendar as well as sent Rarity an online invite and a list of supplies she'd need for the party.

Katie was a graduate student at Northern Arizona University in Flagstaff studying literature. She'd told Rarity last month that she was also writing her first novel. The woman played recreational volleyball and basketball and ran marathons. Every time they talked about what they were doing over the weekend, Katie won the discussion. She made Rarity feel like a slug.

But not today. Rarity had marked off the exercise part of her day and it wasn't even nine. Now, to get everything else done on her ever-expanding to-do list. Including figuring out how to fit the backpack stuffing in the building on the same day as the high school club party.

She wrote an email to her staff and stopped debating the issue with herself. Then Rarity matched up her calendar with the ongoing book clubs, making sure there were no other conflicts. Hiring more staff had taken some things off Rarity's plate but added others. Like this coordination.

Satisfied with the results, she checked her email one more time before getting ready to go open the shop. Katie had already replied. The email was short and Rarity smiled as she read it aloud. "We'll make it work."

That was another reason Rarity admired Katie. She never seemed to get rattled. At all.

When Rarity got to the bookstore, both Shirley and Katie were already there and waiting outside in the shade. Having all three of them there for at least one day a week had been amazing all summer. They'd planned for future events and come up with monthly themes for the clubs, as well as making sure the new books were shelved and in the system. And if they ran out of things to do, Rarity had them read advance reader copies of upcoming books and write reviews.

She unlocked the doors and they got the shop ready for the day. Rarity took Killer off his lead and hung it up behind the sales counter. He took a drink of the water after Rarity filled his bowl, then went to the fireplace to curl up in his bed. It was time for his morning nap. Or a second nap that morning. Rarity had stopped keeping track. The little tan Yorkie had come to her as a foster and she'd been unable to let him go. Of course, Drew had known that Rarity wanted a dog so he'd asked her first when Killer had needed a home.

Now she couldn't see her life without the little guy.

Shirley was setting up her craft station for the Mommy and Me class. Rarity went over to help. Shirley looked up at her. "I wanted to apologize for last night."

"What are you talking about? Nothing happened last night." Rarity felt confused as she rewound their conversation after the club.

"I was on edge and took it out on the book. The book wasn't that bad, it just struck a nerve with me." Shirley laid out the crochet hooks she'd found at yard sales and thrift stores. She'd been planning this session for a few months now.

"I find the best books bring out the reader's emotions. Sometimes that's a good thing if you didn't realize what you were feeling around the subject." Rarity watched as Shirley pulled out three different colors of skeins of yarn. Yellow, blue, and pink, they stacked the yarn into their specific color. Rarity tried not to look at her. The book had made an impact and Shirley obviously wanted to talk.

"You know Terrance and I have been having coffee in the mornings." Shirley sat down and looked around to see where Katie was working. Not finding her, Shirley lowered her voice. "I need a favor."

Taken aback by the quick change of subject, Rarity sat next to Shirley. "Anything you need, I'll do. You really saved the book clubs when I was underwater a few months ago. You're always helping other people. What can I do for you?"

"Terrance asked me to go with him to the grand opening of a new art gallery on Friday. Moments? I guess the owner is a friend of a friend and Terrance wants to support him." She hadn't met Rarity's gaze yet.

"I think that's wonderful. I love gallery openings. You really get a feel for the artists and the gallery's message. Archer and I went there on Monday night. You're going, right?" Rarity didn't understand yet why Shirley was upset.

"That's where I need you and Sam to do me a favor. Can you and Sam and Archer and Drew come with us? That way it doesn't look like a date?" Now Shirley was staring at Rarity. She could see the fear in Shirley's eyes.

"You want Sam and me to come with you and bring the guys." Rarity paused, trying to think of how to explain to Shirley that what she asked for was impossible. At least right now. She must not have felt the tension between all of them last night. She might be able to talk Archer into going, but Drew and Sam? She'd just need to explain why this was impossible and everything would be fine. "Shirley—"

She stood and hugged Rarity. "Exactly. Thank you for understanding. I want to go with Terrance, but as you know, I'm a married woman. What would that look like if we just started going out at night? Together."

"I'm not sure if—" This time she was interrupted by a young mother with a screaming child in a stroller.

"Shirley, I'm sorry to bust in like this, but Henry's teething. What can I do to get him to stop screaming? It's driving me crazy." The young woman pushed the stroller closer to them.

With one look at the stroller, Killer took off for the safety of the sales counter and his second bed tucked behind the register desk. Just in case.

Shirley smiled at Rarity. "Duty calls. Thank you so much. This means a lot." Then she rushed over and picked up the screaming child. She smiled at his mother. "Oh, my. You look exhausted."

As Rarity made her way over to the counter and a shaking Killer, she tried to replay the part of the discussion where she'd said she'd help. Had she really agreed to convince not only Archer to go on this group outing, but also to get Sam and Drew to spend a couple of hours together not fighting while they all viewed expensive art and drank cheap champagne?

This was going to be a disaster. Maybe her calendar already had something that night and Rarity could gracefully back out. But even as she looked up the art gallery and the date of the party, she knew she couldn't back out now.

Her friend needed her.

# Chapter 3

On Friday, Terrance Oldman rang Rarity's doorbell promptly at six thirty. Rarity knew it was him because she'd watched him through her window in the den as he went out to his garage, inched out his Suburban, then pulled out of the driveway. He rolled the car a few feet down the road, then pulled into Rarity's driveway and turned off the engine. He adjusted his shirt as he walked to her porch.

She opened the door. "I could have walked over."

He shook his head, peering around her. "Not on my watch. Shirley asked me to pick you up before we roll to her house and that's what I was going to do. Are you ready? Where is everyone else?"

"Archer's picking up Sam and Drew's meeting us there. His mom and dad came up from Tucson so they're coming as well." Rarity grabbed her clutch purse. Shirley had wanted the night to look like a group outing, and she'd gotten more than she'd bargained for with the addition of Jonathon and Edith Anderson. Rarity liked Drew's parents.

"Okay, then let's go get Shirley and we'll be on our way to infuse some culture into our lives. If you'd told younger me I'd be going to an art gallery, I would have busted a gut laughing. I guess we all change." Terrance held the door open for her.

Rarity called out to Killer, who was lying on his bed, his back to them in protest of being left behind. Killer hadn't even come out to see Terrance, and he liked his next-door neighbor. "I'll see you later, buddy. Be good, okay?"

"You left the television on." Terrance pointed to the Disney movie playing on the screen.

"I know. I read in a book that having the television on makes them feel like someone's home. So he watches movies while I'm gone." Rarity closed the door and checked the locks. No use making it easy for a random robbery or break-in. Especially since several of the police force members would be at the open house this evening. Jackson Sanders's family had donated liberally to the fire station, the police station, and the city. They were well known for their large donations to local causes in towns where they opened businesses. Sedona was now one of those towns. Rarity followed Terrance down the few steps to where he stood by the car.

"Front or back?"

"I'll look like you're chauffeuring me around town if I get in the back." Rarity considered her words. "But I'd rather have Shirley up front, so I guess it's back."

"Okay, then we'll play 'driving Miss Daisy' for a little while. Make sure you call me Jeeves." He opened the door and held out a hand to steady her if she needed it.

After they'd gotten onto the street, Rarity leaned forward. "I think this is the only time I'll get to ask this, at least tonight, so don't freak out on me."

"Depends on what you're going to ask." He glanced at her using the rearview mirror.

"You're not going to like it, so I'm just jumping in. What are your intentions with Shirley?" Rarity had been rehearsing the question for days now.

He stared at her for a long minute. "I get it. The two of you are close and you care for her. Not as an employee or customer, you really care about what happens to her."

The conversation stalled for a second. "Shirley's one of my best friends," Rarity admitted. "Even with the differences in our ages and life experiences, I do care about what happens to her."

"All I'm looking for is company. And, with her situation as it is, that's all she can offer anyway. Shirley is deeply committed to her relationship. Unfortunately, she's the only one who remembers it." Terrance sighed as he stopped at a light and waited for it to turn green. "Rarity, I have to admit, I care about her. And if the situation was different, I'd be fighting for her tooth and nail. But it's not different and she can't move on, even though he's gone in all but his body."

Rarity didn't respond for a few minutes. Then she reached up and squeezed Terrance's shoulder. "Just make sure you don't break your heart while you're trying to heal hers."

He reached up and patted her hand. "Rarity, that's the nicest thing anyone has ever said to me."

When they arrived at Shirley's house, she was waiting on the front porch. Terrance parked, then went to greet her. Rarity stayed in the car. She opened her window for some fresh air and realized she could hear them talking.

"You look lovely tonight," Terrance said and held his hand out for Shirley to help her down the stairs.

"Thank you. Where's Rarity? You didn't come here alone, did you?" Shirley froze like a deer in headlights. Rarity thought she was going to faint or run back onto the porch.

Rarity held her breath. She'd gone through a lot to keep this night going only for Shirley to be having second thoughts at the last minute. She stuck her arm out the window and waved at her friend. "I'm right here. I thought I'd leave shotgun for you."

"Well, isn't that nice of you?" Shirley started walking again. She moved to the car and let Terrance open the door for her. Once in her seat, she turned around and met Rarity's gaze. "Thank you."

As Terrance drove to the art gallery in the hills, the conversation went from the weather to the drive and the road until finally, Rarity stepped in and talked about the visit that she and Archer had made to the gallery. "The view from the gallery takes your breath away. You can walk right out to the vortex and sit to take it all in."

When she'd first arrived in Sedona, Rarity had studied the mythical vortexes. Sam had taken her to visit several of the swirling energy spots in the area to help Rarity heal from the side effects of her cancer treatment. The area was known for spiritual retreats and healing practitioners. The visitor center had a self-guided tour map of the different spots. Rarity had felt something visiting the different vortexes, but she wasn't as convinced as Sam was of their metaphysical power. Since they were in Sedona, Rarity had added books about the power of vortexes to her natural healing section in the bookstore. Everyone had their own path to wellness, even if Rarity didn't believe in the magic.

"I was up here when they were building it. Sanders spared no expense. I hear he's calling in the local Native American tribe to bless the site tonight. You can tell he's been coached by an Arizona native. No New Yorker would have thought about that." Terrance snorted as they pulled into the parking lot. "Here we are. I'll pull up to the valet so you all don't have to walk in this heat. The gods must be working against him. It's hotter tonight than it has been all week."

*And we're back to talking about the weather.* Rarity slipped out of the air-conditioned truck and immediately felt the stifling heat. As she breathed, the warm air heated her body. She took Shirley's arm and walked toward the doorway. Terrance joined them as soon as the valet gave him a ticket.

Even though they only had to walk a few steps, Rarity felt sweat start to glisten on her forehead. So much for makeup. She held the door open for Shirley, feeling the chilly air trying to escape around her.

"I'll get that," Terrance said as he motioned her inside. Another man who had come in the next vehicle took the door from him.

As soon as they were in the lobby, a waiter held out a tray filled with cold towels. Rarity took the towel and dabbed at her face, then used it to wipe her hands and arms. The effect was refreshing. Setting the towel in a basket near the gallery entrance, she took a glass of champagne from a second waiter. "I'd say someone in charge at least noticed the heat forecast. I've never been given a cold compress at an event before."

Shirley nodded. "It was a common practice when George and I attended the Flagstaff Opera. I haven't been in years, but I'd heard they'd stopped doing it."

Terrance dropped his cloth in the basket. "Maybe we should drive up there one night and check it out. I have to say, I've never been to an opera."

Shirley giggled. "Terrance, you don't have to subject yourself to that just for me."

Rarity turned in the direction of her friend, watching the interaction.

He took her arm. "I'm not doing it for you. I've never been to one. How can I decide if it's something I've missed in my life if I never try it? Rarity, help me out here. You must be a fan of new adventures, especially since you turned your life upside down to move here."

*Terrance was right about that.* "I have to agree, you don't know what you're missing until you try it. He might hate the opera, which gives you a reason to say 'I tried to warn you.'" Rarity smiled at Terrance. He had asked for her support.

Shirley pretended to think about the idea, then nodded. "I do like to be right."

"Rarity, it's been too long." Edith Anderson suddenly appeared at her left and pulled Rarity into a hug. "Jonathon has kept you all to himself for the last few trips. I had to sneak into the back of the truck so I could come this time."

Rarity laughed as she squeezed Edith. "You're always welcome, you know that."

"She's just pulling your leg. No one could have dragged her away from that new grandbaby until now." Jonathon gave Rarity and Shirley hugs, then reached his hand out to Terrance. "Good to see you again. I didn't think art galleries were your type of thing."

"Oh, Terrance was just telling us all about his willingness to try new things." Rarity winked at Shirley, who blushed.

Luckily for her, no one else seemed to notice Shirley's discomfort, since right then Drew Anderson walked up to the group at the same time as Sam and Archer. Handshakes went around as well as hugs. Only Sam and Drew kept their distance from each other. They limited their contact to a polite nod, which wasn't missed by the rest of the group.

Archer came over and put his arm around Rarity. She leaned closer. She didn't know if all was forgiven after their fight, but if he was willing to act like everything was fine, she'd do the same. Not like her friends, who were actively seeing how many people they could put between the two of them. Edith sighed and looked at Rarity. Then she rolled her eyes. Everyone felt the tension between the two.

It was at that moment that Jackson Sanders joined the group. Ignoring or not feeling the unease in the group, he put his arms around Sam and Shirley, who stood next to each other. "I'm so glad you could come to my open house. Moments is a project that I'd dreamed about for years. I'd assumed the gallery would be in the city, but this is a terrific second-choice site. And it gives me the chance to work on my leadership skills at Red Rock."

Eleanor had joined the group as Jackson talked. She stood next to Drew. "Don't mind Jackson. Sedona is a beautiful place for Moments. The scenery, the natural vortexes, and of course, such amazing people who live here."

"We have a vortex just outside the gallery. Once the representative from the reservation blesses the building, I hear the vortex is going to help pour money into this place. My family is going to be so happy." Jackson brightened as he glanced around the room.

"The blessing from the local tribe elder doesn't quite work that way," Eleanor started, but Jackson cut her off as soon as a new arrival walked in the door.

"And finally, the mayor has arrived, so everyone's here. Let's get this party started." He kissed Shirley and Sam on the cheek. "Thanks again for helping me celebrate. I'm sure I'll see you all later. And if there's something you want to buy, Eleanor will be happy to help. It is what I pay her for, not for interrupting me."

Jackson left the group and headed over to where the mayor and his wife were standing in front of the painting Rarity had noticed on Monday.

Eleanor glared at Jackson but then took a breath to reset and smiled at the group. "If there's one thing Jackson's great at doing it's starting a party. Excuse me as I let the band know they can take a small break while Mr. Sanders talks."

As she walked away, Rarity heard Eleanor mutter, "Hopefully, he won't alienate every Sedona resident in the next five minutes."

\* \* \* \*

Rarity had more to worry about than the fact that Jackson and Eleanor clearly hated each other. She did wonder how long the gallery's attractive manager would stay in the area, but maybe Jackson would be the one to leave. He didn't seem to be the kind of guy to stay for the day-to-day work. And as Rarity knew, opening a small business was a lot of work. Eleanor, on the other hand, seemed willing to put in the effort to make Moments successful.

Shirley grabbed her arm after the blessing and asked Rarity to go to the restroom with her. Rarity handed Archer her glass and followed her friend. When they got there, Shirley grabbed her arms. "What was I thinking? This is a total disaster."

"What disaster? It's going well. Except Sam and Drew keep moving around like they are those atoms that are oppositely charged. Do you know what I mean? It's been a while since I took science class." Rarity checked her makeup in the mirror and adjusted her hair. She looked fine, even with the wet cloth she'd used earlier to cool down.

"Atoms like that cause explosions." A woman came out of one of the stalls. It was Eleanor. She'd been crying, and as she stood in front of the mirror, she took makeup out of her clutch. She smiled at Rarity. "Sorry about overhearing your conversation. I'm just trying to survive tonight so I can decide how royally I've messed up my life by moving here."

Shirley came over with a box of tissues from the counter. "You and me both, sister. But as I always say, things look better after a good night's sleep.

And you look amazing in that dress, so you should definitely find some hot guy out there to dance with. That might make tonight a little easier."

Eleanor tucked her makeup away and took one last look in the mirror. "A man is not going to solve this problem. But maybe one could make me forget for a night. Thanks for the suggestion."

After Eleanor left, Shirley took Rarity's arm. "I'm being a drama queen, aren't I?"

"A little bit. I get that you're conflicted, but you're not doing anything wrong. If you were, I would tell you. Go have fun. Talk. Dance. And then get a good night's sleep. Everything will be better in the morning."

"It's not fair to use my own advice against me." Shirley held the door open, and they went back to the party that was just getting started.

Rarity and Archer stood at the table the group had claimed as their own, and for a second they were alone. He took her hand. "I'm an idiot. I don't want to fight anymore."

"I can be a little insistent, so I'll take my blame in the argument. But I agree. I don't want to fight." Rarity watched Eleanor as she glared at Jackson, who was now dancing with someone Rarity thought worked at the local library. "Besides, there are enough couples here throwing icy stares at each other. Maybe we could make up and be *the* solid relationship."

Archer came closer and followed her gaze. "I figured you were talking about Sam and Drew, but who's Eleanor angry at?"

She turned his head toward Jackson. "Him. Are they dating?"

Archer shrugged. "I don't know Jackson that well anymore, but from the look she's giving him, I'd say yes. I guess I can ask him tomorrow when we're hiking. We'll have a lot of time."

"That's my take as well." She turned to him and put her hand on his chest. "I'm sorry."

"You already said that, and we're past the making-up part. Well, unless you want to go sneak into my Jeep in the parking lot." He ran a finger up her arm.

"We'd die of heat stroke before anything happened." Rarity laughed.

Archer leaned back and stared at her. "I have to say, Miss Cole, you're not as adventuresome as I'd come to expect."

She started to say something, but Terrance and Shirley came back to the table. "Hey, you two, are you enjoying the party?"

Shirley nodded. "We are, but Terrance is taking me to coffee at Carole's. Do you want us to drop you off at your house or can you find a ride home?"

Archer held up his hand. "It will be a terrible inconvenience, but I'll take Rarity home."

Rarity threw a piece of ice from her empty drink at him.

\* \* \* \*

The next morning Rarity got a call from Archer as she was enjoying her coffee on the deck. "Hey, I'm surprised to hear from you this morning. Don't you have a tour that you need to get to? And don't forget to find out if Jackson and Eleanor are dating. She kept throwing ice daggers at him all night. Even when she was dancing with that hot guy at the end."

"I'm at Moments. Jackson asked me to meet him here and not at his condo." Archer sounded out of breath.

"What's going on? Why are you breathing so hard? Did you run over there?" Rarity still didn't understand why he'd called her. "Don't tell me you want me to come on the hike with you. I've got a ton of work to do at the shop, especially since we're rotating books on all the monthly book clubs this next week."

Archer took a breath loud enough that she could hear it on the phone. "Rarity, Jackson Sanders is dead. He's naked and sitting in the middle of the stone vortex circle with an arrow in his back."

# Chapter 4

Rarity waited on the phone with Archer until the police arrived. Archer had called them first. Then she told him she loved him, hung up, and called Drew.

"I don't know what's going on." Drew answered the call with a statement. "Look, I'm not even at the gallery yet. I'll have Archer call you as soon as I get there."

"I already talked to him. Who would do this to Jackson?" Rarity thought for a quick second. "Someone was arguing with him in his office on Monday about the time Archer and I were leaving the party."

"Good to know. I'll check it out. But Rarity, I really don't know anything," Drew repeated.

Rarity shook her head, even though Drew couldn't see her. "That's not true. You know one thing."

"What's that?" Drew's voice sounded strained.

"Your friend Archer didn't kill Jackson Sanders. You know that." Rarity waited, but Drew didn't answer. "Drew?"

He let out a long breath. "I hope that's true. Look, I'm at the gallery. I'll come by the shop later."

"Let me know if I need to come get Archer. He sounded pretty shook up when he called." Rarity said goodbye and tossed her phone across the table. Killer jumped at the noise, then barked, hiding his initial fear.

Rarity leaned down and snapped her fingers, calling Killer to her. "Come here, little guy. I'm sorry I scared you."

He came and she picked him up on her lap. Then she reached for her phone and called Shirley. It was time to activate the Tuesday Night Sleuthing Club. Hopefully, they wouldn't need to do anything but talk about poor Jackson's death during the club meeting, but if Drew even thought about questioning Archer's innocence, it would be better to be prepared.

Shirley agreed to set up the phone tree as well as new murder investigation books. "Do you want me to call Jonathon? I mean, since he's in town. I know Edith's here too, but he's part of the group."

"Call Jonathon. Maybe he can keep us informed on Drew's progress with finding the killer." Rarity paused. "I'm a horrible friend. How did coffee turn out?"

"You're not a horrible friend. You just had a shock." Shirley knew just how to comfort anyone from any kind of trauma. She'd been named Sedona's grandmother by the local paper just a few months ago. "And coffee was nice. Thank you for arranging the gallery visit. I know I was being a bit clandestine with the whole group there, but it made me realize that no one cares what I do with my life. Well, except the kids. And I need to tell them about my friendship with Terrance."

"He's a good man." Rarity bit her lip, hoping to keep the tears from flowing. Archer was a good man too. "I can't believe I'm getting this upset over nothing."

"It's not nothing. We both know that Archer didn't kill the man, but he did find him. And maybe he saw something that will put him in harm's way. He needs to come to the meeting and tell the group exactly what he saw."

*If he's not in jail by Tuesday.* Rarity pushed the thought aside. "I'll talk to him as soon as I can. Thanks, Shirley."

"Don't even worry about it. Do you need me to work today? It's middle school book club today, isn't it?"

Rarity thought about Shirley's suggestion. "If you could. That would give me the flexibility to go and see Archer."

"I've got a stop to make but I can be there by ten." Shirley paused. "Rarity, it's going to be all right. Once you stare death in the face, other problems don't seem so dire."

When Rarity got off the phone, she realized Shirley was right. She was worrying about something that might not even happen. This kind of worrying was against Rarity's personal rules that she'd set for herself during her treatment period. New wasn't all bad and you couldn't react until you knew the whole story. She only knew that Jackson was dead.

Which was sad, but not in her circle of concern. She rubbed Killer's ear. "If I'm going to get a swim in, I better go now."

Killer licked her hand, watching her face for signs of trouble. Rarity hugged the little dog and set him on the floor. "Let's get this day started."

\* \* \* \*

When Rarity got to the bookstore, Katie had opened the shop and there were already several of her book club members milling around and chatting. With the addition of several youth book clubs, the shop had gone from really, really quiet to a gathering place for the Sedona community. And Rarity loved it that way. She wanted to be the place where kids came and hung out on a rainy Saturday. She waved at Amy, who was chatting with several girls by the fireplace. Killer ran over as soon as he was let off his leash to greet Amy, who had become one of his favorite people.

Katie was at the register, talking with a woman Rarity had seen in the store before. One of the moms, as she thought about them. Katie waved her over.

"On my way," Rarity called back. She needed to chat with Amy first. "Hey, if you leave or go outside, let me know and I'll have Killer come and hang out with me at the desk."

"No problem, Miss Cole. I won't let him get out and get lost." Amy beamed as she looked around at her new friends. Amy loved the fact that Rarity trusted her with Killer.

When Rarity got to the checkout counter, Katie turned to the woman standing with a bag filled with books in her hand. "Rarity Cole, this is Nancy Christy. She's the guidance counselor at the high school."

"Miss Christy! So nice to finally meet you. Staci and Amy tell me you've been helping them with everything they need to know for the backpack drive." Rarity wanted to reach over and give the woman a hug, but she didn't look like the hugging type. In fact, she didn't look like a guidance counselor at all. She was younger than Rarity'd expected and dressed in shorts and a halter top. "We're so happy to be able to give back by sponsoring this event."

"Are you kidding? This is exactly what this town has needed for years, someone to start the project. I've tried to get other fundraisers going but they always seem to get stuck in committee. And call me Nancy. All my adult friends do, unless they attended Sedona High in the last five years."

She looked down at her clothes. "And I know, I'm out of uniform, but I didn't realize that you have book clubs here most Saturdays. I know Staci mentioned that she has one next week, so I wanted to get in here before I'd run into all my students."

"It must be hard being a role model in a small town. Do you live in Sedona?" Rarity had already realized she was the "bookstore lady" for anyone who lived here. Especially the kids.

"Actually, I lived in Flagstaff, but my boyfriend just got a job out at the gallery, so we moved to Red Rock last month." She lowered her voice. "I love the condo, but the people are a little rah-rah for my taste. They keep leaving flyers at our door for events. Like the monthly barbeque and the crafts classes. It's all free, which is nice, but Harry and I like hiking and camping. He's a photographer and sells his stuff at the gallery."

"I just met Eleanor Blanchet this week." Rarity knew that Nancy must not have heard about Jackson. Rarity wasn't going to be the one to tell her that the gallery might shut down and she'd have to move.

"I thought I saw you at Monday's party. All of the Red Rock folk were invited. Harry had a couple of pieces they highlighted." Nancy glanced at her watch. "Anyway, I need to get to Flagstaff and get the shopping done. I love the warehouse store there on Idaho Street."

"Nice to meet you, and I guess we'll see you when we drop off the backpacks." Rarity waved as Nancy headed out of the shop. Then she turned back to Katie. "Are you ready for your book club? I can take over the register if you need to set up or anything."

Katie flung her straight blond hair over her shoulder, her blue eyes still watching Nancy Christy through the front window. "That was weird."

"Do you know Nancy?" Rarity felt her skin crawl on her neck, something that always happened when she found out something unexpected.

"She just wasn't what I'd expected. The kids in the book club talk about her. A lot. She's dating this photographer, like she told you, but she wasn't a few years ago. I guess someone saw her leave school on the back of a Harley and rumors flew about her dating someone in a motorcycle gang." Katie shook her head. "I guess it's all about perception when you work with kids, right? And that's reason ninety-five why I'm not going to work in a school district. I don't need the judgment."

Rarity thought about the dress code and strict rules at the corporation where she'd worked in St. Louis. She stowed her tote and put her phone on the counter just in case Archer called. "What I've learned is there's judgment everywhere."

The look on Katie's face made Rarity laugh. "Except here. The Next Chapter is a judgment-free zone. I don't care what you read as long as you use a bookmark. Now, that's the sign of a real monster, not what you wear or who you date."

Katie laughed as she grabbed a box that was sitting behind her. "And that's why I love working here."

As the day went on, Rarity checked her phone more frequently. Shirley had come in and helped Katie with the book club and now they were working on putting the new book shipment on the shelves and in the computer. Rarity was at a table on her laptop. She was supposed to be working on a budget for the next quarter, but she wasn't getting very far.

The door opened and Jonathon Anderson walked in. He scanned the room and went to sit at the table with Rarity.

"Did Drew send you with the bad news so I wouldn't hit him?" Rarity asked, but inside, her throat was starting to close up. There was no way Archer had killed anyone. And not with an arrow. She was a better shot when they went to the atlatl range at the local park. Atlatl was a spear-throwing game invented by the Native Americans. She didn't think Archer had ever handled a bow. He said he'd been teased about his name too much as a kid to even think about taking up the hobby.

"No, Archer called and asked me to tell you he's on a hike with another client this afternoon and not to worry. He'll be here at six to take you to dinner." He pulled a laptop out of his tote. "Okay if I work here this afternoon?"

"Of course. But are you working here because it's too crazy at Drew's or because you've been asked to watch me?" She glanced around the almost empty shop. "If you thought there might be ninja assassins in town, you should have come when the middle school book club was going. Those kids are ruthless."

"Which is why I don't show up during youth book clubs. I had my share of kids when Drew and his sister were young. I've done my sentence. You all can deal with the little monsters and not me." He opened his laptop. "Edith keeps talking to me if I stay at the house. So I gave her my credit card and told her to go crazy."

"You may regret that." Rarity thought that maybe there was more to the story, but she liked having Jonathon around, so she didn't look too closely at the gift horse. This time when she went back to working on the quarterly budget, she actually got it done. And when it was time to close up shop, she had crossed several things off her list.

Somehow, just having Jonathon around had eased her anxiety about Archer. She put the laptop away and said good night to Shirley and Katie, who were heading to the Garnet for a quick dinner together.

"Jonathon, I wish you lived closer. I'd pay you to write in the shop every day," Rarity called out as she dumped the coffee and turned off the machine. She double-checked the lock on the back door to the alley since Katie had taken the trash out just a few minutes before she'd left. It wasn't that Rarity didn't trust her, it was just one of those OCD things that if she didn't do it, she'd have to come back later to check the lock before she could even think about sleeping.

Jonathon didn't answer her, so when she went back to the front of the building she glanced around. He was standing by the register, his tote over his shoulder, looking at his phone.

"I thought you might have left. I said something but you didn't answer." Rarity took the key out of the cash register and filled her tote with her laptop and a couple of advance reader copies that had caught her eye. She didn't know if she and Archer were doing anything tomorrow, so she was stocking up on reading material.

He looked up from his phone. "Sorry, just catching up on email. They're still at the crime scene. They haven't been able to totally rule out Archer. Yet."

Rarity met Jonathon's eyes. "You're not funny."

"I'm not meaning to be funny. I have an email from my son explaining that the cameras at the gallery have been down since Monday night. Someone disconnected the part that does the daily recording. The system looked like it was working, but they didn't record anything. They can't verify when Archer came and found the body."

"Archer didn't kill the guy. He didn't even have a reason to kill him." Rarity leaned down and clipped the leash on Killer. "He barely knew Jackson."

"Actually, that's not completely true." Archer stood just inside the door to the bookstore. "We went to boarding school and college together and Jackson was a jerk. On the night of high school graduation, I think I told him if I ever saw him again, I'd kill him. Or something like that."

"Okay, so that was just the ramblings of a kid against another kid." Rarity felt a pit growing in her stomach.

"Except they caught me trying to get into Jackson's dorm one night. He wasn't even there. He'd gone home with his folks, but I thought I needed to avenge the way he'd dumped my sister. She'd thought he was the one. She was just a placeholder until he got back to New York and all the hot models he usually dated." Archer leaned against the doorway. "Anyway, Drew wants me to come to the station and explain all this history between us. I came to see if Jonathon would do me the favor of walking you home."

Rarity went over to him and took his face in her hands. "I know you. You didn't kill Jackson."

"I didn't kill him. But I look like a great suspect." He leaned in and kissed her. "Don't be mad at Drew for this. I'm the one who was a stupid kid. And when he finds out who did kill Jackson, the beer's going to be on Drew. For a week."

She kissed him back. "For a month."

Jonathon stayed and helped her finish closing up. As they walked to her house, she turned and looked at him. What would she do without her friends? "Are you coming Tuesday night?"

The older man smiled and squeezed her hand. "I wouldn't miss it for the world. We'll find out who killed Jackson. I promise."

# Chapter 5

Sunday morning, Rarity had finished her swim, made coffee, and was considering making banana bread to keep herself busy when someone knocked on the door. She went to open it and Archer stood there, a grocery sack in hand. "Hey, what are you doing here this morning? No tour today?"

"I've got an evening one with a client Calliope sent me last week. I decided I wanted to spend the morning with you." He leaned in and kissed her, then grinned at Killer, who was jumping on his leg. "Don't worry, big man. I bought your favorite treats. I figured your mother had forgotten to put them on the shopping list."

A bark was the only response as they all went into the kitchen. Killer sat and watched as Archer unpacked the grocery bag. "Bacon, eggs, cheese, butter, cream. If you have flour, I'll make us a quiche."

"Probably healthier than the banana bread I was considering making." Rarity took her stand mixer out of the cabinet and plugged it in. Then she got out the ingredients she needed to make homemade crust.

Killer whined from his spot on the floor and Archer leaned down with a chewy bone for him.

"I told you I didn't forget you." He went over and poured himself a coffee. "I'll fry off the bacon and do the mise en place while you get the crust ready."

"I hope you're not starving, or you should have bought a premade crust. The dough needs to sit in the fridge for thirty minutes." Rarity measured out the flour, not watching Archer.

She heard when he turned on the stove to fry the bacon. He hadn't responded, so when she turned to see if he'd heard her, he shrugged. "I don't know if I'm hungry or not. I'm going crazy thinking that some stupid, angry, revenge stunt when I was a kid is coming back to haunt me now. Jackson and I cleared the air about Dana years ago. The last time I saw him was in New York. I didn't want him dead."

"Drew must know that." She hoped that was true. Sam had said the same thing a few months ago about Drew thinking her brother was a killer. Now they weren't even talking, even though Drew had found the guilty party.

Archer laid the bacon in the hot pan. "He does, it just looks bad on me. I hate that I'm making his job harder."

"Seriously? You're worried about Drew?" Rarity cut the butter into the mixer and turned it on, watching the machine do its magic. "He just needs to clear you and get on with finding out who wanted Jackson dead. Like that guy he was fighting with on Monday."

"How do you know it was a guy?" Archer went and washed his hands again, then got out a plate and covered it in paper towels. "It could have been anyone in that office."

"He looked big. It could have been a woman, but it's unlikely. But truly, I don't know who he was talking to." Rarity gently poured a little water into the mixture and the dough quickly started to form. "Besides finding the body, there's nothing that ties you to the murder."

Archer looked at her. His glance seemed to be trying to tell her something, but then he laughed and went to stand at the stove to turn the bacon. "You're right as always. Drew just needs time to clear me."

Somehow Rarity thought she'd missed something. A clue had been dropped between them and she'd said the exact wrong thing to continue the conversation. As she wrapped the dough in plastic wrap, she asked, "You'd tell me if there was something to find, right?"

His arms caught her as she moved to put the dough in the fridge. "I promise. I told you about Dana and Jackson. That's the only smoking gun in this story. So stop hugging on me or the bacon will burn."

"You grabbed me, Mr. Chef Head." She closed the refrigerator door and refilled her coffee cup. Then she went to the sink to wash out the mixer bowl. "Are you going to want to use this mixer?"

He shook his head. "No, I'll be fine with a regular mixing bowl and a whisk. So what's on your agenda tonight?"

She ran water into the bowl and squirted dish soap into it too. "Well, since you've got a tour, Killer and I are going to do laundry and clean out the linen closet. It's been on my list since I moved here, since I just stuffed things into it when I unpacked. Now that I've lived here a few years, I can get rid of some stuff I don't use."

"Sounds like a fun evening." He took the bacon out of the pan and added more.

"I didn't even mention that I'm putting Les Mis on the television to work by." She finished washing the bowl and dried it. "I bet you're really jealous now."

"Yeah, not so much." He sipped his coffee. Clearly, something was on his mind. "You and your club may want to stay out of this murder investigation. Jackson had some questionable funding sources for the gallery."

"Oh, sweet. You're worried about me." She sat down at the table and watched as he turned bacon.

"I'm not kidding, Rarity. Maybe this is one that you just stay out of." He turned and met her gaze. "Drew will find the killer."

"Yeah, people keep telling me that." Rarity thought back on Jonathon's words. "The club has already been called into session. We'll be talking about it on Tuesday if you want to join us. Jonathon is participating."

"That will make Edith happy. Not." He finished cooking the bacon and turned off the stove. Then with his cup in hand, he moved to sit by Rarity. "I'm serious about being worried. Jackson liked to take shortcuts. And he didn't care who he slept with as long as he wasn't lonely."

"Dana's not in town, right?" Rarity lifted her cup and sipped.

Archer saw the smile in her eyes, though. "You're horrible."

"I've been told that. Should we still go to Art in the Park and see if we can find some reasonably priced art after the quiche is done?" She opened the paper and flipped to the page where the promoter had taken out an ad. "According to this, they have over fifty art booths signed up. Maybe one of the pictures for sale will look like an actual landscape."

\* \* \* \*

Rarity was making framing decisions with a representative from Framed in Arizona, a local company that had been smart enough to have a booth at Art in the Park, when a woman touched her arm.

"That's a nice piece. I just reviewed the artist's work and he's coming next week to the gallery to see if we can get some pieces on commission. It's nice to see he's selling here." Eleanor picked up a sample of matting and quickly matched it to a frame. "I'm not sure if this will fit your home decor, but if I were you, that's how I'd frame it."

Rarity nodded. She'd seen the matting but hadn't known what frame to use. And the guy helping her had been guiding her to a more expensive setting. "Thanks, Eleanor, that's perfect." She finished up with the framer, paying his deposit and getting a card with a pick-up date, then turned to Eleanor. "I didn't expect to see you here."

"A good gallery manager gets to know the local art scene." She moved to glance into the next booth, which held a variety of black velvet paintings. "And we just stepped back into the nineties."

Rarity laughed at an old Elvis-on-tour painting. "I was going to say the seventies."

Eleanor pointed to a woman on a beach towel, naked but posed so you didn't see much. "Jackson would have bought that in a second and hung it in his living room. His condo was full of impulse purchases. The man had no clue about art."

"I'm sorry for your loss," Rarity said. She didn't look at Eleanor as they walked to the next stand. Archer was getting them drinks and should be back any minute, but she could still see the framing booth and he'd have to walk right past her. "Are you staying at the gallery?"

"Thank you. That was nice to say." Eleanor nodded as she flipped through a box of prints at the next stall. "I've talked to the family attorney. They've asked me to stay on and manage the gallery. I report to someone at the law office, so I guess it depends on how much money I make for the estate. Of course, now that I don't have to run everything past Jackson, the gallery has a shot at being profitable. As I mentioned, the man didn't know his art or have a lick of business sense. That first party he threw? It was stupid, but you couldn't tell him that. He liked showing off for his friends."

Rarity could actually see that about Jackson, but it wasn't her place to say it. At least not to one of his friends. "Well, I'm glad you're staying. I was serious about you coming by to help me pick out some art books to stock. I work with a lot of businesses in Sedona and we do this joint bookmark—"

Eleanor cut her off. "Whatever you want. I'll send you the book list. Just don't go overboard on the marketing costs. My budget's pretty tight. I've got to go. I've got a meeting at the gallery this afternoon."

Rarity watched Eleanor walk away as Archer came toward her with two bottles of water. He said hello as they met, but Eleanor didn't respond. Either she hadn't heard him or she didn't realize who he was.

"Was that Eleanor?" He handed her a bottle of water.

Rarity opened it and took a long sip. "It was. She helped me pick out the framing materials for the picture I bought. Then we chatted about bad art. But as soon as I brought up Jackson, she clammed up and took off."

"She didn't even acknowledge me." Archer drank some water. "I'd feel hurt but it's too hot to even try. Are we done looking?"

"Yes, please. Let's go home and watch a movie until you have to leave." She fell into step with him. "Are you going to be okay on the hike?"

He nodded. "I think so. We start in the shaded area, so by the time we reach the top it should have cooled down a bit. The guy wanted to see the lights of Sedona, so we'll be hiking back in the dark."

Rarity glanced over at him. "That doesn't sound safe."

"The trail's well marked, and we'll have flashlights. Besides, there's a full moon tonight. We should have plenty of light." He took her hand as they walked to the parking lot. "I can see you're worried about me. Do you want me to call when I get home?"

"Would you laugh or freak out if I said yes?"

"I would be honored that you're concerned about me. I'll give you a call. And don't worry. I don't often do evening hikes and as such, I got paid a crazy high rate."

*Money's not everything.* Rarity didn't express the thought. She just bumped Archer's shoulder. "Just be careful. Please."

He met her gaze and smiled. "I'm always careful. It's kind of in the job description."

Later, at the house, when Archer stood to go get everything ready for the hike, Rarity handed him a piece of paper and a pen. He frowned at her. "What's this?"

"Write down the trail or hike you're taking this guy on and his name." Rarity tapped the paper. "That way if anything happens, I know where to send Drew to find you."

"Rarity, it's just an evening hike." He started to put the paper down but something in her eyes made him stop. "You're that worried?"

Rarity shook her head. "I don't want to be. And maybe it's because of the whole Jackson thing or I've just got a bad feeling, but can you humor me? Just this time?"

"Honey, I'll send you my weekly schedule from now on if it makes you feel better." Archer scribbled something on the paper and set it down on the coffee table. "But right now, I really have to go and get ready."

She watched him leave the house and Killer came up on the couch and curled in her lap. She rubbed the little dog's belly. "I know it's silly, but I'm nervous."

He snuggled in closer. Apparently, he didn't share her concern.

After a few minutes, Rarity started the movie. Then she got up and started taking boxes out of her hall closet. Killer stayed on the couch, watching her. "If I'm going to have all this nervous energy, I might as well use it productively."

Rarity got to work. After she got the closet cleaned out, she started laundry. Then she made a bowl of soup for dinner from the homemade soup she had frozen last week. She warmed up a slice of the quiche. There was just enough for one more breakfast, and she'd eat it tomorrow before she went into the bookstore.

After dinner, she opened her laptop and worked on some marketing ideas.

It was already dark and Archer hadn't called. She glanced at the clock. She'd give him until nine. He'd have to take the bus back to storage if he drove it. Archer hadn't said when he'd be back.

A pit started in her stomach.

She changed into her swimsuit and took her phone out to the deck. She turned up the volume and started to swim. By the time she was done, Archer would call. She knew it.

With her laps done, she climbed out of the water and checked her phone. Maybe she'd missed the call.

Nothing.

She went back inside the house and changed. It was fifteen minutes until eight. She'd said she'd wait until nine.

She kicked herself for not asking when he thought he'd be back. That would have been smart. She was probably worrying for nothing.

She made a cup of hot cocoa and curled on the couch to watch *Grease* while she waited. But even Danny and Sandy's teenage love ups and downs couldn't distract her. Even as she sang along.

Her phone rang, the ringer on high, and made her jump out of the couch and knock the phone off the coffee table. She grabbed it and answered it without looking at the display. "Archer?"

A silence held on the other end of the line. "So he's not there?"

Drew was the one who'd called. She sank onto the couch and muted the television. "No, he went on a late hike with a client. He was supposed to call me when he got back. Why?"

"Did he tell you who he went with? And maybe where?"

Drew's questions bothered her. "Is this because of Jackson? Did he miss some meeting with you?" Rarity was just about to tell Drew exactly what she thought of that when he spoke.

"Calliope called and said that they should be back by now. She was supposed to go to dinner with this guy at seven thirty. They're not back yet. Do you know where he's at?"

# Chapter 6

Archer's Jeep pulled into her driveway at midnight. By then, Shirley, Sam, and Terrance were all sitting around her living room waiting with her. Holly and Malia were working but they'd called three times, checking in.

Killer heard the car, and ran to the door. Archer opened it and Rarity let the worry fall off her. She walked over to give him a hug as he said, "Hey, I hear there's a party going on without me."

"Not much of a party without you." Terrance stood and patted Archer's arm. "You all right, buddy?"

"My client twisted his ankle on a rock on the way back. He didn't want me to leave him to get help, so it was a slow hike out of there. Drew said Calliope called to let him know we were missing." Archer looked down at Rarity. "I would have thought that you would have had Drew on speed dial."

"I didn't know when to expect you so I didn't know what late was. Killer told me not to worry and call at nine. Otherwise, I'd look clingy." She stood close, letting his arm pull her even closer.

"I think maybe sending you my schedule isn't such a bad idea." He kissed her on the head.

"Well, since you're safe, I better head home." Shirley patted Archer on the chest. "There's a cranberry loaf in the kitchen for you."

Terrance and Shirley left. Sam stood and unkinked herself from the couch. "I'm out too. Stop scaring us, dude. It's not funny."

Archer pulled her into a hug with his free arm. "I didn't mean to scare anyone."

As Sam left, Archer held the door from closing. "I've got to meet Drew at the office so he can close out this call. My client is on the way to the hospital. I told him I needed to see you before he debriefed me."

Rarity kissed him. "Maybe hiking in the dark isn't worth the money."

He held her arms and grinned at her. "You don't know what I charged him."

"Call me tomorrow so I can yell at you then." She followed him to the door and watched as he climbed into his Jeep. Killer went out and did his business, watching the Jeep pull away. Then he came back to the porch and sat with Rarity as she tried to calm herself.

That was the problem with caring for people. Sometimes you worried. She went back inside and closed the door. Then she turned off all the lights and headed to bed. The other good thing about letting people into your life: she didn't have to worry alone. Shirley had been here within minutes of when she heard the news from Sam. Who'd been called by Drew to come to sit with Rarity.

As she tried to go to sleep, she thought of those nights during her treatment when she couldn't sleep. Back then, she had Sam. That had been her entire support system. And Sam lived several states away. Now she could be here in minutes. Rarity didn't want any more close calls, but it was nice knowing she had people to help her get through the rough times.

\* \* \* \*

Monday morning, Rarity was up earlier than she needed to be. Especially after her sleepless night. Even though Archer was fine, last night's activity had made her hyperaware of what could happen. During treatment, when she went down this rabbit hole, she either called Sam or wrote in her journal. Sam wasn't much of a morning lark, and she'd been at the house until Archer showed up, so Rarity pulled out her journal and started writing.

When she looked up, her coffee was cold and Killer was at her feet, whining to be let out again. Now that she'd written down all her worries and got them out of her head, she opened her laptop. It was time to find out more about the new gallery and what books she should order. Yesterday at Art in the Park, she had been inspired by all the local artists with booths. Her nonfiction section kept growing as she learned more things about Sedona and the surrounding area. When she opened the bookstore, she had started the collection with several local healing books, including Sam's favorite crystal books.

Then Archer had suggested several hiking books. And with each business she joined marketing forces with, the nonfiction section continued to grow. Last month she added several books on Southwestern-style cooking. Archer had bought the first cookbook out of that section.

Pulling up the website for the gallery, she noticed it still had the open house notice on its main page. Maybe Jackson had been the web guru or, more likely, Eleanor hadn't gotten around to changing it yet. She paged through the tabs and found the painting she'd liked so much. The one Eleanor had kept her from touching.

As she had mentioned, it was from the pre–Civil War era. The kids in the painting were all dressed in their Sunday finest. As was Mom. Dad was nowhere in the picture. Had this been commissioned by the father, who was living somewhere else? Something to remind him of what he was missing during his travels? The painter wasn't listed, and from the information on the web page, Moments gallery had purchased it from an estate sale in New York.

Maybe Eleanor had been the one to find it.

As Rarity scanned the paintings, she wrote down several art terms and periods. While she waited for Eleanor to send a list of art books she should stock, Rarity would try to find the best books that represented the gallery's holdings. She wanted to have a couple of kids' books on art available too. The gallery didn't look kid-friendly during the open house, but maybe Eleanor would be open to having school tours come through.

Glancing at the clock, she saw it was time to go open the store. She tucked her notebook into her tote along with one of Killer's favorite toys, then went to get ready for her day. It was still cool enough, barely, for her and Killer to walk to the store if they left now. Rarity tucked his folding water dish and a bottle of water into her tote.

He was waiting at the door when she came out of her bedroom. "Yes, it's time to go. Happy puppy, happy life."

Killer barked, telling her to hurry. As soon as they passed by Terrance's walkway, Killer paused to do his business. Terrance was on the porch and held up his cup in greeting.

"Did he drink too much coffee this morning, like me?" Terrance called from the shade.

"Sorry, I didn't realize he had to go." Rarity tried to not let Killer water the neighbors' lawns if she could help it.

"No worries. I'm not grumpy like old Mrs. Crabtree on the corner. How's Archer's client?" He set the paper down on his table and walked to the edge of the porch, staying in the shade.

Rarity blinked. Archer hadn't called this morning like he'd promised. And she'd forgotten after writing down all her worries in the journal. "I don't know. Archer probably slept in today."

"That boy works too hard." Terrance waved and went to sit back down and finish reading the paper.

As she passed Mrs. Crabtree's house, she saw the curtains in the front window move. Apparently, the woman had been watching for her. She hurried Killer across the street, just in case he wanted to mark his territory or something. She didn't want her neighbors complaining about her dog.

After they arrived at the store, she checked her messages. Shirley had texted and begged off work due to last night's events. She did promise to make treats for Tuesday's meeting. The door opened as she put down her phone and Katie came inside with two coffees and a bag from the Garnet.

"I didn't know you were coming in today." Rarity took the bag and pulled out two large sub sandwiches.

"Shirley texted me. So I brought lunch. I hope you like Southwestern turkey." Katie set the coffee on the counter as well. "And I bought an extra roll for Mr. Murder down there."

Katie was always changing Killer's name, but he knew enough to come when someone said bread. Which was his favorite food in the world. "Let's eat and I'll catch you up on the gossip before you hear it from someone else and think I'm holding out on you."

Katie pulled up a second stool and unwrapped her sandwich. "Shirley said you would be better able to explain things. Did she really go on a date?"

Rarity shook her head. No wonder Shirley had wanted the gallery opening to be a group event. Rumors were already flying. "No, we went as a big group. And the next morning, Archer found the gallery owner dead. I would have thought you heard that on Saturday?"

"The kids were talking about a local murder, but I shut the discussion down. The book we read was a YA mystery. I thought they were just getting into the topic. I didn't realize it happened this week." Katie set down her sandwich. "That's creepy."

Although Rarity agreed with her assessment of the creep factor, she decided to change the subject. She told her about Archer's client getting hurt on the trail. "So that's why Shirley's not here."

Katie took it in stride. After she finished her sandwich, she looked around. "So what can I help you with today? I've never worked on a Monday before."

Rarity explained that the store probably would be quiet, so she wanted Katie to take on looking up books for the new art section. "Including kids' books. I'm thinking about ten to fifteen different ones. Make a list and if I agree with you, I'll show you how to order them."

"We could make up a welcome for the gallery shelf that also has fiction that deals with art. Like the Dan Brown one or that women's fiction you had me read last month."

Rarity was catching Katie's excitement. "We could ask Eleanor for marketing handouts from the gallery and maybe a picture or two of the paintings."

"I know just where to set it up." As Katie led Rarity over to the nonfiction section, Rarity tried to think of more novels that either were set in an art museum or the main character was an artist. It was going to be fun to curate the selection.

Archer showed up right at five. He held the door for Katie, who was leaving to meet up with friends before classes started next week. He walked toward Rarity as she closed up the register. They'd only had five walk-ins that day. And most of those were locals wanting to know about the gallery murder. The good news was they all bought at least one book. And the last visitor brought her two kids so they both loaded up on books. It hadn't been a slow sales day, even though they'd had little traffic.

"Your boyfriend is the worst. He was supposed to call you today." He picked up Killer and gave him a cuddle.

"He's forgetful at times." Rarity took the key out of the register and looked around. "All I need to do is turn off the lights and grab my tote."

"The back door?"

"I checked it just before Katie left. We're good to go." Rarity pulled out her keys and set her alarm. Then she locked the door. Turning around, she saw Killer was now on his leash and on the ground, sniffing. "How was your day?"

"I spent a lot of it with yesterday's tour client, Clint. He was so embarrassed by his fall. He apologized several times. I'm just thankful I make all customers sign a liability waiver. I don't want to get sued by some guy who made up all the rules, then didn't like the result." He took her bag. "Do you want to go to the Garnet for dinner?"

"Actually, no. I've been thinking about waffles all day. I guess I'm in a breakfast kind of mood." She leaned into him and took his arm. "Besides, I'm going to be peopling all day tomorrow. I'd like tonight to be just about us."

He didn't say anything.

"Unless you want to go to the Garnet." She turned to him and stopped.

He pulled her close. "I just want to go home and relax."

"Oh, well, I can make soup if you need to leave."

He frowned and then laughed. "No, I want to go home with you and have waffles. That's what I meant. Sorry. Should I not call your house home? I guess that was a little presumptuous of me."

She squeezed his hand. "It wasn't at all. I'm not sure why we're tiptoeing around each other tonight."

"I know why. We had a stupid fight. I need to be more in tune with your feelings." He pulled her close. "Let's start over. What kind of waffles are we making?"

"Wait, there are different types of waffles?"

He laughed and they started walking home again. "Oh, dear. You have so much to learn."

\* \* \* \*

The next morning, Rarity took the time to swim, even though she knew she would be a little late opening the shop. With the book club tonight, she needed to stretch her muscles now as she'd be sitting all day. After she dressed, she checked Killer's food and water. "Terrance is coming over at noon to walk you so don't bite his ankles or anything."

Killer jumped off the couch and went to his bed. He knew he stayed home on Tuesdays, but it didn't mean he had to like it. Or make it easy for Rarity to leave. Terrance would come by at least twice to see Killer, and Rarity suspected that he came more often and stayed longer to make sure the dog wasn't lonely. She had wondered if Terrance had been the lonely one, but now with his coffee dates with Shirley, her neighbor was happier than he'd been in years.

The group meeting started promptly at six and everyone was there. The book they were supposed to have started reading was *The Last Thing He Told Me*. As a suspense, it was perfect to talk about before they started talking about the murder.

Rarity always had the book club discussion first, as there were a couple of stay-at-home moms who enjoyed the club but didn't want to be part of the sleuthing. When Jonathon showed up, the tone of the chatter changed. At the break, Ginny and Deb walked over and handed Rarity the book they'd be talking about next week. "You're already ready to go?"

"I can see that you're all champing at the bit for the sleuthing discussion. Jonathon being here just puts a whole mystery vibe on the room. Although he is very insightful about the book discussions." Ginny took her credit card back from Rarity. "I appreciate that."

Deb giggled. "It's nice to have a man's perspective on a book. Tom isn't interested in reading or talking about books. At all. Sometimes I think I married the wrong man. I should have found someone who loves books like I do."

Rarity rang up Deb's purchase. She'd also grabbed a couple of romance novels off the shelves before she came to the register. "Although, the best stories are when opposites attract. Maybe you just have something else in common."

Deb actually blushed, then nodded. "He is a good man."

After they left, Rarity watched the door. Relationships were hard. And what was going on with Archer calling Rarity's house home? Was it more than just a slip? Should she be thinking long-term in the relationship? Was she just being…

She didn't get to finish asking herself the rest of her thousand questions about her and Archer because Shirley waved her over to where she was sitting and crocheting. "What's going on?"

"Terrance just sent me a picture of him and Killer sitting on your couch. I think they're watching a movie together. You need to be careful or that man will just move in."

Rarity took the phone and looked at a smiling Terrance. He did look comfortable on her couch with her dog curled up on his lap. But she knew that Terrance wasn't trying to impress her. He'd sent the picture to Shirley.

The man was in love. And Rarity knew that all Shirley could do right now was break his heart.

# Chapter 7

Holly started off the sleuthing part of the meeting. "Since Archer is a suspect, Rarity asked me to run the club meetings until we find the killer. Just so the investigation isn't tainted."

"If my son were here, he'd say all of our investigations are tainted since we're not actually officers of the law." Jonathon paused, looking around at the group. "But I know you're going to investigate, no matter what Drew thinks, so count me in. I miss the thrill of the chase."

"Okay, thank you for that off-topic confession, Jonathon." Holly walked over to the flip chart. "First, we need to establish a timeline. Research the victim. And list any suspects, like Archer, who might have done the deed. Then we'll examine their access and motives to see if we can trim it down to one or two people."

"We need to find out more about Jackson." Rarity held up her hand. "I heard him arguing with someone Monday night. He was talking about the gallery. Archer said that Jackson liked to take shortcuts. Maybe this was one of them."

"That's a good clue." Jonathon smiled at her and wrote something in the notebook in front of him.

"Oh, wait. I forgot to hand these out. I thought about them earlier, but Ginny and Deb were still here." Shirley handed a loose-leaf binder to each person. They had their name on the front along with a cartoon character of either a male or female investigator. "Aren't they cool? Terrance helped design the cover sheet."

"Oh, Terrance did this, huh?" Holly grinned at Shirley, who'd turned beet red. "You've been spending a lot of time with him."

"Stop teasing Shirley. We all know that she and George have a complicated relationship." Rarity stepped into the discussion.

Holly and Rarity locked gazes, but then Holly broke eye contact, backing down first. "Anyway, we're here to figure out who killed Jackson Sanders. Does anyone besides Rarity have information to get out there to the rest of us?"

"Drew told me that the gallery is Jackson's second attempt at running a business. His family bankrolled him both times. He lost the restaurant about a year before they started getting permits to build the new gallery. His family's construction company built the Red Rock neighborhood. Mostly to give the employees somewhere to live here in Sedona. You all don't have a lot of rental housing available." Jonathon stopped talking as he noticed everyone was staring at him. "What? I asked him some questions on the way to the gallery open house. This was all before Jackson got himself whacked, so Drew was more open about what he knew."

"Is whacked a technical term from the law enforcement community?" Rarity asked, trying to keep a smile off her face.

"It is when you get an arrow shot into your back." Jonathon leaned forward. "What I'm not supposed to know is that the end of the arrow was dipped in some sort of drug, which is what really killed him. I overheard the coroner telling Drew this while I was waiting to take him to lunch today. The coroner said he was guessing that the drug was pentobarbital, but he sent it to the state crime lab to confirm. It's typically used in assisted suicides."

"So where does someone get a drug like that? Is assisted suicide even legal in Arizona?" Shirley got out a new skein of yarn from her bag.

"Actually, no. But you can get the stuff on the internet pretty easily." Holly was writing on the flip chart. When no one said anything, she turned around. "What? I did a paper on it in college. Ethics in legal issues or something like that. I got an A."

"Well, you're our expert then," Malia teased her friend.

Rarity stared at the flip chart. Someone killed Jackson with an arrow dipped in a drug. Did they think the arrow would lead investigators to the blessing ceremony Jackson had hired the local Yavapai Apache tribe to perform? And what was the significance of the death being at the vortex circle?

"Rarity? What are you thinking?" Holly's voice cut through the questions floating in her head.

"I'm not sure, but this death looks staged. The killer wanted the attention on anything but the real reason for killing Jackson. Like Archer showing up to take him hiking. Who knew that plan? And why the ceremony around the vortex and with the arrow? The killer is trying to confuse us." Rarity looked around the group and saw the same questions on their faces. "So why was Jackson murdered? I think once we have the real reason, the killer will be obvious."

"So right now, we just have to keep knocking down the fake walls the killer built up. Like pointing the finger at Archer. Who changed their meeting place for Saturday morning? Or was it always supposed to be at the gallery?" Holly wrote down the questions.

"I can answer that." Archer stepped into the circle and sat down by Rarity. He took her hand. "At first, Jackson and I were supposed to meet at his condo. Calliope pulled me aside on Monday night and told me that he wanted to meet at the gallery."

"Calliope," Rarity whispered. Why did that woman always show up at the worst times?

\* \* \* \*

On the way home, Archer was quiet. Finally, he spoke. "You can't think that Calliope set me up to look like I killed Jackson."

Rarity looked up at the sky filled with stars. She had been thinking just that, but Archer knew the woman better than she did. "I don't know. I just think it's something that Drew should look into."

"Believe me, I told him the same thing I told your group. It was when I left you for a minute at that Civil War painting you liked so much. Calliope had texted me and asked me to meet her at Jackson's office. I knew you wouldn't be happy about me talking to her, so I didn't tell you. Now, I wish you'd been there so you could have heard what she said too."

A voice called to them as they walked by Terrance's house. "Rarity, don't freak out."

She turned toward his porch. She was thankful for the distraction. "Now, why would I freak out?"

"I've got Killer over here with me. I felt bad leaving him in the house alone, so I brought him over after my last check-in. He's on a lead out here. I'll bring him over to you."

Before she could reach the porch, she could hear his barking. Terrance stepped down and handed her the Yorkie. "Hey buddy, did you have fun with Uncle Terrance?"

Killer didn't respond except for licking Rarity's shoulder. She could feel he was tired. She took his leash from Terrance. "You didn't have to do this."

"I know, but he keeps me from being lonely too. Or looking like an idiot talking to myself. This way, I can always talk to Killer. You're doing me a favor." He reached out and shook Archer's hand. "You've had a couple of exciting days."

"More excitement than I want." Archer actually laughed. Something Rarity hadn't seen him do for a few days. "I like my life to be a little calmer."

"Don't worry about it. It will settle down soon enough. We all know you didn't kill that guy." Terrance turned around and headed for the porch. "You're not the killer type."

As they entered the house, Archer went to the kitchen and turned on the fire under the tea kettle. "I would be offended by Terrance's description of me if I didn't just come in here and start making tea. Maybe I should be more careful of my actions. The powers that be might revoke my man card."

"You can play macho on your guys' nights with Drew. I know you happen to like apple cinnamon tea. And it doesn't make me see you as less of a man." Rarity put her arms around him. "But if you'd rather have a beer, I've got some in the fridge."

"They're probably IPAs and not mass-produced, good-old-boy brands." He sat at the table. "Besides, I think my choice of beverage is the least of my problems right now."

Rarity got down the tea bags and cups. Then she set everything on the table. "Are you hungry? I could warm up some soup or make eggs."

"Drew fed me tonight before I came over to collect you from the meeting. He's worried about me." He met Rarity's gaze. "He doesn't think I'll do well in prison. There's no honey for the tea."

"Then let's keep you out of there. Look, the only thing they can prove is you listened to the wrong person. We need to find out what Calliope knows about Jackson's death." She watched Killer curl up on his bed. The little dog was ready for his day to be over.

Archer stared at her. "What's your day look like tomorrow?"

"Mommy and Me class and book ordering. Shirley's doing the class but I need to run the register." She frowned as the kettle went off. As she poured hot water into the cups and took them over to the table, she waited until she sat to ask, "Why?"

"Calliope wants to meet for lunch at the Garnet at one. Come with me."

She thought about normal traffic for a Wednesday. "I'll call Katie to come in for the afternoon to back up Shirley. But yeah, I can be there."

He handed her a tea bag as he unwrapped his own. "Good. I think it's time for us to deal with the Calliope problem as a couple. Which I'm sorry we didn't do earlier."

"At worst, I'll have a report to take back to the sleuthing club next Tuesday." She put the tea bag in her cup and started dunking it.

"That's the spirit." He reached over and squeezed her hand.

\* \* \* \*

The next morning, Rarity was unpacking the week's shipment of books when Shirley came in, followed closely by Katie. She glanced at the clock. "Thanks for coming in, but I thought you had something to do this morning."

"It's done. I had a meeting with my advisor, and it took all of ten minutes. He hates my book idea. It's not literary enough. And he said my choice of classes for this semester was all wrong. So now I need to fit another class into my schedule because it's not going to be offered for two years. If I don't take it this semester, I won't graduate next May like I'd planned." She tucked her tote under the counter, then pulled her straight blond hair into a pony. She might have looked like Janey, one of Rarity's former employees, but she was a spitfire to the other woman's calm demeanor.

"Are you going to be able to fit it in?" Rarity asked.

She nodded. "I think so, but I'll need tomorrow off to go get forms signed so I can start next week. I just hope the extra homework isn't going to kill me."

Shirley had dropped a bag off in the book club area. "If you need more study time, I can take your middle school club for a few months. I've been banned from seeing George."

"What? When did this happen?" Rarity set down the book she'd been getting ready to shelve.

"Last week. Apparently, he has a girlfriend in the home. Or he does when he remembers her. So when I showed up with cookies, she got jealous and started tearing up her room." Shirley went into the break room and poured coffee. "I guess the universe is paying me back for spending time with Terrance."

"No, that's not what's happening." Katie took the cup of coffee from Shirley's hand and set it on the counter. Then she wrapped her arms around the older woman and gave her a long hug.

Shirley met Rarity's gaze with a question, and she answered with a "I have no idea" shrug. When Katie stepped back, tears were filling her eyes.

"Look, I don't talk about this a lot because I don't like to be sad, but my grandmother was like your husband. She forgot all of us over a period of a year. We'd go in to see her and it was a different woman each time we visited. None of them was the grandmother I remembered. But my mom kept telling us to go and visit. The woman in front of us at the home didn't even like kids. Mom would tell her about what we were doing in school, then Grandma would turn to her and ask, 'So these are your kids? Are you Sarah's daughter?' Sarah was her roommate. That she remembered."

"Oh, honey, I'm so sorry. That must have been devastating." Shirley reached over and squeezed Katie's shoulders.

"Well, to get back to the point of my story. Grandma died a few months later. Then Grandpa married this woman from church. In the space of about a month. Everyone talked, but he was lonely when Grandma went into the facility. They bonded since Grandma Alice had lost her husband a few years back. Now, I remember and love Grandma, but Grandma Alice comes to all the family events. And she remembers my name."

"People come into your life for a reason," Rarity added.

Shirley nodded. "I'm not replacing or cheating on George. Terrance and I are just friends."

Rarity nodded as she thought about Terrance bringing Killer over last night to ward off the loneliness. "We're not saying anything like that. Just that the universe is not punishing you."

Shirley sniffed and looked at the clock. "Oh, my. I need to get everything ready. The babies will be here soon."

After Shirley was out of hearing range, Katie whispered to Rarity, "I didn't say the wrong thing, did I?"

Rarity patted her new employee on the shoulder. "Not at all. I think you said exactly the right thing. So, do you have a list of art books for me to order?"

As they worked on next week's book order, the moms came inside with strollers. Shirley fell into her element. She was Sedona's grandmother. She remembered each mom's name as well as the babies and the talk in the room centered on feeding issues, nap times, and enrichment activities. Today, they didn't have a craft to do after they read the book, so Shirley had invited them all to bring a dessert to share.

One of the mothers brought over a plate for Rarity and Katie. "You two look like you need some sugar."

"I never say no." Rarity thanked her for the cookies. "Are you enjoying the club?"

"Mommy and Me is the highlight of my week. Don't get me wrong, I love my son, Alex, but I need adults to talk to as well as reading *Funny Little Monkey* ten times a day." She held out a tiny hand. "I'm Selena, and I live over in Red Rock."

"Your husband works for the gallery?"

She nodded. "He's in security, and they're all freaked out that Jackson was killed on their watch. Someone turned off the recording function of the video cameras. Probably Jackson. He didn't like to be watched. Especially since the rumors were that he was seeing a married woman."

"Someone in Red Rock?" Rarity asked as Shirley called the group back to read the book aloud.

"No, I heard she was from Sedona." Selena started to walk away. "Apparently, she was a cop's wife or something. Jackson liked to play with fire."

Rarity filed that bit of information away to tell the sleuthers' group. She took a cookie and pointed it at the screen. She moved Katie over to stand in front of the laptop. "You key in the book order and I'll watch this time. That way I can eat more cookies."

As Katie keyed in the book order, Rarity thought about the Sedona police department. Most of the guys were older with wives, who didn't seem like the cheating type. Drew was always saying that they did their hiring from retirement notices from other departments around the country. People retired, moved to Sedona, then got bored and got a part-time job. The younger officers, of which there were three, besides Drew, were all single.

And then there was Drew. Who was kind of dating Sam. If Sam had found a new boyfriend, would she have told Rarity? Rarity thought their breakup was temporary. That Sam would forgive Drew sooner or later. But what if Sam had been seeing Jackson? Drew had just investigated Sam's brother in an investigation. What would happen if she became a primary suspect? Sam wouldn't kill anyone, especially Jackson. Rarity wasn't even sure they knew each other. But if they *had been* having an affair, it might explain a lot of questions Rarity had about the facts of the case.

Her best friend or her boyfriend. There were no good choices in this investigation.

# Chapter 8

Archer and Calliope were sitting in the foyer and waiting for a table when Rarity arrived. Archer stood and gave her a kiss. Out of the corner of her eye, she could see Calliope narrow her eyes into a glare that disappeared as soon as Archer turned. He still had his arm around Rarity. "Rarity, I think you know Calliope."

"We met at the gallery last Monday. I think that was the first time." Rarity held out her hand. "Nice to see you again."

"Likewise." Calliope turned to the hostess. "Can we get a table now?"

"Oh, we're waiting for one more." He turned toward Rarity. "Jack, my new assistant, is joining us. I'm going to turn over Calliope's clients to him for tours and such. That way, I can focus on the larger corporate clients."

From the look on Calliope's face, that was totally new information to her. Rarity put a hand on his chest. PDAs would be the style for today. Lots of Public Displays of Affection between her and Archer. Maybe sooner or later, Calliope would catch the hint. Rarity felt like she was back in high school again.

Thankfully, Jack had followed Rarity into the restaurant. Archer waved him over, then nodded to the hostess. "We're all here now."

"I'll put you in Malia's station," the hostess said, acknowledging Rarity and Archer's friendship with one of the servers. As they sat, Malia rattled off the specials and dropped off menus. In a few minutes, she was back with four glasses of water and a breadbasket. She winked at Rarity. "I'm supposed to ask if you want water and bread, but you guys are mostly regulars. So I took a chance."

"Thank you." Rarity glanced at the menu. She knew it by heart but didn't know what she wanted to eat. Especially sitting across the table from Calliope. "I'm thinking soup and a half sandwich. The moms brought in cookies for their Mommy and Me class earlier."

"I don't eat carbs. Especially processed carbs." Calliope pushed the menu toward the edge of the table.

"I eat a lot of protein too. My trainer has me on this Keto thing to try to build muscle. And then I get to carb load before competition days." Jack directed his comments to Calliope, who was ignoring him. "I work out at the CrossFit gym out by the highway. Barbells?"

"What?" Calliope looked over at him, confused.

Jack blushed and Rarity knew he was trying to impress her. "Barbells. It's the name of the gym. You should stop by. There's this one chick there who can press more weight than a bunch of the guys."

Calliope paused and really looked at Jack. She took in his handsome face, tanned, sculpted arms, and trim body. She blinked twice and Rarity could see that she realized he was a total hottie. "Maybe I will. So you're taking over my hiking clients? Tell me about yourself."

For the rest of the meal, Jack talked about his love of hiking in the Sedona area. When his watch beeped, he looked at Archer. "Dude, I've got that guy coming in so he can book tours for his church group. I need to go."

"I'll take care of your meal." Archer waved him away as Jack pulled out his wallet. "It was business-related."

After Jack left, Archer turned to Calliope. "I'm sure you'll enjoy working with him."

"I'm sure I will." She set her fork down from the salad she'd special-ordered without any croutons or cheese and dressing on the side. "So this was the message you wanted to send? You're off-limits?"

Archer glanced at Rarity. "One of them. I have something else we need to know. Tell us why Jackson wanted to change where we would meet. And why didn't he tell me himself?"

Calliope sighed and wiped her face with her napkin. "I don't know why Jackson changed the meeting spot. He told me he needed some time to work through the blessing ceremony and how to market it. He was still looking for you to tell you about meeting at the gallery when a waiter came up and told him he had a visitor in his office. I said I'd find you and tell you about the change in pick-up location. I wanted to see you alone."

Rarity hoped her face was serene because inside, she wanted to yell. Instead, her voice seemed to be at a normal level when she said, "You wanted him back."

Calliope nodded. "No use being coy now. Yes, I wanted him back."

"Calliope." Archer looked confused. "You worked for me. There is no back. We never dated."

She snorted. "You didn't think they were dates. I guess I always hoped you'd see me differently. But you don't. And now, you're dating her. I get the point."

"I never knew," Archer said softly.

Calliope stood and nodded. "I guess I was too subtle. Don't worry about it, I'll get over you sooner or later."

They watched her walk out and Malia came up to the table. "I'd ask if you want anything else, but neither one of you look like you've eaten much."

"Just the check. Although now that it's just the two of us, I'm finishing this sandwich." Archer smiled at Rarity, who nodded.

Malia leaned over and stacked the plates from Jack and Calliope. "Did she kill Jackson? What did she say when you asked her?"

"We weren't that direct on the killing Jackson point." Rarity didn't want to tell Archer's business, so she looked at him.

He sighed. "She said I was an idiot and she'd just realized that part. But no, I don't think she killed Jackson or set me up to take the fall. She just wanted to talk to me about us."

Malia set down her tray. "Seriously? You were that blind? Everyone except you knew she had it bad for you. When you came in here for lunch, everyone would watch her try to get your attention. I felt bad for her. Especially after you and Rarity started hanging out."

Archer turned to Rarity. "I'm sorry. I know you kept saying that she was into me, but I thought we were just friends."

Rarity finished her soup and set her spoon down. "The question is, do we believe her story about Jackson? That he asked her to change the meeting place on Monday night?"

Archer leaned back and stared at her. "You're right. Why wouldn't he just tell me? He had days in between. I didn't think about that."

"She said he wanted to work on how to market the blessing ceremony. And I'm starting to wonder who would have told Jackson the story about making his fortunes better?" Rarity turned to Archer. "Why would Jackson even believe it? It was apparent that Eleanor thought he was an idiot for believing that the blessing was anything but a welcoming gesture."

Archer nodded. "Jackson always looked for a shortcut. And he definitely believed in the vortexes around here. He insisted that the gallery needed to be built near one without affecting its magic."

Malia glanced around at her station. "I've got to get busy, but I have an idea. I know a guy who categorizes and identifies vortexes in the area. David even wrote a book about it. He's been doing it for years. I bet Jackson or his people used him to find a vortex where he could build."

After Malia left, Archer whispered, "Vortex hunter? Is that a real job?"

Rarity playfully slapped his arm. "Shut up. She's trying to help. Let's finish lunch, I need to get back to the shop."

"To your job next to the crystal shop. Maybe Sam can help hunt down the vortex sites." Archer took a big bite of his sandwich.

"Oh, you nonbeliever. I'm going to tell Sam you're making fun of her profession." She opened her sandwich and took the last of the turkey out and popped it into her mouth. She was full. The lunch had taken long enough for her body to acknowledge the signs of satiated hunger, something she had been exploring since she moved to Sedona. Listening to what was going on both inside and outside your body was important. She wondered if she had any books on the vortexes. She must. She was in Sedona.

Archer finished his sandwich, then flagged down Malia to take his credit card. As they waited, he leaned into Rarity, laying his head on her shoulder. "If I say I'm sorry, will you not tell Sam? She scares me just a little."

\* \* \* \*

After she returned to the store, she went looking on her Sedona shelf and found a complete guide to Sedona vortexes. The book was written by a local author named David Valles and must have been on Sam's list of books to carry. She sat in the book club area and started reading.

Sam came into the store around three and found her still reading. Shirley had already gone home and Katie was finishing stocking books and making a list of possible book club choices for her two clubs.

"Hey, it looks like it's been a quiet day," Sam said as she sat down next to Rarity. She studied her face. "You look tired. Are you not sleeping?"

"Not well since Friday. I get a few hours, then I lie there awake until I decide to get up and read until I start to fall asleep again." Rarity set the book down after putting a bookmark in to save her place. "Did you close early?"

"Yeah. I've been shortening hours during the week since I'm usually crazy busy on the weekends. Trying to have some of that work-life balance everyone keeps talking about." She was digging in her bag. When she found what she was looking for, she handed Rarity a small velvet bag. "I brought you something."

Rarity opened the bag and took out a silver chain with a cylindrical purple stone on it. "It's beautiful."

"I'm glad you like it," Sam said as she took the necklace and slipped it over Rarity's head. She patted the stone. "That's amethyst. The stone is all about surrounding yourself with possibilities. Its energy holds qualities of purification and protection. I sell a lot of these to help with immune issues, but also to heal addictions."

"I don't think addiction is my problem unless you count coffee." Rarity smiled at her friend. Sam was a true believer in natural healing and had sent her books and charms during her cancer treatment. "But it is pretty."

"Amethyst can also affect our dreams and sleeping, so try wearing the necklace at night or keep it under your pillow for protection." Sam picked up the book. "So why the interest in vortexes?"

Before Rarity could answer, Katie stood in front of them. "That's pretty. My mom wears one all the time. She's convinced it's her lucky stone."

"Your mom's a smart woman," Sam said, giving Rarity a side-eyed glance that screamed "I told you so."

"Sam makes lovely jewelry." Rarity tried to change the subject. "What's up?"

"If you don't need me, I'm going to head back to Flagstaff. I need to make sure that the class fits my schedule. Then once I get everything finalized tomorrow, I'll email you my class schedule. I hope we can still work my hours around classes."

"Of course, we can. Just send me the schedule and also put it on our work calendar. We'll deal with whatever we need to." Rarity hoped that Katie believed her. She didn't need her to push herself too hard and wind up quitting. Katie was great at the store. Rarity would probably lose her once she graduated, but for now, she loved having her here.

"Cool. Thanks. And I'm taking two of the books in the back to read. I'll write reviews this weekend when I have a minute. Once I get back to classes, I'll probably only be able to read one or two books a week." Katie stopped and rubbed Killer's head. "Good night, Dexter. I'll see you Saturday."

After she left, Sam looked over at Killer. "She knows that's not the dog's name, right?"

"He's some sort of serial killer. She likes showing off her knowledge of different killers and changing his name each time she sees him. It's their thing." Rarity smiled over at her dog, who was now watching the front door to see if Katie was coming back. When he decided she wasn't, he curled up into a ball and went back to sleep. She returned to the subject of the book. "Do you know this author?"

"David Valles," Sam responded. "You might have met him. He was probably at Darcy's going away party last spring. Malia hangs out with his group now and then. They go hiking off trail to try to find new vortexes."

*Okay, now she saw the connection.* Rarity rubbed the smooth stone hanging around her neck. "Malia's going to talk to him and see if he 'certified' the vortex by the gallery."

"Since you actually made air quotes around the word *certified*, I'm taking it you don't believe in the power?" Sam held the book close to her chest and watched as Rarity tried to phrase her answer correctly.

"I know there are things that science can't quantify. But vortexes might be one step too far on my belief ladder." She took the book from Sam and stared at the picture of the man who'd written the book. Had she met him? He looked like a lot of other academics on the more esoteric studies side. His hair was just a bit too long, he wore John Lennon–style wire glasses, and he had a bit of a five-o'clock shadow proving he was too cool for an author photo. "He's cute. I can see why Malia hangs with him."

Sam chuckled as she looked over Rarity's shoulder at the photo. "Our Malia is a Rapunzel, just waiting for her prince to save her."

"No, she's not. She's an independent woman who is living her best life. Besides, isn't she dating Dane O'Conner?" Rarity snuck a second peek at the author. "This guy is cute, though."

Sam laughed as she stood. "As an independent woman, I'm heading home. If I don't do laundry, I'll have to wear a cocktail dress to work tomorrow."

Rarity set the book on the table and stood to hug her friend. "Hey, are you dating someone new?"

Sam pulled back from the hug and looked at her. "Is this coming from Drew?"

Rarity shook her head. "It's nothing, just something someone said. And not Drew," she added quickly.

Sam leaned against the fireplace as she looked out the window. "No, I'm not dating anyone. I haven't completely ruled out a relationship with Drew. Things are just complicated right now. We both need some time to heal. We said some horrible things to each other the last time we spoke."

"Do you want another hug? Or a double-date invite?"

Sam smiled and stood up straight. "Neither. So unless you want to do my laundry for me?"

"Go, do your adulting. I'm here for another couple of hours until five. Archer's coming to walk us home." Rarity sat back down and picked up the book. "And I need to understand the power of the vortex."

"Have fun." The bell rang, announcing Sam's departure, and Rarity was alone in her shop.

She looked around the room. Her bookstore. How far she'd come from that late morning in the radiologist's office where the doctor had told her they'd found a lump. She wasn't sure exactly what else she'd said because the ringing in her ears was too loud. When the biopsy had come in, she'd taken the call at work. It was a Friday. After listening to the woman on the phone explaining that she had cancer, Rarity asked what her next step was. She could deal with the next step. Then she'd taken a break and left the building. And called Sam.

One step at a time. One treatment at a time. Now, she was healthy and miles away from that third-floor office painted bright white. Sometimes she wondered if Sedona had drawn her here because of all the colors. Red rocks, deep blue sky. The colors had wiped out the memory of that cold white room. Or did most of the time.

Rarity returned to reading and wondered again if the vortexes had called her to this place along with the colors. She rubbed the stone on her necklace absently as she read, and had finished the book by the time Archer arrived to take her home.

That night Archer made dinner while Rarity swam. They didn't talk about Calliope, or Jackson, or even what was going on in their friends' lives. They just enjoyed being together. Rarity stood up in the middle of the movie that Archer had found and headed to the kitchen. "Do you want some hot cocoa? Or something else?"

"Cocoa will be fine," he answered as he followed her into the kitchen. He'd paused the movie when she'd first stood. He sat on the stool on the island bar and watched her. "It's been a nice night."

She smiled as she used the Keurig to make individual cups of cocoa. She had whipped cream in the fridge that she would put on top. "I know we're ignoring the world tonight, but I don't care. I wanted a night where nothing was wrong. Nobody we know is either dead or being investigated."

"Including me," Archer added and met her gaze.

"Yeah, I guess that's been bothering me more than I've let myself realize. Sam must have realized I wasn't sleeping, so she brought me this." She held up the necklace. "It's supposed to help me mold my own reality out of all the possibilities."

"That sounds nice," he said as he reached for the stone to examine it. "Maybe I need one. Will it help me sleep?"

"I'll let you know in the morning." Rarity switched out the cups and started the second one. She added a heaping serving of whipped cream and sprinkled cinnamon on top of it. Then she handed the cup to Archer. "Served with love."

He stared at the cup, then looked up to meet her gaze. "You're the best, Rarity Cole. I'm so glad we met."

"Yeah, life led me down a crazy path to get here, but I don't think I'd trade any experience because if I did, I might not wind up here. With you." Rarity looked over to where Killer was supposed to be sleeping in his bed. Instead, the Yorkie was watching them to make sure food wasn't coming out of the kitchen. Killer loved food just about as much as he loved Rarity. Sometimes, she thought it was more. She finished putting the toppings on her hot cocoa then held the cup up to Archer for a toast. "Here's to us."

"I'll drink to that."

# Chapter 9

Jonathon showed up on her doorstep first thing on Thursday morning. He held up a bag of what smelled like donuts. "Do you have coffee going?"

She opened the door and let him inside. "The machine's already warmed up. I'm on cup number two. Why are you here this morning?"

"I told Edith I was going to work on my book at the shop. She's heard me brag about how much work I got done the last time I was here. At home, it seems like I'm always standing up in the middle of a thought and going to clean the basement. Or clean out gutters. Or wash the car."

"You need discipline," Rarity said. She pulled out napkins and Jonathon set donuts out on the table like they were plates. Rarity started a cup of coffee for him. "Now, don't be thinking I know anything about writing a book, but I brought in a local author last month for a talk and she said to treat it like a job. Maybe working somewhere else kicks in that 'job' mentality you can't find at home."

Jonathon took a bite of one of the donuts, then waved it at her. "You are a wise woman, Rarity. I wish my son had fallen for you rather than your friend Sam."

Rarity turned away and watched the coffee finish, hoping her cheeks wouldn't be flushed when she turned back. Drew had tried to see if there was any spark between them, but she'd never felt more than friendship. With Archer, sparks flew hot and fast between the two of them. "Sam's just trying to get past what happened. We actually talked yesterday about Drew, and she's not saying no."

Jonathon took his cup from her. "She's just not saying yes right now. I'm an old man. I'd like to see more grandchildren around the Christmas tree before I'm gone."

"You really know how to layer on the guilt. No wonder Drew doesn't like you visiting." She sat down at the table and took a bite of the donut. "These are really good. But I'll be on a sugar high until lunch."

"Well, now that we got that subject off the table, what did you find out about the murder?" Jonathon pulled out his murder notebook with his name on the front that Shirley had refilled and handed out on Tuesday. "Did Calliope set up Archer to take the fall?"

Rarity thought about yesterday's luncheon. The woman was clearly in love with Archer. But like Drew's feelings toward her, it was one-sided. "I don't think so. But it's not clear yet." She went on to tell him what Archer had told her about Calliope wanting to talk to him and how she'd admitted she'd asked Jackson to let her tell Archer about the change of plans for Saturday's hike. "But I think it was because she needed an excuse to talk to him."

"What does Archer say?"

"He was oblivious. He thought they were friends. They both love hiking. And she knew he was dating me. He assumed that would be enough to keep them in the friend zone." Rarity sipped her coffee, thinking about Calliope's face yesterday. "He assigned Jack to be her hiking contact from now on. Maybe that will help. Except it's clear that Jack has a crush on her. Everyone has bad timing."

"Dating was so much easier in my day. You found someone in high school or college that you clicked with, and you got married. By the time you even questioned if you were in the right spot, you had three or five kids and had to stay anyway. Life was simpler." He glanced at his watch. "Shall we take these coffees and the rest of the donuts to go? I'd hate for you to miss customers because you're chatting with an old geezer."

"Let me pack my tote and get Killer ready. Can you grab travel mugs from the cabinet over the coffee machine and make two fresh cups? There are baggies in the drawer on the island for the donuts."

"Go get ready. I'll get our treats going."

Terrance was on his porch when they walked by and Jonathon waved at the retired naval man. "I'm glad you have good neighbors. That way I don't worry when we're home in Tucson."

"I'm a grown woman," Rarity reminded him.

Jonathon shrugged. "You're part of our pack now. You'll always be worried about."

Rarity realized she didn't mind that. Not at all.

Once they were at the shop, the day seemed to fly by. Jonathon ran to the Garnet and grabbed them lunch. Shirley had the day off so it was just Rarity at the register, but she'd run this business all alone for years now. She could do it for one day. Especially if she had Jonathon around, looking for excuses to not write.

When five o'clock came, he closed up his laptop. "I've written more today than I did all last week."

"I'm surprised," Rarity said from the counter, where she was closing up the register. "You were up and down and pacing a lot."

"It's part of my process. I get stiff sitting so much. So thank you and I'll be back tomorrow unless Edith needs me to drive her somewhere."

The bell over the front door sounded, and Edith along with Archer came inside. "I heard that. I'll have you know that I'm going to Flagstaff with the girls tomorrow so you can come and write all you want. Unless Rarity doesn't want you hanging around, that is." Edith walked over and gave her a hug. "How are you, my dear?"

"I'm good. Better today since I actually got a good night's sleep." She kissed Archer. "We were just closing up so you're right on time."

"Actually, Jack and I have a presentation to the men's group at the local church. They want to set up a hike for their teen group. I forgot about it until today when Jack came to work." He made a face. "I came to walk you home, though."

"Why don't you come to dinner with us?" Edith squeezed Rarity's arm. "It's been a while since we caught up or have even seen each other. I'd love to hear how everything's going."

"I'd have to take Killer," Rarity started but Archer held up his hand.

"I'll run Killer home. Jack's not expecting me for a few minutes anyway since he knew I wanted to walk you home. You go with Jonathon and Edith for dinner." He kissed her on the cheek. "If you want to, that is."

"Are you kidding? I haven't even seen any recent pictures of the grandbaby." Rarity tucked her laptop and notebook into her tote. "And, as Sam reminded me the other day, I need to do laundry tonight."

"Sam's always thinking of others," Edith said, glancing over toward where Sam's shop sat. "Maybe she'd want to come to dinner too?"

"I'll call her." Rarity didn't think she'd show, but it didn't hurt to ask.

Sam turned down the invitation. Which didn't surprise Rarity.

Edith, on the other hand, wasn't giving up. As soon as they got to the restaurant, she pulled out her day planner and made a note. "I'll just stop by Sam's house in the morning with donuts. Jonathon's already seen her at your crime-fighting book club meeting. I'm heading home on Monday."

"Oh, then I'm glad I got to spend time with both of you before you leave." Rarity set the menu aside. It was Thursday, so she was having the special, Southwestern chicken. She could tell she was a regular now because she knew the menu by heart and knew most of the specials. In St. Louis, she'd gone to the same lunch spot for years. And special occasion dinners were always at a local steak house. She tended to know what she liked.

Jonathon leaned closer. "I'm staying around. I should have some new information for Tuesday night."

Edith sighed. "I caught him trying to access Drew's home computer this morning. I don't know what's got him so riled up, but I'm not sticking around to see Drew putting his dad in jail for obstruction."

"I'm not going to jail. Drew loves me too much." Jonathon kissed his wife's cheek. "Don't worry."

Edith met Rarity's gaze, "You see he didn't deny what he was doing, just the outcome. I hope Archer doesn't learn these husband communication tricks too quickly."

Rarity felt the heat warm her face. They hadn't really talked about marriage, but if she was going to take the plunge, she hoped she and Archer would be as happy as the couple sitting at her table.

"You made her blush, sweetheart," Jonathon said, but then he turned to the waitress, whose name was Candice. "I think we're all ready to order and this will be one check. I'm paying the bill, so don't let that one trick you."

"Works for me." Candice grinned at Jonathon. "You just missed Malia, Rarity. She's heading out with some group to test a vortex tonight. Something about a full moon."

Rarity saw Candice roll her eyes. "She's supposed to be at the shop on Saturday, I'll have to ask her how it went."

"I think David just uses the group events to sell books. Although I did hear he was going to give a talk at the university on Sunday night. I bet you'll be able to pick up his book on the subject for the low price of thirty-two dollars." Candice finished taking their orders and left the table.

Edith excused herself to go talk to a friend who'd just walked in.

Rarity sipped her wine. Then she asked, "Do you believe in vortexes?"

Jonathon straightened his silverware while he responded. "I know that there are places of power on this earth. Good or bad, you can feel the energy sometimes. What about you?"

"Valles makes a solid argument. Yes, I read his book. Sam asked me to stock it for the crystal shop referrals. I know I've felt that energy you talk about. But I think there are too many here in Sedona for all of them to be real."

"Especially for one to be found on the land Jackson got for a song because you couldn't build anything residential on it?" Jonathon looked around the room. "I got on the tax record site earlier today when I was taking a break."

"It was zoned commercial?" Rarity reached for a roll and buttered it while they were talking. She was starving and this dinner was so much better than soup and bread at home.

Jonathon shook his head as he watched his wife walk back to the table. "Industrial. Jackson talked the county commissioners into changing the zoning for him. He made a few enemies who were trying to set up some sort of a technological park in that area."

"Interesting, do you think—" Rarity didn't get to finish the question as Jonathon stood and waited for his wife to sit down. He shook his head and promptly changed the subject.

"Edith and I are considering getting a dog. Tell her how much Killer has changed your life. I need some support here." Jonathon smiled at his wife.

"Now, dear, you don't need to get Rarity involved in our squabbles." Edith tucked a book into her purse as she sat down. "But since you did, he wants a husky. Can you imagine me walking a hundred-pound dog while he's up here playing cop with Drew and your book club?"

Rarity saw how Edith's use of the word playing had wounded Jonathon. But he brushed it off. "Huskies are very loyal and protective. I'd feel better if you had something that could protect you if I was up here visiting with Drew."

Candice delivering their food saved Rarity from needing to take sides. As they were leaving the restaurant, Gay Zelda, or Madame Zelda to her clients, walked in the door with a young brunette who Rarity assumed was her daughter, Heather.

Edith hugged Gay and then Heather. "I'm so glad to see both of you. I'm only in town for a few days."

"Heather came into town to get me out of the house. I've been a little reluctant to be out in the normal world for the last couple of weeks," Gay explained to Edith.

"Mom thinks something bad is going to happen at the vortexes and she doesn't want to run into someone who might be hurt later." Heather met Rarity's gaze. "Sometimes she lets the visions take over her life."

"The visions are my life," Gay said in a low tone. "Anyway, we're getting dinner. Are you coming or going?"

"We just finished," Rarity said. And the thought followed that if she could really tell the future, she should have known that.

Gay's eyes turned a dark brown. "I did know, Rarity. I was being polite. Much like you in just thinking the thought rather than saying it."

"Mom," Heather warned, and took her arm, but Gay shook her off and focused on Rarity.

"Come see me tomorrow when Shirley arrives at the bookstore. We need to talk." Gay met Rarity's gaze with an intensity she hadn't seen before.

The moment broke as the hostess held out the menus. "If you'll follow me."

Outside, Jonathon turned to Rarity. "What was that about?"

"I'm not exactly sure," Rarity responded, looking back at the restaurant. She could see Gay and Heather at a table by the window. Gay was still watching her. She turned back to Jonathon and Edith. "I guess I'm getting my fortune told tomorrow. Thank you for dinner. It was so nice to see you."

"I'll be over at ten. Edith and her girls are going antique shopping." Jonathon nodded to his car parked across the street. "Can we drive you home?"

Rarity looked up at the full moon and shook her head. "I think I'm going to try to walk off some of this dinner. Thank you again, and Edith, I hope I see you again before you leave on Monday."

"I'm coming to the shop on Saturday to help stuff the backpacks," Edith said as she kissed Rarity's cheek. "I love back-to-school shopping."

Jonathon gave Rarity a hug. "She bought me ten new spiral notebooks and some index cards. And two sets of pens. I think I'm in love."

Edith swatted his arm. "You better still be. Two kids and almost forty years of marriage and he gets excited about some new writing supplies."

"You knew I would, that's why you bought them. That's true love." He nodded to Rarity. "I'll see you in the morning."

As Rarity started walking home, she wondered if Drew was behind Jonathon hanging out at the bookstore. Did he think she was in danger for some reason? She pushed the question away. If he did, Jonathon wouldn't have let her walk home by herself.

She loved being able to walk to work, to dinner, and basically anywhere she wanted to go here in Sedona. There was even a small market on Main Street where she could get milk, bread, or eggs if she needed them. She still did her major shopping in Flagstaff, but in a pinch, she could get everything she needed without even starting her car.

She heard someone calling her name and saw Terrance coming up behind her from town. They were almost at their section of the street. She waited for him to catch up. "What has you out and about tonight?"

"I met some of the guys for a drink. I thought I saw you in front of me, but I wasn't sure until you turned back there." He fell into step next to her. "How was work? Where's the little guy?"

"Archer took Killer home for me so I could have dinner with Jonathon and Edith." Rarity let her shoulders down. If Terrance had been assigned the task of watching her, he would have known about her plans. Maybe she was just being a little paranoid.

"That must have been nice. I don't know Jonathon or Edith well. I guess having a son who's in the police force tends to limit your circle of friends. Jonathon came to a neighborhood watch meeting last year before they moved." He paused at the intersection of his driveway and the sidewalk. "But he seems to be around a lot. Shirley says he's helping with your sleuthing thing."

"He's part of the Scooby Doo Crew as Drew would call us." Rarity yawned as she stood with him. "I'm beat, so I better go take care of Killer. He's going to be mad enough without him hearing me talking to you outside when he's stuck in the house."

"He likes being with you." Terrance started walking up the driveway. "Maybe I should get a dog so I don't keep borrowing yours."

# Chapter 10

Friday morning, Rarity decided to spend some time updating her murder book. She'd be busy this weekend with the backpack project and Katie's high school book club. Several of the kids had parents who showed up to drop their kids off, then strolled through the bookstore and bought something that they took over to the coffee shop to read while they waited. It was like a parental time-out corner over there. At least that's what Shirley had called it one day when she'd run over for coffee and treats for the staff.

Rarity was happy that her events brought customers into town and those customers also bought books. It helped her bottom line as well as the coffee shop and the Garnet, since a lot of people stopped there for lunch after the book club was over. Sam said she'd even seen an increase in walk-in traffic at her crystal shop during and after a book club event.

As she tried to focus on the murder book, her mind went back to the discussion with Gay last night. She'd been less than coherent. Was there something going on with the woman that Heather hadn't wanted them to know? But why would she allow her to work if she wasn't feeling her best?

All Rarity knew was as soon as Shirley arrived, she was going over to see what was on Madame Zelda's mind. And to see if it had anything to do with Jackson's death.

She wrote down a list of questions and included an asterisk near Malia's name. Maybe she'd know more about the gallery's vortex and its validity. If Jackson had faked the vortex to bring people to the gallery and someone who believed in vortex lore had found out, would that be enough to want Jackson dead? It was a valid question.

That was the reason she liked doing these murder club investigations. Because sometimes, the questions they asked themselves, the police hadn't considered. Like, were vortexes real?

As she thought about the place where Jackson was killed, she wondered if Drew would tell her anything about the means of death. She dialed his number. He didn't answer before his voice mail picked up. Rarity started to leave him a message, then saw he was calling her back. She picked up the call and said, "Good morning, Drew."

"No, I don't know where my dad or mom are and you just interrupted my first long shower alone in my house for days." He shut a door behind him. "What do you need, Rarity?"

"I'm still thinking about that long shower," she teased, but then added, "Kidding. Anyway, was Jackson killed by the arrow or the drug?"

She heard the sigh. "Despite my better judgment, I'm going to try to answer that question. The coroner said it was six of one, half dozen of the other. If the arrow hadn't caused him to bleed out, the drug would have stopped his breathing about the same time. Why?"

"It all seems like overkill. The method and causes of death. The setting. Having Archer be the person who found him. Especially if they knew about Archer's history with Jackson." Rarity listed off the things that were bothering her.

"You mean about Archer's sister or how Jackson tried to get Archer kicked out of college by stashing drugs in his room?" When Rarity didn't respond, Drew let out one word. "Crap."

"Bingo. I didn't know about the second incident," Rarity responded. She thought she and Archer really needed to have a long talk about all the possible hurdles in their relationship. Including not telling her things. "Anyway, especially knowing that, don't you think it's overkill?"

"I agree with you. And if the cameras hadn't been turned off, this investigation would be done and Archer cleared of the murder. But they were off." Drew paused. "Rarity, I wasn't going to tell you this, but Archer was seen near the security room on Monday at that party. Tell me he was with you the entire time you were there."

"He was with me," Rarity said.

Drew slapped something loud. "I knew it. Thank you for helping me keep my friend out of jail for something he didn't do."

"Except," Rarity started. "Drew, he left me for about ten minutes. I was over by the Civil War painting, and he left for a few minutes. I thought it was a trip to the restroom, but I found out that he met Calliope during that time. And he didn't want me to know they were talking."

"You know this or you suspect that's why?"

"We talked a couple of days ago with Calliope." Rarity hated airing their dirty laundry, even in front of Drew. "He knew I didn't trust her. And she admitted over lunch that she'd been trying to get him back. He was clueless. He even told her there was no back because they'd never been an item. She was pretty upset."

"When was this?"

Rarity told him the details, then when she was done, she asked, "You don't really think Archer did this, do you? He doesn't hold grudges. We both know that."

"I know, Rarity. I'm just trying to find things I can prove." He had put her on speaker and she could hear him moving around his house. "I've got to get ready for work. Tell my dad hi when you see him. I hear your dinner with the folks was nice. They really like you."

"I think they miss talking with Sam," Rarity admitted. They liked Rarity but they had assumed Sam was eventually going to be part of their family.

There was a long pause on the line. Then he said, "I miss talking to Sam too. I've got to go."

The bell over the door rang as Shirley and Jonathon walked in together. He had four coffees and Shirley had a bag of treats. Rarity groaned. She was going to have to do more than swim and walk to get rid of all the sweet-treat calories she'd been eating the last few days.

Stress eating. It wasn't a spectator sport.

"What's wrong?" Jonathon asked after one look at Rarity's face.

"Nothing. Your son says hi. Is Edith over at Sam's shop?" Rarity took a sip of the coffee and felt rejuvenated. It was funny how fast it helped. Of course, it could all be a placebo effect.

"We stopped there first with more coffee and treats. Your coffee shop owner loves me and my wallet today." Jonathon took off his shoulder tote and set it on the table. "You're sure you're okay? Did Drew say something?"

"Drew says a lot of things. But nothing that upset me." Rarity walked around the counter. "Shirley, Katie's not coming in today so can you help me by setting up a staging area in the kitchen for the backpack stuffing project? And maybe Jonathon can help you pull out an extra table from storage. I think we'll need more working room. We've got a lot of people coming to help."

"I can do that. Where are you going?" Shirley asked as Rarity walked to the doorway.

Rarity checked that Killer was still asleep in his bed. "I'm getting my tea leaves read."

Jonathon chuckled. "I don't think Gay's talents lie in that type of fortune-telling."

"Whatever floats her boat." Rarity opened the door. "If I'm not back in two hours, send the cops in to find me."

"Drama queen," Shirley called after her. "Besides, I'd just send Jonathon. That way we save our tax dollars."

Madame Zelda's shop was in the building next door. The bookstore was bookended by the fortune-teller's shop and Sam's crystal shop. Rarity should put a sign on her door saying that she had books on both topics. Maybe she could get walk-in traffic from both stores.

Rarity had a large selection of books in the store on alternative healing options. Personally, she still felt the typical Western medicine tools and treatments had saved her life during her cancer bout, but some people wanted to have options. And with the chemo treatment being so toxic, Rarity couldn't argue with their wishes. She played with the stone around her neck. She had been sleeping better since Sam had given her the necklace, but she didn't know exactly why. Had her fear just run its course, or was the stone actually helpful? She decided to give it the benefit of the doubt. Just like she would Madame Zelda.

The bells over her doorway tinkled like a cascading waterfall. Rarity wondered where she got the melodic chime. She'd have to ask her a different time. Today she was here to see what Madame Zelda felt a need to tell her. "Hello? Madame Zelda?"

Even though Rarity knew her real name, in the woman's workplace, her theatre, so to speak, it seemed disrespectful to pull off the veil and show her true face. "Hello?"

No answer. Rarity walked around the small shop, looking at charms and necklaces and bottles of moon dust and dried rosemary. Maybe she was too early? But the front door had been unlocked and the window sign turned to Open. A pit was forming in Rarity's stomach. "Madame Zelda? Gay? Where are you?"

She turned toward the doorway that led customers to the reading room. And there, in the hallway, she saw what looked like Madame Zelda's feet sticking out of a doorway. She ran to the room, wishing she'd brought her cell phone rather than leave it on her register. When Rarity touched her arm, Madame Zelda groaned and looked at her. Then she grabbed Rarity's arm tightly.

"Things aren't what they seem. Be careful in the light of the moon." Madame Zelda slumped back and closed her eyes.

Rarity felt the woman's wrist, then realized she didn't know what she was looking for. She looked around and found a cordless landline. She dialed 911 as she returned to kneel by Madame Zelda, watching the woman's chest for movement. She was breathing. That was good. From what Rarity could see, it looked like the fortune-teller only had a head wound, as blood seeped out from under her head wrap.

"911. What's your emergency?" a female voice crisply asked.

"Please send an ambulance to Madame Zelda's Fortune Telling shop. She's been hurt but she's alive." Rarity tried to speak slowly but she felt like she was screaming.

The voice on the other end of the call verified the address and Rarity tried to focus. "Yeah, I think that's it. The street number sounds right. It's right next to my shop, The Next Chapter. The bookstore? Do you want me to go outside and check for the street numbers?"

"No, just stay with Ms. Zelda. Is this Rarity Cole?" the voice asked her.

Rarity blinked, surprised at being called by name. "Yes."

"I visit your bookstore often. Jennifer Baker, I read a lot of historical romance." The woman, Jennifer, had a really calm voice.

Rarity tried to picture her. Dark hair, a cute smile, and short. She'd always come in shorts and a tank top and they never talked about work. "I remember you. Last time you were in, we discussed how there couldn't be so many dukes in England but you said you didn't care. You loved reading the genre."

"That's me. In love with love. So, Rarity, tell me what happened this morning. How did you find Ms. Zelda?"

Rarity realized Jennifer had been trying to calm her down, talking about their common love of books. She told Jennifer about being asked to visit the shop this morning. And that the door was open but no one was in the shop, until she went back to the reading room where she saw Madame Zelda's legs and feet sticking out into the hallway. "Then she spoke to me."

"What did she say?" Jennifer asked.

Embarrassed, Rarity recited Madame Zelda's warning to her. "I'm not even sure she knew it was me."

"Well, I'd say be careful walking at night," Jennifer responded. "The ambulance should be pulling up now. Do you hear or see them?"

"Sedona Emergency Services," a man's voice called out as the door banged open.

Rarity stepped out of the hallway and waved them toward Madame Zelda. "Over here, she's in the reading room."

She moved back to let the EMTs into the small hallway. The gurney just barely fit and Rarity tried to stay out of their way. She realized that Jennifer was still on the phone. "They're here. Should I leave?"

"Why don't you stay on the phone with me until they leave? They may want to talk to you first." Jennifer paused. "Drew Anderson said to tell you he'd be there soon."

Rarity nodded and went over to a small table where she could see the patio between this building and the bookstore. Jonathon stood out in front, watching the building. He saw her and waved. She waved back, holding up a finger to tell him she'd be back in a few minutes. He saw she was on the phone and nodded, then he walked toward the curb. Rarity moved so she could see better and saw Drew's truck pull up. "He's here. I'll let you go and I'll meet Drew outside. That way if there's something here, I'm not contaminating the scene any more."

"Probably a good idea. Make sure to take care of yourself. Finding someone who needs help can drain your own energy." Jennifer said goodbye and hung up.

Rarity put the phone back on the cradle by the register and went to meet Drew and Jonathon.

"What happened?" Drew asked as soon as she walked out the door.

She shrugged and rubbed her arms. "I don't know. We ran into Madame Zelda, Gay, last night at the Garnet. She asked me to come by when Shirley got here. That she had something to tell me." She met Jonathon's gaze.

"That's right. Your mom and I were there with Rarity when Gay and Heather came up to us as we were leaving. Gay didn't look good, but Heather thought it was just she'd been housebound for too long." Jonathon rubbed Rarity's shoulder. "Are you okay?"

His hand felt so strong on her arm. Like he was taking away some of the fear. She smiled, grateful for the calming influence. "I'm fine. I think. Jennifer said it might affect me, just to find Gay like that. Anyway, this morning, after Shirley and Jonathon arrived, I ran over to see what she wanted and found her on the floor. She must have fallen and hit her head. Or maybe someone hit her. I don't know. She told me that things weren't what they seemed and that the moonlight was dangerous. Or something like that. Then she blacked out. I need coffee. And sugar."

"And you probably need to sit down." Drew nodded to his father. "Take her back to the bookstore. I'll be over after I see what's going on."

Drew rubbed Rarity's back. "It's going to be okay."

She nodded, then let Jonathon lead her back to the bookstore. She was going to be okay, but what about Madame Zelda? The woman must be in her late sixties. Would a crack on the head kill her? Had she fallen? Or had someone attacked her? One answer made Rarity look like a gift from the universe, saving the woman after a random event. The other made Rarity a possible suspect in her attack.

She sank into the couch as Shirley brought her the cup of coffee she'd left on the counter. Killer jumped up and curled on her lap, watching her face to make sure his friend was okay. "I'm not the one who got hurt. I shouldn't be upset."

"You found her and called 911. That's traumatic." Jonathon held out a bear claw. "Eat some sugar. You'll feel better."

"Do you feel like talking?" Shirley asked.

When Rarity shook her head, Jonathon told Shirley what she'd told him and Drew. He nodded to the window. "The ambulance just left."

"Someone should call Heather, her daughter," Rarity said.

Shirley jumped up. "I can do that. You just sit there and relax. I'll handle the store, too. I need to keep busy."

Rarity sipped her coffee and ate all of the pastry before the bell over the door announced Drew's arrival.

He came over and sat across from Rarity. "How are you?"

"Better than Madame Zelda. Tell me she fell." Rarity leaned forward, watching his face.

He shrugged. "I don't know what happened. Maybe the doctor can tell us more when they examine her. Right now, I've locked up the store and put a sign on the door." He handed her a key on a string. "I told Heather that she could come get this as soon as she was free. Can you hold it for her?"

"Of course." Rarity took the key and thought about the homeless people she'd seen on the streets of Flagstaff. Sedona hadn't had much of an influx yet. Mostly because the shops were focused on tourists and the restaurants catered to either townsfolk or the tourist craze. Drew had talked about chasing people out of the park when they tried to set up a tent or shelter. "What does your gut tell you?"

He sighed and looked out the window. "I want it to be a fall. It would make everything easier. But I don't think so. Now, we need to find out if she was just robbed or maybe surprised by a robber, or if something else is going on. We've already had one murder in town this week. It would be a huge coincidence if this wasn't related. You don't know what she wanted to talk to you about?"

Rarity shook her head. "It could have been nothing. Or about the backpack project. I don't know. And what she did tell me didn't really clear the air. 'Nothing is what it seems.' Did she mean Jackson's murder or something else? All I know is my head's killing me."

"Why don't you go home?" Drew looked at Jonathon and Shirley. "They can keep the bookstore open."

"We've got a big day tomorrow." Rarity rubbed Killer's head. "Besides, if I'm home alone, I'm just going to worry. I'm going to stay and work. Work helps everything."

"You sound like my dad," Drew mumbled, glancing over to see if Jonathon had heard him.

"Watch it, kid," Jonathon teased. "Besides, I've been retired for two years now. Work is not my go-to anymore."

"Except now you're writing a book and you've drunk the Kool-Aid on how to be an author. Don't think I don't know where you go every Wednesday night when you're in town. I'm pretty sure you have a group in Tucson now too." Drew stood and faced his father.

"I didn't think you knew." Jonathon stared at his son.

Drew laughed and slapped him on the back. "I'm a detective, Dad. I put things together. And before you ask, Mom knows as well. She's just waiting for you to break the news to her. But she doesn't care. It keeps you busy and out of her hair."

"Well, I guess I wasn't as stealthy as I thought." Jonathon looked at Rarity. "You're staying around?"

When she nodded, he turned and sat down at the table. "Then I better get my words in before something else distracts me."

# Chapter 11

Saturday morning, Rarity was ready for the back-to-school backpack project to be over, but she knew that today was going to be a long day. All day Friday, people had stopped by the store to drop off bags, supplies, and money. And to ask what was going on with Madame Zelda. Word must have gotten around that Rarity had been the one to find her. Heather had called from the hospital and told them that her mom was going to be okay and released later that day. She thanked Rarity for finding her.

Rarity wasn't sure it was all over, but at least on Monday afternoon, when Staci, Amy, and she went to the elementary school to drop off the backpacks, one thing would be off her plate. With Katie going back to school full-time, she needed one less worry.

Archer had come over early to make breakfast since he'd been out on a hike until late afternoon the day before. He hadn't heard about Madame Zelda until he'd called Drew. By that time, Rarity was already tucked into bed with a book and a cup of tea. Killer was curled on her feet when Archer called. The dog kept giving her dirty looks when she moved. Archer told her he'd come and make her breakfast before her big day at work.

He'd arrived before she'd gotten in the pool, but he didn't mind if she swam while he cooked. At least she hoped he didn't, because she needed the stress release that the swim would give her. Especially after yesterday.

Drying her hair with a towel after getting out of the pool, she sat in the kitchen, drinking coffee and watching him finish cooking the bacon. "Did Drew say anything about Madame Zelda when you called him last night? Did she remember anything? I forgot to ask."

"She can't remember what happened. She remembers that you were coming over and that she had two readings on Friday that she'll have to reschedule, but she said she was sweeping the shop floor, then the next thing she knew she was in a hospital bed." He took the bacon out of the pan and put two slices on each plate along with a waffle with melting butter. He took the plates over to the table, then turned back to get the warm syrup from the microwave. "So neither one of you is a good witness."

She poured syrup over her waffle, then took a bite. "This is really good, thank you."

"You're welcome. I've got a hike that starts at ten, but I can come over to the bookstore to help after I get back." He waved a slice of crisp bacon at her. "And we're either grabbing takeout for dinner or eating out. Your choice."

"Neither. Let me cook. I've been wanting to try this Korean fried chicken dish and I bought all the spices for it last week." She finished off the bacon. "Unless you really want to eat at the Garnet."

"Nope, I'd love to be home. Arizona's playing tonight." He shrugged. "I just want you to take care of yourself."

"Football, I get it. I'm surprised you said you'd go shopping tomorrow for the rest of the supplies." Rarity finished her breakfast and went to refill her coffee.

"The Cowboys don't play until the late game. We have plenty of time." He picked up the plates and looked at the clock. "Is the dishwasher empty?"

"Yes, but you can leave those in the sink. I'll clean up when I get home." Rarity headed to the bedroom.

"You're kidding, right? My mother would shoot me if I left dishes in the sink." Archer started the water running. "I'll get everything in the dishwasher and run it. Go get ready and I'll walk you to the shop."

When they arrived at the bookstore, Archer kissed her at the doorway, then turned to the sidewalk. "Make sure you delete that from your security feed. I don't want people watching us on some sort of kiss cam."

Rarity waved goodbye, then she and Killer went inside and set up the store for opening at nine. She went into the security closet and ran the feed backward for a few minutes. She saw their kiss. Then she froze the feed after he'd walked away. Over her shoulder, she could see Madame Zelda's front door.

She still had ten minutes before she was supposed to open the shop, so she carefully reversed the security feed. When she saw Drew at the front door, she slowed down the recording until she saw herself go into the fortune-teller's shop. Then she slowly reversed. Someone tall, dressed all in black, left the shop a few minutes earlier. And they had something in their hand. She let it run backward until she saw Madame Zelda enter her shop yesterday.

Then she called Drew. "Can you come over now?"

"I'm not even dressed," he muttered, but she could hear him moving around. "Where's here and why am I coming over?"

"My security camera has a view of Madame Zelda's front door." She paused for effect. "I wasn't the only one to visit her yesterday."

\* \* \* \*

Drew got in and out of the shop before Katie or Shirley arrived. He sent himself a download of yesterday's feed and as far back as the backups went, which was almost a month. "If he or she came before, maybe I can identify them from their shape on the recordings." He hugged her before he left. "Thank you. I know I keep telling you to stay out of investigations, but this was a smart find. I had people checking the street cams, but I didn't realize your security camera covered that view. I should have at least checked."

She shrugged. "I didn't think about it until Archer told me to erase the kiss he gave me outside the door. I knew he was kidding, but then I got to wondering if the security camera would have even picked it up. So I checked and saw Madame Zelda's entrance."

"Now if I could just figure out why the cameras at the gallery were turned off, it would at least point me in some direction." Drew hesitated, then asked. "Does your group have any theories?"

"It almost killed you to ask that, didn't it?" Rarity teased. But she was going to have to let him down. "Not yet. Malia's tracking down vortex certifications. Other than that, we're kind of lost. The problem is Archer has all this history with Jackson, but we know he didn't kill the guy."

"Yeah, that's the problem." He paused at the door. "I'm going back to grab the donations from the station for the backpack project. If I can't get them here by ten, I'll send someone down with them. If you don't see anyone doing a drop-off, call the station and remind me."

"Sounds good. We'll get those kids ready for school, no matter who's trying to stand in our way." Rarity waved as he got into his truck. She saw Shirley coming down the sidewalk and she had coffee. "I'm going to have to pay you back for this someday."

"Don't worry about it, the bookstore is buying. Just tell me if I'm charging too much on your account." She handed her a to-go cup. "I brought one for Katie too. Is she here yet?"

Rarity glanced at her watch. "Not yet, but she has ten minutes still. And traffic might be an issue from Flagstaff."

"Did Drew drop off the donations from the station?" Shirley asked as she tucked her tote bag under the counter.

"No, he was here to get a copy of our security feed. Someone went into and left Madame Zelda's before I did yesterday." Rarity sipped her coffee.

"And the feed caught it?" Shirley looked back at the entrance. "I didn't realize the camera picked up all of that."

"Drew didn't either. He has people checking out the street cams, but he didn't check this. I found it this morning." Rarity grinned. "Archer was worried we were showing too much PDA on the street."

"PDA?" Shirley asked.

Rarity booted up her laptop and checked their online sales channel to see if they needed to mail out any books. "Public displays of affection. I really pushed my comfort zone in that area on that Monday at the gallery when we ran into Calliope. I guess I was feeling a little jealous."

"I don't understand why everything has to be shortened down to just initials nowadays. I saw some singer named their kid with initials. And someone else used words to name a child that more accurately described a job. What's wrong with full, traditional names? Those kids are going to be teased at school." Shirley carried a box of donations back to the break room where they'd set up the backpack station.

"I'm pretty sure there have been many names that people considered weird over the years including my own." Rarity thought there was a certain megastar singer who had named his son Blanket back in the day. She decided not to bring it up. "Many authors use initials to hide their gender when they're writing in a genre that has predominantly either male or female authors."

Shirley came back out and grabbed another box of supplies. "I guess you're right. But it's just weird. What's wrong with a nice Meg or Beth? Or Nick or Henry for a boy?"

"You need to stop reading your junk mail in your email account. Or is it the magazines on the checkout line?" Rarity asked as she scanned through her own promotions tab, deleting as she went.

"Both, I'm afraid. I'll sit down just to check email and then I'll look up and an hour has gone, just like that." Shirley glanced around the counter area. "Any more bags or boxes in here?"

"Not yet. I've had some emails saying they'll be dropped off before noon, so keep an eye out. The high school book club starts at one." Rarity stood and looked at the setup. "Do we have enough to start working on them?"

"We do, but if there's not anything to do when Amy and Staci arrive, we'll be in trouble for starting early. I'm sure we'll be done by three at the latest, even if we start right at noon." Rarity picked up a pink sparkly backpack from one of the boxes. "This is cute. My backpack was always black, but I put pins and badges on it to brighten it up. And I got a BeDazzler one year for Christmas so that helped."

"I can't see you with a BeDazzler. You're so reserved." Shirley picked up a blue plaid backpack. "This one's cute and classy."

"I've become more of a class act since high school." Rarity looked up when the bell rang and saw Katie hurrying in with a box. "Anything in your car we need to help with?"

Katie kicked the door shut behind her. "Nope, I've got it all. And locked my car with my remote. I'm getting great at multitasking."

The chaos started at eleven forty-five.

By three, the backpacks were all lined up against the wall, and the ones that were still missing something had a sheet of paper with the item or items listed on it taped to the front. Staci went around and wrote down all the missing supplies on a sheet of paper. She took the list to Rarity. She was just finishing up at the register with the high school group as they were buying next month's book along with the second and sometimes third book in the series from this month's chat.

"Here's what we're missing. Do you have enough actual money to buy the supplies to finish these bags?" Staci frowned at the list as she held it out.

Rarity handed the receipt and the three books she'd bought to the last girl in line. Teenagers had a lot more cash than she did back in the day. It was going to be a really good week for the bookstore. "Let me see." She reached for the list and reviewed it. "I think we'll be fine. And Miss Christy told me that she'll use any leftover donations to fill in what each specific class requested. Thank goodness we didn't have to personalize each backpack. We'd still be here working to get these together."

"Miss Christy says that we're helping out a lot of families who have more than one kid and can't afford all the school supplies." Amy stood next to Staci, a cookie in her hand. Shirley had brought some in for the backpack party. Her eyes widened as she had a thought. "We should do this every year."

"Hold on," Rarity laughed. "Let's not get carried away. We'll meet in May next year and see if you two want to spearhead this project again. I'm keeping a folder with all the things we did this year. Maybe each of you could make me a list of the things that went right and what didn't work. And what ideas you have for next year if we do it again."

Amy nodded. "I'll go get started now. My mom's picking me up at four. What time do you want to drop off bags on Monday?"

"I'm thinking we'll meet here at ten? Then I'll take you both to lunch, my treat to thank you." Rarity smiled at the two girls. Staci should get a medal for putting up with the overly energetic Amy. But Amy did a lot of work to make sure this went smoothly. And it was originally her idea.

"That sounds great." Staci grinned as Amy ran over to a table and climbed up on a chair to make her list. "I'll bring you my list on Monday. I'm meeting some friends who were at the book club for ice cream over at the Garnet. I loved next month's book and need to talk to someone about it."

Rarity pulled a bag out from under the counter. "Well, here's the rest of the series and the following month's book. My treat for all the work you did on the backpack project."

Staci took the bag and looked inside. "Rarity, this is amazing. Thank you. Did Amy—"

Before she could ask the question, Rarity answered. "Yes, I have a bag for Amy, but I thought I'd wait to give it to her until after I got her list. She can be distracted easily."

Staci laughed. "That is so true. Thanks again, Rarity."

Rarity found herself in a bear hug from the teenager. She patted her back. "You guys did all the work. I was just out here selling books."

"I know that's not true, but thanks. My mom says I can put this on my college applications. Can I use you as a reference?"

"Of course." Rarity watched the girl head to the door, stopping to give Amy a hug before she left. "They grow up so fast."

Shirley laughed. "Just wait until you have one of your own. That seems like a speed track. They're born, they go to school, then they leave you and build a whole new life. It's depressing, actually."

"Well, aren't you a cheery version of Sedona's favorite grandmother?" Rarity teased as she looked around the almost empty bookstore. She waved Katie to the counter. "When you finish cleaning up the book area, come and help me with the backpacks. Shirley, you can hang out at the register, just in case we get a customer or two."

Shirley sat on the stool. "Thank goodness, my dogs are barking."

Rarity laughed as she headed to the back room. "Now you sound like a grandmother."

# Chapter 12

With one project almost completed, Rarity focused on looking at next month's plan. With school back in session, she had more events coming up than during the summer lull. She'd scheduled three author events in the next month and still had to do marketing and the administration bits, like ordering books. She needed one more employee, especially now that Katie was back in school. And since she wouldn't be coming on full-time after she graduated or at least after she got a real job, Rarity needed to build some depth in her employee roster. She watched Archer and Jonathon talking while she finished her closing chores.

It was too bad Jonathon didn't live closer; she'd hire him in a second, even just for part-time hours. But he lived in Tucson, and really he just wanted to sit in her store and write. She tucked everything she needed into her tote, went into the back room to check the lock on the back door and turn off lights, then snapped her fingers at Killer. "Time to go."

"I guess I'm done writing then." Jonathon stood and put his laptop bag over his shoulder. "The other good thing about working here is it helps my work-life balance, since Rarity won't let me work all hours of the day."

"Edith would kill me." Rarity clicked on Killer's leash. "I'm making Korean fried chicken if you guys want to come over tonight."

"Edith got tickets to the ballet over at the university tonight. I'm avoiding going home to get into a suit. I thought I gave those up when I retired." Jonathon kissed Rarity on the cheek. "Thanks for letting me hang out today."

"You're kidding, right? You packed backpacks and wrangled teenage couples out of dark corners of the shop. I didn't realize how many places there were to hide here." She locked the door as they stepped out. "And tomorrow, Archer and I will fill up the rest of the bags and get them all tucked into boxes so we can drop them off at the school on Monday with Amy and Staci."

"You did good by those girls, letting them lead the troops today and getting all the credit for this event. But we all know you were the driving force behind it." Jonathon waved and started toward his truck.

"It was fun. Except now, Amy wants to do it again next year. Can you believe it?" Rarity juggled her tote. With a book to read, her laptop, and the file for the backpack event, her tote felt heavy tonight.

"Let me carry that." Archer reached over and took it off her shoulder.

"It's pink with a princess crown in rhinestones on the front," Rarity pointed out.

He looked at her, then at the bag. "You're so right. It doesn't go with my cargo pants. I should have worn my ballet tights and shoes. Or are they called something else? I forget."

"Fine, you're macho enough to carry a pink bag, I get it." She took his arm and leaned into him as they walked. "I got a call from Madame Zelda's daughter today."

"Heather? How is Gay?" He checked her face for a clue to what she was going to say.

"Fine, I guess. Heather said Gay was furious that Heather wouldn't let her open today. She said she was losing money, hand over fist." Rarity smiled as she remembered hearing Madame Zelda complaining in the background. "But she said that she wanted to see me tomorrow night if I could swing by around seven."

"Works for me. Do you want me to go with you?" Archer turned them down Rarity's street.

"If you want to. But I know you have a football game, right?"

He nodded. "I could record it."

"No, why don't you go home after we finish the backpacks? And I'll go to Madame Zelda's. Then if there's time, I can watch a movie." Rarity rolled her shoulders. "Or read."

"Or fall asleep on the couch?" Archer teased.

She nodded. "It's been a long week."

"Which is why I wanted to go out tonight for dinner," he reminded her.

"I like to cook. Especially when I'm thinking about something. I've been wondering about Jackson and if he was really meditating or if he was posed after he was killed."

"You're just saying that because you hate yoga." He held his hand out for her house keys as he stared at her on the porch.

She laughed and dropped the keys into his hand. "Probably true, but at least it's a question."

Archer opened the door, then handed her the keys. "The problem with this case is Drew has ten questions for every answer we get."

"I'm beat. Let's not chat about murder or business or even the future as we cook tonight. Let's just talk about nothing and no one." Rarity looked around the living room for Killer and found him sitting on the couch, ignoring her.

Archer turned on the music. "Unless we want to list songs to dance to at our wedding."

"You're such a romantic." She leaned into him and kissed him.

\* \* \* \*

The next afternoon, while they were in the store, she remembered she had a painting still at the framing shop. She checked the address as they waited to check out and realized the shop, Framed in Arizona, was in the same strip mall as the Target where they were shopping. "Hey, the frame shop is here. Can we stop in and see if my painting is ready?"

Archer glanced at the line. And then the clock. "Why don't you head down to check, and I'll deal with this and bring the car around?"

"Sounds like a plan." Rarity handed him the envelope with the donation money. "Just put the receipt and change back in the envelope."

"I hope your painting is ready," he called after her.

Rarity nodded. It wasn't that she didn't like visiting Flagstaff, she just liked being in Sedona better. There were fewer people and less traffic. And it felt calmer there. She giggled at her next thought. *It must be because of the vortexes.*

Now she was doing it.

When she entered the small shop, the clerk was talking with a woman. When she turned to leave, Rarity realized it was Eleanor. The shock on Eleanor's face must have matched her own. "Hey, what are you doing here?"

"Dropping off a few paintings from the gallery we need to get framed," Eleanor answered. Then she frowned. "What about you?"

"I bought a piece at the Art in the Park, remember? You helped me pick out the mat and frame." Rarity reminded her.

"And saved you some change." She turned and looked at the clerk. "Tim was steering her toward a mat that cost ten times as much and wasn't even a good match. You need to send April to those events. She has a good eye and doesn't just want to jack up the price."

"Thank you for telling me how to run my business," the clerk said. He turned to Rarity. "I'm sorry about Tim. I'm Mike Kelly, and you are?"

"Rarity Cole. I run the bookstore in Sedona." She reached out and shook his hand. "I was in town and thought I'd check to see if my painting is ready."

He flipped through a pile of papers. "It's right here. And Eleanor was right about the matting. This turned out beautiful. Hold on and I'll go get it. Here's the full invoice. Cash or charge, I take both. I'll be right back."

Eleanor stepped toward the door. "I'll see you later."

"Hey, thanks for the help. Did you give any thought to the books I could be stocking to highlight art and bring people to the gallery?" Rarity asked as she took out a credit card.

Eleanor stopped and shook her head. "It doesn't much matter. Whatever you think."

"Are you focusing on local artists or going after older stuff, like that Civil War portrait?" Rarity wasn't having much luck in getting Eleanor to participate in her marketing plan. Which meant she wouldn't be pushing clients to check out the bookstore.

Eleanor looked at her watch. "Look, it doesn't much matter unless Jackson's family changes their mind about closing the gallery."

Rarity watched her leave, then heard a noise behind her.

"Here's the painting," Mike said as he walked toward the counter. "I think it's nice."

Rarity stepped forward and handed him her credit card. "It's perfect. I mean, I liked it without a frame, but now it looks like it should be in a gallery somewhere."

"So you approve? Good, I'll wrap it up." As he secured the painting in a cardboard box to protect it, he talked about the artist and what an up-and-coming talent he was. Rarity saw Archer pull up and park in front of the storefront. She held up a hand, letting him know she was almost ready.

"And we're done," Mike said as he handed her the box. "I put your credit card receipt in the box."

She took the box and tucked it under her arm. "Thanks for your help with this."

"No problem. Any friend of Eleanor's is a friend of mine. She's a little tough to get used to, but she's always had my back, even back in art school." Mike turned to make notes on the canvases that Eleanor had brought in.

Rarity noticed the Civil War painting was among them. "Oh, are you reframing that one? I really love it."

"No, I'm going to try to restore the paint." He waved her closer. "Do you see how that section is muddy? I suspect that they painted over something sometime after the painting was finished. Maybe another kid or a husband they didn't want to acknowledge anymore. If he's famous, it might make the painting worth more."

"You're taking off paint to see what's under it?" Rarity shook her head. "That has to be dangerous to the original painting."

He winked at her. "Not in the hands of a master. I'll call you when I'm done and you can see the difference. I promise you, it will look amazing."

Rarity nodded and headed to the car. She put the wrapped painting gently in the back seat. "Thanks for letting me stop. I didn't want to fit in time to go back into town next week. Now I can get this hung tonight."

"Not a problem. Let's take these supplies to the bookstore and get those backpacks finished. The game starts in a couple of hours." He pulled out of the parking lot and headed back to Sedona.

When they got to the bookstore, they unloaded the Jeep. She looked at her watch. "Why don't you drop off the painting at my house and then go home? I'll do the backpacks."

"Are you sure?" He glanced at the bags. "It will go faster with two of us."

"Yeah, but then you'd have to drive me back to the house. If you go now, you'll make it to your apartment before the game even starts." She nodded toward Madame Zelda's shop. "And I think Heather must have had her stay home today, the shop isn't open. I'll call her next week and see if she still wants to meet up."

"You're very thoughtful." He kissed her and headed to the door. "You're the best."

She followed him and locked the door after him. "I am the best."

By the time she finished she was starving and Madame Zelda's shop was still dark. So she called in a to-go order from the Garnet and picked up the food on her way home. Malia was working and brought her bag to the front.

"Hey, are you by yourself?" Malia looked past her to see if Archer was with her.

Rarity held up her hands. "Just me. I have a quick question. Have you heard any rumors about the gallery closing?"

Malia's eyes widened. "No. In fact, I heard the family is going to keep Eleanor on as a managing partner. They gave her part of the business."

"But she told me—" Rarity was cut off by another waitress.

"Malia, table four wants another round."

"Sorry, I've got to go. I'll update you on Tuesday." Malia waved and disappeared into the crowd at the restaurant. The bar was filled and the televisions were all on the game. Football season had arrived in Sedona.

As Rarity walked home with her food in one hand, she thought that maybe Eleanor was playing games. It also occurred to her that Killer paid a lot more attention to her while they were walking when she had food in her hand.

\* \* \* \*

On Monday, Amy arrived promptly at ten, dressed in a cute plaid skirt and white shirt. With her black Mary Jane shoes, she looked like she attended some swank private academy and not the public middle school down the street. Staci was in a typical teenager outfit of shorts, a cropped T-shirt, and new tennis shoes. When Rarity was in school, the unofficial dress code had been jeans and a full-length shirt. She would have gotten sent home for wearing something that showed her abs. And in Illinois, the weather would have dictated sweaters more often than just T-shirts.

Archer helped them load the boxes of backpacks onto his bus, and soon they were off to drop the filled bags at the high school. Miss Christy would work with a local charity to get the bags where they needed to land.

Rarity sat in the front seat behind Archer. Amy sat next to her. Staci was in the next seat. She turned to look at the kids. "You two have done a really wonderful job with this. I know I keep saying it, but you should be proud of yourself."

Amy looked down and shrugged. "I just know how it is for some kids whose parents can't afford a new backpack each year. Kids can be mean."

Staci looked over at her and grabbed her hand. "They can be mean. But mostly they're just jealous and insecure. And when you get to high school next year, I'll show you around the first week, so you'll have someone to ask questions. But no dumb questions, at least not where other kids can hear us. I have a reputation to keep, you know."

Rarity met Archer's eyes in the rearview mirror. The two girls were so cute that Rarity wanted to cry. Amy drove Staci crazy at times, but here she was, acting like a big sister. She glanced out the window and saw the high school on their left. "Well, just don't think that since you're back in school and both so busy with friends and classes that you can't spend some time with me at the bookstore."

"I wouldn't do that," Amy declared. She glanced over at Staci. "But Staci might be cheerleading or on the dance team. She'll probably forget us in a week."

"I'm just trying out, twerp. It doesn't mean I'll get in. Besides, you'll be starting dance class next week too." Staci looked over at Rarity. "Amy got a scholarship into the Sedona School of Dance last week. She's really good for a kid."

"That's great." Rarity pulled Amy into a sideways hug. "Why didn't you tell me?"

Amy beamed. "It's no big deal. I'll have class one night a week, then we'll do performances closer to Christmas. Do you want an invitation?"

"Of course, I do." Rarity thought about her conversation with Shirley. The girls were growing up, and soon they'd be off to college and just stopping in on school holidays. Her bookstore was going to collect people who were going through different stages in their lives. Like when she hired staff from the college. First Darcy, one of her original employees, had left to study abroad. Now she was already seeing the future with Staci and Amy. *Learn to live in the present*, she reminded herself.

"Miss Christy's out in front waiting for us." Amy pointed to the door that led to the gym. "And she's got a lot of kids with her."

Staci's eyes widened as she leaned down to see what Amy was pointing at. Her voice came out in a squeak. "That's the junior varsity football team. Nick's on the team."

"Nick? The guy you think is so adorable? Which one is he?" Amy's voice got louder as she leaned over Rarity, trying to study the boys waiting behind Miss Christy.

"Hush. Never you mind," Staci said, then she pulled out a makeup case and checked her hair in a mirror. She muttered, "I knew I should have worn the pink shirt."

"You look cute," Rarity assured her, then stood as the bus stopped. "Okay, everybody off. We'll drop the bags off then we're heading to the Garnet for lunch, my treat."

# Chapter 13

When Archer came to pick her up at the bookstore that night, he waited for her to complete her closing ritual. "Man, hanging out with those two today made me feel really old. I thought it was just yesterday that I was playing JV ball, but those kids made me look like an old man as they carried in all the boxes. I felt like the old guy who used to drive us to games."

"You're probably the age that old guy was back then." Rarity went back to the break room to lock the back door. When she had so many people running around in the store, she always double-checked the locks herself. It probably was just superstition, but she didn't want to drive back and check the door in the middle of the night. Okay, probably not superstition but OCD. She'd accept that.

He pulled her close as she came out of the back room. "So, I've been thinking today."

"What did you come up with?" she asked, relaxing in his arms.

"Maybe we should talk about the future. Before I get too old to even think about being the bus driver." His voice lowered and Rarity could smell the soap he'd used in the shower after finishing his afternoon hike.

"The future? Our future?" Rarity had been expecting this talk, but not after they'd spent the day with teenagers. She'd thought that might make Archer run away, screaming down the street. Especially after having lunch with Amy, whose hobby seemed to be asking personal questions of anyone who came within fifteen feet of her. Staci had been on cloud nine during the meal since Nick had talked to her at the school and said he'd see her later. Oh, to be fourteen again and in love. "You're telling me you still want kids? With me? After today?"

"You sound like Amy." He let her go and called to Killer. "Let's go, big guy. You may be the only one I get to try my cool parenting skills on since your mom doesn't want to marry me."

"I didn't say I didn't want to marry you." Rarity followed him out of the building, turning off lights and locking the front door. She glanced over at Madame Zelda's. The building was still dark. Heather had said she was staying in town for a week to try to keep her mom from working. Rarity was thankful that the shop had been closed. She needed to get over to talk to her sooner than later, but today had been packed and tomorrow she had the book club and the sleuth investigation. She caught up with Archer on the sidewalk. "How did we even get on this subject?"

He grinned at her. "When you went to the bathroom at the restaurant, Amy asked me why we weren't married. Didn't I love you? What was I waiting for? So while I was leading today's hike, I tried to answer her questions, at least for me."

"And what did you find out?" Rarity pulled her jacket closer. It was chilly tonight. She looked up and saw the waning moon. Madame Zelda's prediction made her shiver.

Automatically, Archer pulled her closer. "Well, I found out that yes, I love you. But I never found the right answer to why I was waiting, so I thought maybe you knew the answer."

Rarity didn't respond immediately. When she did, she nodded. "I think some of it is me. Kevin hurt me when he left. Worse, his leaving made me feel like I was alone in the world. My world was pretty scary just then. I had one real friend, Sam, who lived several states away and no one else."

"That could never be true." Archer shook his head. "You are the most open and friendly person I know."

"I didn't know that back then. When the man you thought you were going to marry turns his back on you, well, it causes a scar." She took his hand as they walked. "After treatment, I moved here and you came along. I started to open up. I'm just not sure if I'm ready yet. Can you give me a bit so I can think about what life would look like if we took the next step?"

He brought her hand to his lips and kissed it. "You can have all the time in the world. But *you* get to tell Amy what's going on with us the next time she asks."

Rarity laughed and Killer stopped and turned back to look at them. "That sounds fair."

When they got home, Rarity pulled out her murder book. She wrote Malia's name on a sticky note and pressed it to the page. Something was going on at the gallery and she wanted to get the full story. She looked over at Archer, who was making dinner. The television was on and he was waiting for the game to start. "Do you know Jackson's family at all?"

He stopped chopping. "Not really. They didn't like me, especially after that thing between me and Jackson. Why?"

"I'm hearing different stories about the gallery. Eleanor told me that the family might be closing it. And Malia heard that Eleanor is actually taking over the full management of the place." She made a couple of more notes in her book. Given that the murder occurred over a week ago, they didn't have much on who might have killed Jackson. Except for why it couldn't be Archer. Maybe they were looking at the whole thing wrong.

"Drew might know. But it makes sense that Eleanor would run the gallery. She has experience working with Jackson's dad at the New York museum. I think that's how she found out about the job." He dumped the veggies into the wok and started stirring. "I'm just glad my alibi works with the time of death."

"I thought you were sleeping."

He nodded. "I was. But there was someone in my apartment. Calliope needed somewhere to crash so she popped in after we got home from the party, about ten. We talked for a few hours, then I went to bed and she crashed on the sofa. I told you this, right?"

Rarity felt a headache coming on. "No, Archer, you didn't. I'm beginning to understand why Calliope didn't get that you weren't interested. She asked to stay over. Really?"

"Rarity, it's not a federal case. She lives more than an hour away. She's come over several times after she'd been drinking and slept on the couch. Or at least she did when she worked for me. I don't like the idea of her driving after she's been drinking." Archer turned down the stove. "Nothing happened and it's a good thing she was there. Otherwise, Drew would have me in a cell right now for something I didn't do."

Now it felt like a phantom knife had been stuck in her gut. On one hand, Archer was right. Calliope was a perfect alibi. On the other hand, he hadn't told her that Calliope had even been there. And now, he was acting like it was no big deal. Which it wouldn't be if it was Drew on the couch. Or even Malia. It wasn't that Calliope was a woman. It was because she was in love with Archer. And if he couldn't see the difference, maybe... She paused; she didn't want to go on in her head. Not down that path. Not until she really understood their relationship. "You're right. We are lucky she was there, but Archer, can you send her here the next time she asks to stay over? I think I know why she's getting the wrong idea."

He sighed, turning back to the stove. "I think you're overreacting."

Rarity hoped he was right. That she was overreacting. But there was one fact. They were looking for a killer. Not a boyfriend stealer. She put the book away and went to change so she could swim. She needed some time to think.

When Archer left that night, he pulled her close to say good night. "Apparently, I was an idiot thinking that Calliope was only a friend. I'll do better, I promise."

She squeezed him. "That's all I can ask for."

\* \* \* \*

Archer had an early hike Tuesday morning, so Rarity got ready and gave Killer a hug. "You're in charge of the house today."

He frowned and looked away, not liking her wording.

"I'll leave the television on, just in case you want to watch a movie or something." Rarity had heard that having a radio or television on helped a dog not feel lonely. But right now, the looks Killer was giving her made her think that he wasn't going to buy it. Kind of like the way she now felt about Archer. He had to have known that Calliope wanted more. Archer was a good man and Calliope was taking advantage of his good nature. But it wasn't Rarity's issue unless she made it a problem.

He'd promised that it wouldn't happen again. Rarity would just have to take him at his word. In order to trust him, she would just have to let it go. No matter what, neither he nor she could go back and change the past.

She locked the door and waved at Terrance as she walked by. "I'll see you tonight."

"I'll be sure to go visit with him at least twice. I'm on patrol tonight. Okay if he goes walking with me?"

She smiled and nodded. "Killer would love that. Thanks, Terrance."

"Not a problem. I'm sure as soon as that man of yours moves in I'll be losing my babysitting job, so I'll take the time when I can get it." He held up his coffee in a salute and went back to his paper.

She didn't want to tell Terrance that they'd gotten into another fight last night. And that his assumption of them being a couple might be overreaching. At least for right now. She pushed the idea out of her head. She was the one overthinking this, not Archer.

If he didn't come to get her tonight, she'd call him after the book club ended and they'd hash it out. She'd tell him how it made her feel and she'd ask that he didn't do it again.

With that decision made, she hurried off to open the store. She had a lot to get done before the book club that night. And both Shirley and Katie were off. Shirley would be back at six that night and on the clock during the meeting. That way she could help random customers or even club members if Rarity was tied up. It was a win-win.

Rarity only hoped that the rest of the day would go smoothly.

\* \* \* \*

Later that night, Jonathon was updating the group on what he'd heard from Drew. When he told the group that Archer had a verified alibi, the group cheered. Jonathon glanced at Rarity, who smiled at him. She tried to let him know that she knew who had talked to Drew.

Holly was still leading the group, so she was the one who asked the burning question. "So who was Archer's alibi?" She stole a sly wink at Rarity. "Was he at your house that night?"

Rarity shook her head. "No, I'm not his alibi."

Jonathon held up his hand. "I'm not sure it's important who cleared Archer."

"Don't tell me it was that Eleanor. I'm not sure I like that woman," Malia said. "I told Rarity what she'd told me about taking over the gallery and then found out that she's been saying other things too. Like the family was going to kick her out of her job."

Holly leaned forward. "I think if we're going to completely rule Archer out, we need to know his alibi too. Isn't that what we're here for, a second set of eyes for law enforcement? No offense to Drew, but if we're just going to let them investigate, we should get back to reading books."

Jonathon started to speak, but Rarity waved him down. "Look, Jonathon's right. Archer has an alibi. Calliope Todd was in his apartment from ten that night to when he left that morning to pick up Jackson."

The room was deathly quiet.

Finally, Shirley said, "Oh, Rarity, I'm so sorry."

Rarity shook her head. "No, you don't understand. Calliope had been drinking and she didn't want to drive back to her house in Flagstaff. She'd stayed over before, on the couch, so Archer let her stay again. It's all innocent."

The looks on her friends' faces told a different story. One where she was being foolish for taking Archer's word for the late-night visit. She smiled and met everyone's gaze, one by one. "Look, the good news is he's been cleared. Now we just have to find out who actually killed Jackson."

"Rarity," Malia started, but with one look, Rarity stopped whatever she was about to say.

She stood and walked over to the treat table. She picked up a cookie. "Look, I know what this looks like, but I trust Archer. He's a good person. As a human, however, sometimes he makes mistakes. Anyway, it's done and the fallout is between the two of us. What else do we need to talk about? Or should we take a quick break?"

"I vote for a break," Holly said as she put the lid on the marker and set it down. "We'll reconvene in ten minutes. I want reports back from everyone else, if Jonathon was done, that is."

"I'm done." Jonathon stood and walked over to the table where Rarity was now eating the cookie she'd used as a pointer earlier. "You could have left her name out of it and off the report. I was planning on it."

"Now what sort of crime fighter only lets the good stuff come out when they're investigating a murder?" She squeezed Jonathon's hand. "Seriously, I'm fine. I know Archer and he's got a kind heart. Which gets him in trouble, I'll grant you that. But I trust him not to do the wrong thing."

"Drew was so mad at him, he really laid into Archer when he found out. He told him that he was messing things up with you big-time. Drew has your back, Rarity." He squeezed her hand back. "And so do I."

When the group returned from break, Rarity could feel the tension. They believed that Archer had made a mistake. It wasn't Rarity's job to defend his actions. She hadn't been happy when he'd told her, but like she'd told Jonathon, if they were going to find out who killed Jackson and why, they needed all the facts. Not just the ones that were convenient for her.

Malia stood and gave the next report. "I talked to David Valles about the vortex certification Jackson was bragging about. Apparently, it was a lie. David did scout out the site to see if there were any vortexes, but they didn't find anything. And he told Jackson that months ago. He was really mad that Jackson was claiming to have a site outside the gallery."

"Whoa, that's crazy. So the rock circle was just a decoration?" Rarity asked.

Malia nodded. "David said he'd heard that Jackson was claiming he had a vortex on Monday, after the party for the Red Rock people. He has a friend who lives in Red Rock with his girlfriend, who works at the gallery."

"Did he confront Jackson?" Jonathon was leaning forward, scribbling in his notebook as Malia talked.

"He said he went to talk to Jackson, but he wouldn't step away from the party. He told Eleanor that he would sue the gallery if they continued to make the claim. David thought he could get a judge to stop the gallery from using it in their marketing. It's a big deal around here." Malia glanced through her notes. "And before you ask, David was in Flagstaff at a retreat the weekend Jackson was killed."

Jonathon nodded. "Do you mind if I relay this information to Drew?"

"I told him we were investigating and anything he said might be used against him." Malia rolled her eyes. "Do you know what he said?"

"No, what?" Rarity could see from Malia's expression it hadn't been well received.

"He just laughed at me and said, 'Do your worst. People laugh at me for looking for vortexes, so a book club looking for a killer is probably treated the same.'"

"He doesn't know the power of the Tuesday Night Sleuthing Club," Holly exclaimed, and held up her marker like a medieval sword as everyone laughed.

Jonathon shrugged. "I don't know, you guys are pretty good at figuring these things out."

Holly looked at the flip chart. "Maybe he's right this time, though. With Archer off the list, which is what we wanted, at least before tonight, we're a little short of suspects."

"Not so fast." Jonathon flipped through his notebook. "I have three. This guy David was upset at Jackson for lying about certification. Sometimes people get really upset about things that don't mean a lot to others. I also have Jackson's financial issues and then there was whomever he was yelling at the night Rarity heard him."

He paused and looked at the next page.

"Who's the final suspect, in your eyes?" Rarity asked. She'd been so worried about getting Archer off the list, she hadn't thought a lot about who had killed Jackson.

"Eleanor Blanchet. The gallery manager." He looked around the room. "Now don't tell me that she didn't ring any bells for the rest of you?"

"I've only met the woman once, that Friday night." Shirley pondered the question. "I could see she was angry at Jackson because of the way he was treating her. But it's a long way from being annoyed at your boss to killing him."

"Not if you were sleeping with your boss in New York and found out he was with someone else here," Jonathon replied.

# Chapter 14

As soon as Archer arrived to walk Rarity home, the final few members of the sleuthing club left. Rarity wouldn't say they were rude to him, but they had been quick to leave. He stacked chairs after Jonathon offered to walk Sam home.

Archer had brought Killer to the bookstore with him and the dog got more attention than he did.

When Rarity joined him in the club area, he tucked the chair holder into the closet. "I take it they're all mad at me?"

"Your alibi came up," Rarity clarified. "I thought it was better that they know the truth than even think you might have killed Jackson."

"You told them about Calliope." Archer blew out a long breath.

She picked up a cookie and broke it in half, sitting down on the couch. "Have a cookie. This might be a long conversation."

He sat next to her and took the cookie. "It's a yes or no question."

"Actually, yes, I told them, but I also told them that you'd let Calliope stay there before when she'd been drinking. That I knew about it and that I believed you didn't do anything with her." Killer jumped on the couch and sat for a bite of cookie, but she shook her head at him.

"I'm either a murderer or I'm cheating on you." he sighed, eating his cookie. Then he made an all-gone motion with his hands so Killer would know he wasn't getting a bite from him either. "So much for just being a kind person."

"Calliope made no bones about her interest in you. Everyone except you knew how she felt. Because of that, her staying over, well, it looks bad."

"Except I was her boss." He ran his hand through his hair. "Man, you should have heard Drew yelling at me when I told him. He said I was either stupid or lying."

"He's a good friend." Rarity rubbed Killer's head.

"To you," Archer mumbled, but then he shook his head. "No, that's not true. I expect my friend to be up-front with me about how my actions look. I guess I just assumed everyone knew that I wouldn't do that to you."

"They'll get there. Right now, they are dealing with it." Rarity shrugged. "You're just going to have to prove yourself to them."

"No, I can deal with them being mad at me." Archer stood and pulled Rarity up into his arms. "As long as you believe me. Do you, Rarity?"

She stared into his eyes for a long time, wondering what exactly to say. Then she nodded. "I do believe you were just being kind. However, in the future, if Calliope or any other single female who is interested in a relationship with you, or not, needs a place to stay, drop them off at my house."

He laughed and hugged her. "I should have thought of that. Of course, Calliope would have sobered up quickly if I'd given her that option."

"Or smothered me in my sleep," Rarity mused as they walked around and finished closing up the bookstore. "I guess I need to remember to push the dresser in front of the door if that scenario occurs."

"I could install a dead bolt on your bedroom door," he suggested.

As they locked up the bookstore and headed home, he put his arm around Rarity. "Or I'll just stop trying to be a nice guy all the time to all people. Drew says I've got a problem with wanting to be liked."

"You could probably say the same thing to our friend Drew. That's why I respect you both. You are kind souls who believe the best of everyone." The moon had come up and was trying to give them some light as they made their way home. It wasn't a full moon, but it was pretty.

The moon made her think of Madame Zelda's warning. She shivered and Archer turned to look at her.

"Do you need a coat?" He pulled her closer. "Maybe I should start bringing the Jeep to pick you up on Tuesday."

"No, I was just thinking." She smiled at him. "Anyway, what's for dinner?"

\* \* \* \*

When Rarity arrived at the bookstore Wednesday morning, she saw Madame Zelda's front door standing open. She tucked Killer into her shop and relocked the door before heading over to check on her neighbor. She knocked on the door before going inside. "Hello? Madame Zelda?"

Heather was standing behind the register. "Oh, hi, Rarity. Come on in. My mom's in the back, getting ready for a reading. I wanted her to stay home for a few more days, but what can you do."

"I'm glad you're with her, at least." Rarity shivered as she remembered the last time she had been in the shop. She tried not to look in the direction of the reading room, where she'd found the owner. "So how is she doing?"

"I'm just fine and my hearing is even better." Madame Zelda came out of the reading room in full costume. "I'm glad you stopped by, Rarity. I wanted to thank you for helping me out a few days ago."

"Mom, she had to call the ambulance because someone attacked you," Heather clarified the situation.

"Now, dear, Drew Anderson hasn't told us that I was attacked. At least not yet. I might have just had a low blood sugar event and fell." Madame Zelda smiled at Rarity. "So anyway, I'm glad you're here. I wanted to tell you that I've been having dreams about you and some painting."

"I bought one at the art fair a few weeks ago. Was it valuable?" Rarity asked.

Madame Zelda shook her head. "It's not that painting. You got that from a local artist. I'm not sure they're going to be worth investing in."

"It's a lovely painting anyway," Rarity said to Heather.

"You're not listening to me." Madame Zelda grabbed Rarity's hand. "The painting is the clue. You need to find out what's under the paint. Then the situation will become clear."

"Mom, are you all right?" Heather grabbed at Madame Zelda as she started to slip toward the floor.

"What?" Madame Zelda's eyelids fluttered and she pulled herself upright using the counter. "Oh, Rarity, so nice of you to stop by."

Rarity and Heather exchanged a glance. Rarity asked, "Are you okay?"

"I've never felt stronger. I wanted to thank you for helping me the other day." Madame Zelda was repeating herself.

"You're welcome," Rarity answered. Then she turned to Heather. "I was just seeing if everything was okay, because the door was open."

"Oh, yeah, I left it open to air the place out." Heather nodded, letting Rarity know it was okay to leave. "Mom wants to do this reading, then we'll probably be closed again until Monday."

"Saturday. I'm reopening on Saturday, so please let people know that. Heather's going to make me a sign." Madame Zelda turned to her daughter. "Aren't you, dear?"

"Yes, Mom." Heather rolled her eyes.

"Well, if you need anything, just let me know. I'm opening the bookstore now." Rarity stepped toward the doorway and saw Heather mouth *thank you* as she left.

She'd had a second message from the beyond. The painting was the clue. Since the killing was at the gallery, it could have been any of the paintings. Rarity wished the messages came in a little clearer. Like "the painting with little pink elephants is the clue." Or "watch out for potholes on your walk home on moonlit nights."

Madame Zelda's ghost contacts needed to up their game.

She found Jonathon sitting on the bench in front of the store.

He looked up and smiled at her. "I was just texting you. I heard Killer barking inside and wanted to let you know I was here."

"I was checking in on Madame Zelda." She pulled out her keys and opened the door.

"How is Gay doing? I saw Heather in the restaurant yesterday grabbing some food for them but I didn't get a chance to talk to her." Jonathon set his tote on a table and pulled out his laptop. "Head injuries at our age are no joke."

Rarity thought about just keeping the message to herself but then thought better of it. "Well, I think she's doing okay. She had a message for me from the other side about Jackson's killing."

"Oh, should I pull out my murder book so we can write it down?" Jonathon laughed as he walked toward the back room to make coffee.

"I don't know," Rarity responded truthfully. She repeated Madame Zelda's words as Jonathon made the coffee. She stood in the doorway of the break room just in case someone came in the front door. She could see both entrance doors to the bookstore from this spot and it gave her comfort at times. Like now.

"The painting? She couldn't be more specific?" He got two cups out of the cupboard and set them near the now-running coffeemaker.

"That's what I thought." Rarity laughed. "So you don't think I should tell the sleuthing group on Tuesday?"

"Well, I think looking at the gallery's stock of paintings and where they came from isn't a bad idea. Edith picked up a sales brochure that night. I guess we can go through it and see if there is anything that would be worth killing over." He left the break room and went back to his table to dig in his tote. "Actually, I have two. Do you want one?"

Rarity followed him and took the second brochure. "But wouldn't the painting be gone now? Did Eleanor report any missing paintings or money the night they had the break-in? Or the night Jackson was killed?"

Jonathon paused on his way to get coffee. He pulled out his phone and started to text. "That's a great question. I don't think so, but if he was murdered in a robbery, wouldn't something have been gone? I'll ask Drew."

Rarity moved to the cash register and started setting up for her day. "Oh, and if he responds, can you ask him if Madame Zelda fell or if she was attacked? She said she hadn't heard anything."

Jonathon brought her a cup of coffee and set it on the counter. "She was attacked. Drew told her that last week when he visited her. He asked her to check to see if she was robbed that day."

"Was Heather there when he talked to her?" Rarity worried that something else was going on with her neighbor. "I don't think she remembers the conversation."

"I'm calling him now," Jonathon said as he set down his coffee and went outside to call Drew.

When he came back inside, Rarity looked up from the book order she was working on. "What did he say?"

"He's going back over to chat with both Heather and Gay this morning. I guess he just talked to Gay before and he thought she was coherent, but if she said she didn't know, well, he's worried."

"I think Heather's worried about her too." Rarity sent up a prayer for Madame Zelda's health and went back to working on the book order.

When she finished, she realized what Drew had told his dad. "Jonathon, if Drew thinks Madame Zelda's attack was an attempted robbery, do you think I need to make sure there are at least two of us in the store at all times? Would that help or just put both of us in danger?"

Jonathon looked up from his computer and glanced around the still-empty bookstore. "I wouldn't stay open late by yourself, that's for sure. I'll ask Drew tonight to give you a call or stop by and talk to you. If they were targeting Madame Zelda for some reason, you might be safe."

"She does stay open later than I do and takes evening appointments." Rarity walked over and looked at the street in front of her. "Of the three of us, I'm the one with more chance of having someone in the building besides me or a staff member. People wander in and out of bookstores a lot."

"Still, I'd like Drew to talk to you about what happened to Gay. Maybe it was a coincidence or someone she knew." Jonathon turned back to his computer.

For the first time since buying the bookstore, Rarity felt concerned for her safety there. Something she didn't think she'd have to worry about in Sedona. She returned to her counter and pulled up the weekly report.

She pushed off the fear she had felt. Just because someone had attacked Madame Zelda and Jackson, that didn't mean her bookstore was next on that person's list. And maybe they were different people.

She wasn't going to let fear shake her. Instead, she looked up a local employment site and put in an ad for a temporary bookseller. She would just make sure there were always two people in the store for a while.

And she'd talk to Drew about other safety practices.

When Drew arrived close to lunchtime, Jonathon popped out to grab them something to eat. She sat down at a table near the door to talk to Drew. The day had been slow and currently, there was no one else in the store.

"Heather said Madame Zelda gave you a reading but didn't remember doing it," he started the conversation.

"Yeah, it was weird. I thought she was awake, but I guess she was in a trance. Or her short-term memory is toast." Rarity hoped Drew would agree with her.

"I felt the same way when I was talking to her the other day. I would have sworn she was hearing what I was saying, but she swears I never talked to her about the attack at all. Heather's going to make sure she sees a neurologist, but Gay's convinced it's just the spirits taking over and she'll have a talk with them." He closed his eyes. "If you would have told me that dealing with spirits and vortexes and the other side would take up most of my day in law enforcement, I would have listened to Dad and gone to law school."

"It's been a crazy day, that's for sure. But Madame Zelda was attacked? Was it a robbery? Should Sam and I be concerned since our stores are so close to hers?" Rarity wanted to finish her conversation with Drew before someone came in to buy a book and ran screaming out of the store, scared of what might happen.

"I don't know who or why, so I know that doesn't ease your mind. Dad said you were thinking of always keeping two people on-site. I think that's smart. But I can't tell you that they were just going for the fortune-teller because of a bad reading because I don't know yet." He sighed and tapped his fingers on the table. "I know that's not what you wanted to hear. I'm not being very helpful for you lately, am I?"

Rarity knew he was talking about Archer's alibi. "I'm just freaking out a little. I'm a big girl. I've got the baseball bat my uncle sent me when he found out I had opened a bookstore. He said it worked great against all kinds of losers. Boyfriends or robbers."

The rest of the day was filled with kids and parents stopping in for one last bookstore visit before school started. Shirley's Mommy and Me class wasn't scheduled for this week. Staci showed up and delivered a print copy of three reviews for books she'd read over the last few weeks. She was consistently one of The Next Chapter's best customers, especially over the summer. Rarity wondered if now that school was starting, she'd get lost in the social activities. She was a good kid, so if she did, Rarity would be happy for her. And, if Staci was anything like Rarity, she'd come back to books and reading sooner rather than later. It was in their blood.

Rarity opened up her murder book and looked at the three possible suspects that Jonathon had listed on Tuesday night. She decided to find out more about Eleanor Blanchet. Maybe she was the key to this mystery. She opened her laptop and started researching, making notes about Eleanor's past as she did.

# Chapter 15

Sam stopped by after closing her crystal shop. She looked around the empty shop and smiled at Jonathon. "I should hire you to do security at my shop too. I'd hate to have a break-in like Madame Zelda did."

"Dear, if I stay in Sedona too much longer, Edith's going to divorce me. Especially when I tell her I've been hanging out with you two lovely ladies. Maybe you should talk to Terrance and see if you can hire his neighborhood watch to do some walk-bys." Jonathon tucked his laptop away. "Rarity, I'll see you in the morning. Please don't stay late, and if you do, please call Archer to have him walk you home."

"Actually, Archer is doing a tour, so it's just me and Killer." Rarity locked the cash register and pocketed the key. "I'm checking the back door, then I'm out of here. Unless you need something, Sam."

"I wanted to see if you'd have dinner with me. I feel like we haven't talked for days, or even weeks—at least not outside of the book club. I miss you." Sam picked up a book and read the back cover. "Go finish closing up. I can entertain myself."

"I bet you can." Rarity held up one finger. "I'll be ready in a couple of minutes. Do we want to sit outside or take Killer home first?"

Sam leaned down and picked up the little dog. "Let's just sit outside. I've got a jacket, so make sure to bring one for yourself. I know the Garnet doesn't mind if we bring him."

Rarity went over and locked the back door. Then she grabbed one of the jackets she'd left at the bookstore after wearing them on chilly mornings in the fall. She needed to take several of them home, but right now, she was glad they were here. She put on the jacket and headed back out front to meet Sam and say goodnight to Jonathon.

When she came back into the main bookstore, she heard tense words between the two. She couldn't hear what was being said but from the body language between the two, it wasn't warm and friendly. When Sam had been dating Drew, Jonathon and Edith had treated her like family.

Rarity guessed that even family members fought from time to time.

Jonathon said his goodbyes and left before Rarity could say anything. Through the window, she saw him turn like he was walking toward Drew's house. She asked Sam. "What were the two of you talking about?"

"He thinks I should call Drew. I told him that we were on a break. I need time, but Jonathon doesn't agree with my methods. He said couples should fight out the differences in the beginning. That makes them stronger, not weaker." Sam held up a book. "Do you mind turning the register back on so I can buy this?"

"Just take it. I'll snap a picture, then I'll reorder it tomorrow. If I don't, I'll forget you have it and I'll be tearing this place apart. Yes, I'm a little OCD." After taking a picture of the book, Rarity clicked on Killer's leash and turned off the lights. "Let's go get a table. I'm starving."

At the restaurant, Malia had the outside patio as her station. "Hey, guys, I'm glad you came in. You won't believe who's eating inside and with a hot hunk of a guy. My friend says he's an artist. She probably will be hanging his paintings in the gallery sooner than later."

Rarity looked through the window. It was the guy who she'd bought the painting from at the art fair. "I know him. He's really talented."

They watched as the artist put his arm around Eleanor and pulled her into a kiss.

"Well, I guess Eleanor knows him too," Sam said as she took the menu from Malia. "Did we see any of his work at the gallery Friday night?"

Rarity shook her head. "No. And I walked through the entire collection on Monday for the preview. I wonder why Eleanor didn't show at least one of his paintings."

"That's a really good question." Malia wrote something down on her notepad. "Do you remember his name?"

"Daniel Cleary? I have the framed painting at home now. I need to get it hung. Why?" Rarity glanced into the window again and saw the couple now had food that they were enjoying.

"Maybe Daniel was the straw that broke the relationship between Eleanor and Jackson. He attacked her and she killed him." Malia rattled off a theory.

"Except there was no fight. Jackson was found on top of his fake vortex shot with an arrow dipped in drugs. Not something you can find on the spur of the moment." She handed Malia her menu. "Can I have the Baja tacos and a strawberry margarita?"

"Sure." Malia turned to Sam. "What's your poison?"

"Salmon with a side salad and asparagus. And a glass of white wine." Sam handed over her menu. "If I'm going back into the dating pool, I need to lose some weight."

"You're not going back into the dating pool," Rarity countered. "And you look amazing. Malia, can you get Killer a bowl of water too?"

"Sure thing." She hurried away from the table.

"The kid's worried that we're going to fight." Sam nodded toward the retreating Malia.

Rarity leaned closer to her friend. "You're not really going to dump Drew, are you?"

Sam sighed and started ripping a napkin to shreds. "I may not have a choice."

"That's wrong. You have all the choices in the world. He still loves you." Rarity counted off the reasons it would be wrong to dump Drew.

Sam shook her head. "I know all that, but we can't seem to get past what happened with Marcus. Anyway, how are you sleeping? Better with the amethyst?"

Rarity blinked. "Actually, yes. Even with all the crazy stuff going on. My sleep has been good."

Sam held out her hands. "Another case solved by the amazing Dr. Sam's healing crystals."

"You're a nut." Rarity watched as Eleanor and Daniel cozied up together after finishing their meal. Would Eleanor have killed Jackson because she'd found someone new?

\* \* \* \*

Rarity swam when she got home, grateful that she'd turned on the pool heater the week before. Killer lay on the deck watching her. She wondered what the little dog thought as she did laps in the pool. Maybe something about the fact that humans really loved the water. Or at least his human. She grabbed her towel as she got out and wrapped it around her. The sky was clear tonight, and since the day had been warm, the concrete around the pool was still warm to her feet. She rubbed Killer's back. "Hey, kiddo, what's going on in your head?"

A cough came from the other side of the fence. "I didn't know you saw me out here," Terrance admitted.

She looked up, startled, then laughed. "I didn't. Come on in."

Terrance opened the gate on the side yard and walked in, sitting on one of the benches around the pool. "I was watching the stars and heard you come home. I like listening to you swim. It's calming."

"I think so, but I'm doing the swimming." She pulled off her swim cap. "What's got you in a thoughtful mood?"

"Female problems." he chuckled. "I never thought I'd hear myself admit to that. I have to say, Shirley is pretty incredible. I know she can't give me more, but she's an amazing woman."

"Were you ever married?"

He shook his head and patted the top of his arm where Rarity had seen a tattoo before. "I was married to the navy. I've had my share of girlfriends, but it wasn't ever anything serious. I was a bit of a player in my younger days. And now I guess I'm paying the price for breaking so many hearts."

"Shirley loves George," Rarity stated the obvious. "But George doesn't know she exists anymore. I don't think he can make her happy anymore."

"But they are married. A commitment that Shirley doesn't take lightly. I wouldn't want her to be any other way." He brushed off his shorts and stood. "I'm just going to be patient. I can't say I'm hoping for George to recover, but if he does, I'll step aside and let them be happy. Today, I'm going to make her as happy as she'll let me. Rarity, I have to say the songs were right all these years. Love hurts."

Rarity watched as her neighbor went back through the fence to his yard. She didn't hear a door shut so she assumed he stayed outside to continue to watch the stars. Watching and waiting.

She went into the house and locked the door behind her. So many people were hurting around her. Drew and Sam. Shirley and Terrance. George. Well, maybe not George. As she tried to go to sleep, she kept thinking about love and the powerful drive it was for people. Calliope had loved Archer. He loved Rarity. And she loved him back. Not everyone got to be happy in that scenario.

As she started to drift, she wondered if Eleanor had loved Jackson. Was that why his verbal barbs had hurt so much? She hoped Daniel was nicer to her. Sometimes people continued to pick the same type. Over and over.

\* \* \* \*

The next morning, Rarity was at the store already when Jonathon and Shirley came in together. "Look who I found at the coffee shop." Shirley greeted her with a hug. "Can we keep him?"

"I'm not sure Edith would approve of that." Rarity took the coffee Jonathon handed her and turned back to her computer, where she was posting future social media announcements. "But maybe she'd loan him to us for a while."

"I'm sure she'd love that." Jonathon settled at the table he'd commandeered as his own. "As long as I came back in time for the opera and ballet seasons. She hates going alone and our daughter always pulls the kid card since she hates the things."

"Well, there you go." Rarity sipped her coffee. "Shirley, we've got a bunch of new kids' books that came in this week. Can you get them into the system and ready for next month's book club? I'm so glad we plan a week between clubs to get resettled."

"Me too. Although I missed my Mommy and Me group yesterday." Shirley took her jacket and tote into the back room. "Is Katie working tomorrow?"

"Tomorrow and Saturday. She's going to be mostly on weekends until the semester is over. Then we'll have her full-time until classes start up again in January." Rarity thought about hiring, again. Had she even put in an ad? Was this the right time? She looked up at Shirley. "You'd tell me if I'm giving you too many hours, right?"

"Yes, Rarity. I'm happy with more hours. In fact, if you want to move me to full-time until Katie gets done with this semester, I'd love it. Not visiting George as much has given me way too much time on my hands." She stacked the books that were on the counter in a neat pile. "But only if you need help. I don't need charity hours. I can go work at the church rummage sale if you don't need me."

"You're kidding, right? I've been worried that I was going to have to hire someone else. I'd love for you to work full-time. Give me a schedule working around Katie's hours and we'll implement it starting tomorrow. Or next week, whenever you want." Rarity checked off one of the items on her mental to-do list. Then she went to cancel the help wanted ad.

"Drew will be happy about this. He mentioned that he was concerned about you and Sam working alone so much," Jonathon said when Rarity finished her task and went to sweep the sales floor.

"Believe me, finding Madame Zelda like that kind of scared me as well." Rarity smiled over at Killer. "Although, I do have a watchdog. That seems to help scare off robbers, right?"

"In theory," Jonathon said as he also smiled at Killer. "But maybe something a little bigger might be more effective?"

"Talk to Sam about adopting a new pet. Killer and I are just getting into a groove together. I don't want to mess up his rhythm." Rarity held up a finger. "Although I do have an idea for Amy's next charity project. We can do an adoption day here at the store, maybe late next month so it's cooler?"

"I'm sure Amy would love that. Will Staci be interested in helping again? I think the two of them worked well together." Shirley came back from the storage area with a cart filled with books.

"I'll email her. I wanted to let her know I paid her for the reviews she did for the store. She's got a talent for this kind of work." Rarity walked over and wrote herself a note as a reminder.

A man walked into the bookstore. His clothes were dirty, and as he looked around he stepped back, closer to the door.

"Hello, welcome to The Next Chapter, what can I help you with?" Rarity noticed Jonathon watching as well. Nothing over the top, but still watching.

"What is this place?" the man asked, looking around.

"It's a bookstore. Is there a book you need?" Rarity didn't think he was here for a book, but she might be reading the situation wrong.

The man stepped forward and picked up a book off the sale table near the door. Then Killer growled from his bed by the fireplace. The man looked over, his eyes narrowing as he found Killer, then dropped the book. "No, I'm in the wrong place. I thought with that name, this was a shelter or something."

He turned around and, after one last look, left the bookstore. Jonathon stood and walked over to the front windows. "I think I'll go visit Sam and see how she's doing this morning. Maybe you should lock up until I get back."

"Is he headed to Sam's?" Rarity asked.

Jonathon nodded. "And he keeps looking over at Madame Zelda's. She's closed today, right?"

"Heather made her promise to close until Saturday. Longer if her memory doesn't kick back in. I think the spirits are talking to her." Rarity watched as the man turned toward Sam's shop. "I'll lock up."

"Call Drew and see if he can get someone out here to take fingerprints. It's just a guess, but that guy gave me the creeps. Half of the time, intuition solves cases faster than shoe leather." He went out the door, then turned back and pointed to it, reminding Rarity to turn the lock.

Since it was still early and she didn't expect any customers for a while, she followed Jonathon's instructions. Then she grabbed her cell phone. She picked up the book the man had touched by the edges. "Drew? Can you send a fingerprint guy over for a second? Your dad's concerned about someone who just dropped by."

"Where is my dad?" Drew grumbled. "I need to talk to him and remind him that he's not on the job anymore."

"He followed this guy over to Sam's shop. Look, I got the same weird feeling. Can you just send someone?"

"Vic and I will be right over." The line went dead.

Shirley met her gaze. "Is he coming?"

Rarity nodded as she watched out the window toward the crystal shop. "Funny how all I had to do was mention Sam's name and he came running."

Shirley went back to keying the new books into the computer. "I don't think it's strange at all."

Drew pulled up and a man got out of the passenger seat of his car. Then Drew drove off and Rarity saw him park in front of Sam's.

She opened the door. "Hi, you must be Vic. He opened the door and picked up a book. I have it over on the counter. Other than that, I don't think he touched anything."

"Yes, he did." Shirley stepped forward. "The man was holding the door open with one hand when he first arrived."

"And how tall was he?" Vic asked as he set his tool chest on the floor, blocking the door open.

Shirley looked at him. "A little taller than you, maybe six feet. You're five eight, five nine, right?"

Vic grinned and nodded. "You're very observant. I love witnesses like you." He studied the door, then waved his dust on the panel. "And look at that, four clear fingerprints. I think the doorknob is going to have too many samples. Where is the book?"

Rarity nodded to the counter. "Over there. I picked it up by the edge with a napkin."

He looked up at Shirley and Rarity after collecting the first set of prints. "You're both very crime-sensitive for booksellers. Don't tell me, you have a mystery book club that meets here."

Shirley smiled and went back to the stack of books on the counter. "Something like that."

By the time Vic finished getting the prints, Jonathon was back and ready to continue writing. Rarity sat next to him as Drew and Vic drove off. "What happened at Sam's?"

"Nothing much. He was browsing when I got there. I went over and stood near Sam, talking about what she did the night before. She played along fast. She told me about her fictional husband and four boys who were practicing for peewee football." He opened his laptop. "When Drew arrived, the guy left. Drew grabbed some pictures of him crossing the street. He's going to go show them to Gay, just in case. You don't get a lot of transients around here. I guess Drew thought it was worth a shot."

"I hated stereotyping him, but something in the way he looked at me when he came in gave me the willies." Rarity watched as Shirley took a wet cloth over to the door to clean up the fingerprint dust.

"Paying attention to those feelings is smart. So many women I've interviewed after a break-in or a robbery or worse, they all said something felt off. When it does, don't hesitate to get somewhere safe. Or lock your doors. I think it's our primal nature or fight-or-flight reaction that picks up on the negative vibes. Of course, now I'm sounding like Sam and her crystals." Jonathon glanced over to where the shop was located, even though he couldn't see it through the bookshelves and the walls.

# Chapter 16

With school starting on Monday and no scheduled book clubs, the bookstore was quiet on Saturday. Which gave the three of them time to plan for the upcoming fall schedule. Rarity had the group around a table in the back room. Jonathon had offered to watch the front, but so far they'd only had three customers come in, so the planning session had been very productive.

Especially with Shirley on board for full-time hours, Rarity felt comfortable opening up the schedule for things like writer events and more evening author visits. She sent an email to Miss Christy at the school to let her know that someone, probably Shirley, would love to visit with classes or even the librarians. As they took a break to eat lunch, Rarity felt like she'd finally broken into being part of the community. Not just another store trying to make it all on its own.

After lunch, Rarity went through her to-do list and found the list of art books she and Katie had gathered as part of the joint marketing campaign with Moments and now, Eleanor. She decided to mock up a bookmark with the list and take it over to the gallery. When she finished, she made a copy and put it into a folder, along with several of the ones she currently used with other Sedona businesses.

Customers had started coming into the store, but it was still pretty slow, especially for three people on duty. She grabbed her tote and Killer's leash. She'd have to run home to get her car and she could leave Killer there. "Hey, Shirley? I'm heading out to visit the art gallery and show them the bookmarks. If Eleanor's not going to help in the design or even chosing the books, maybe I can guilt her into paying the full price of the bookmarks. I'll be back about four, four thirty."

"Sounds good." Shirley waved at her as she moved toward the door. "We're fine here."

Jonathon looked up and frowned. "Do you need someone to ride shotgun?"

Rarity shook her head. "I'm running home, then to the art gallery, then back here. I think I know my way."

"Okay, but if you break down, you know the auto club isn't in saving range, right?" He pointed to his laptop. "You're lucky I'm in a writing flow or I'd come with you."

"See you in a few." Rarity headed out the door and started walking home. A group of women went into Madame Zelda's shop as she walked past. The local fortune-teller must be feeling better, or at least she'd told her daughter she was, because her store looked packed with people. Everyone wanted to know their future. After surviving cancer, Rarity was happy to live in the here and now. She didn't need any surprises coming from the other side.

The day wasn't too hot and Killer seemed happy to be out for a walk. Typically, he hung around the shop with her most days. Now that fall had arrived, and she'd gotten extra help at the store, maybe they'd do a short walk like this in the middle of the day more often.

Once they were home, he went to his bed after drinking some water. He closed his eyes almost immediately.

"I'll be home for dinner and then we'll snuggle on the couch," she said as she closed the door. She took out her keys and started her car, checking the gas gauge. As rarely as she drove, she didn't want to run out of gas on her way to the gallery. Jonathon hadn't been kidding when he said that the auto club didn't cover that road.

She was in luck, the fuel tank was almost full. She backed out of the driveway and headed to the highway that would take her west of town.

Her phone rang as soon as she passed outside the city limits. Using the hands-free feature, she answered. "Hi, Drew. Do you get an alert when anyone leaves town? Or am I the only one you watch this closely?"

He actually laughed before he answered. "Sorry, that's proprietary information of the Sedona police department. Honestly, I called Dad to see if he was going to be around for dinner tonight and he ratted you out. Why are you going to the gallery? Or do I want to know?"

"It has nothing to do with Jackson's murder. I'm trying to talk Eleanor into participating in my bookmark marketing promotion, but I can't get her to volunteer a list of books for me to order. So now I'm just asking for money to pay for the bookmarks." She paused, letting that settle in. "Madame Zelda's is open today."

"I know. I talked to Heather yesterday and Gay was adamant that she was opening. She didn't recognize the guy from the picture but she still doesn't remember what happened, either."

"Did the fingerprints come back yet?"

"Not yet. I'm hoping for later today. My officers have been watching the guy since yesterday. He's renting a room in the motel out on the highway. So don't pick up any hitchhikers on the way to or home from the gallery."

"Not something I've ever considered." Rarity scanned the road in front of her. No cars, no people, and no houses, but there was the crossroads for the gallery and the large stone sign that pointed the way.

"Anyway, stay safe. Call me when you get back into town. I'd like to know you're okay." Drew disconnected the call and her music came back on.

Rarity usually loved driving alone, listening to music, but the last few weeks had drained her energy supply. Now, following Drew's call, she was beginning to question her decision to come out here alone.

Soon, the gallery was in sight and she let out a sigh of relief. There were several cars parked in front of the building and a few near the edges. Rarity assumed those were employee cars out near the back of the lot. At least it hadn't been a waste of time to drive here. Unless Eleanor was MIA.

Rarity parked in front of the building. A van with Framed in Arizona painted on the side was parked in the next spot. Seeing the van there reminded her about the new painting she'd hung at the house last night. She'd picked out the perfect spot for it on her living room wall. A real painting from a creator she'd actually met seemed like a very adult thing to have in her new cottage. Much better than the concert posters she remembered hanging in her first St. Louis apartment after college. Although the posters had brought back fun memories.

Rarity opened the door and was overwhelmed with the scent of oranges. She scanned the front area for the source, but the scent must have been pumped into the room. Rarity hadn't noticed it on her two other visits to the gallery.

A woman in a power dress stood from the desk where she'd been working before Rarity entered and came to greet her. "Good afternoon. Welcome to Moments in Time, the premier Sedona art gallery. Are you here for something special or just looking around?"

"I thought the gallery's name was Moments?" Rarity glanced over at the wall behind the reception desk. The sign still said just Moments.

"We're in the middle of a rebrand. A lot of galleries do it after a soft launch. Comments from the open house were used to adjust our local footprint." The woman had perfect hair, perfect nails, and was wearing a perfect dress. She looked like she worked at a gallery set in the Upper East Side of New York City, not Arizona. She must be part of the rebrand as well.

Rarity thought about the bookmarks in her folder. Where would people even pick them up here in this white-on-white world with no clutter besides the art on the wall? Maybe this had been a waste of a trip. "Is Eleanor here? I'm Rarity Cole. I own The Next Chapter, the local bookstore. I've been chatting with her about a joint promotion."

"Oh, well, it's not Eleanor you want to chat with, it's me. I'm Jade Williams. I'm the gallery's director of marketing and promotion. I'm just covering the front desk for Allie's break. She's not expected back for almost an hour. Should we sit and talk now or schedule an appointment for next week? I could come into town if that is more convenient for you. I know staffing a small shop is hard." Jade tilted her head to the side, watching the door as she talked to Rarity.

Somehow, the woman was saying all the right things, but Rarity felt like she was being dismissed and put in her place because the gallery was too good to be part of the Sedona business community. Or maybe she was just tired.

Rarity handed her the folder. "This is the information on what I've been doing with other businesses in the area. Basically, the program works like this. You give me a list of several books you believe your customers would be interested in. We make a bookmark with your store's information and the bookshop's. Then you give out the bookmarks to interested customers and they come to me to buy the books. Or if they're in my store and buy an art book, I tuck the bookmark into the purchased book and mention the gallery as a possible tourist stop on their vacation. It's a win-win."

Jade flipped through the folder. Then closed it. "I'm sure we can work something out, but the books you've listed won't do at all. Is your email information in the folder? I'll send you a list of books. Invoice me the cost of the bookmarks and let's get this going."

Rarity hadn't thought it would be this easy. "Okay. My email address is on the business card stapled to the front of the folder. I'll be waiting for your list. Thank you. I think we can work nicely together."

"I'm certain it won't bring us much business, but we do support local businesses through our charity account." Jade turned around to walk back to the desk. "And please make sure you change the name of the gallery on your little bookmarks. Moments in Time."

Rarity turned around. She felt her face warming and she didn't want to argue over the effectiveness of joint marketing. However Jade wanted to code the charge, it didn't matter to the bookstore's bottom line. Except the conversation had a direct hit on Rarity's pride as an effective former marketer for million-dollar companies when she worked in St. Louis.

"Rarity? Rarity Cole?" She turned as she heard her name and realized it was the man she'd talked to at Framed in Arizona. "Hey, I thought that was you."

"Hi." Rarity looked down at the man's shirt and his name tag. "Mike. So good to see you."

"I wanted to see how the painting was working for you. Sometimes when people buy art on a whim, it doesn't even get hung. I'd be glad to purchase the painting for my own collection. The artist seems to be really blowing up. I'd give you a ten percent bump on what you paid, including framing," Mike chatted as they left the building. He glanced back at Jade. "Unless you already sold it to the gallery."

Rarity knew that buying art was subjective, but she'd only owned this piece for less than a month. "No, I was here on a business errand. I'm really not interested in selling."

"Well, if you ever need some fast cash, I'm your guy." He gave her a business card. "Oh, you should come by and see the Civil War painting. My restorer's almost done, and apparently the master of the house must have been a bad boy because they painted over his image. Eleanor's trying to determine who he was. If he was famous, the painting might be worth a fair penny. Especially now that we've restored it."

"They painted over him?" Rarity was trying to remember the details of the painting. "It looked like it had dust on the canvas."

"They didn't match the paint color exactly. It's rare that someone or something is painted out of a family portrait." He grinned as he started the van. "He must have really made his wife mad."

"I guess back then you couldn't just rip a painting in half when you broke up, not like you can now with a photo." Rarity waved as Mike pulled the van out of the parking lot.

She got into her car and texted Drew, letting him know that she was on her way back to the shop. She'd leave Killer at home for the rest of the day. She had just turned back onto the highway when her phone rang. It was Drew. "Hey, that was quick. Do you want a report? Jade someone is now the gallery marketer and boy is she full of herself."

"I was just checking on you. We're looking for Johnny Simmons. The prints we took from the doorway of your shop match those we found at Madame Zelda's. We believe he's our man."

The thought that the man who had attacked Madame Zelda had been in her shop caused a shiver to go down Rarity's spine. "You're sure?"

"He's wanted in Ohio for doing the same thing to three different shop owners. He seems to focus on shops where the women are alone. The women he's attacked, well, he sexually assaulted them. You coming over to the shop probably saved Gay from more trauma. You must have scared him off."

"Is that why he came into my shop? Because he saw me?" Rarity reached over and hit the lock button on her doors a second time. Had she locked the car when she'd parked at the gallery? She didn't remember, but the good thing about driving a small car was there wasn't anywhere to hide. She slowed down and glanced at the back seat.

No one else was in her car. She let out a long breath.

"Rarity, did you hear me?" Drew's voice calmed her a little.

"Sorry, I was checking the back seat. I know, overkill, but I'm freaked out here," Rarity admitted.

"What I said was we don't think so. We think he was just seeing if you were alone and when you weren't, he went to Sam's."

"And Jonathon followed him." Rarity breathed out the words. "I hate being scared in my own shop."

"Well, as soon as we pick this guy up, I'll let you know. Sedona's a safe town. I'm going to make sure it stays that way." He paused. "Eleanor gave me a list of what had been taken from the gallery when Jackson was killed. It looks like Archer must have scared him off as there are only three paintings on the list. Eleanor thinks they were looking for a cashbox from the open house. Although I don't know a lot of people who buy art with cash especially at those prices. Where are you going now?"

"Back to the shop. I know Jonathon is there with Shirley and Katie, but if this guy feels threatened, he might act off-script." She thought about the list of paintings. "Maybe I can come over and look at the list later."

"I'll send you a copy via email. Look, I'm going to hang up and call Sam. If I can't reach her, can I text you to call her? She'll pick up when she sees your number." He paused. "I know everything is probably fine, but I'd like to know for sure."

Sam's store might be bursting with customers or she might be all alone in her shop. Retail was fickle. Even on a Saturday. "Sure, just let me know."

She drove past the low-end motel on the side of the highway and wondered if Drew's guys had been there to check for Johnny. There was no way she was going to stop and check herself. She was done investigating. Especially when it put her and the people she loved in harm's way.

She found a parking spot near the corner of Main Street and Highland Road near the *Open Gate* sculpture. She walked by the sculpture every day and still didn't know what it was supposed to represent. She locked the car and walked down the sidewalk toward her bookstore.

As she passed by Madame Zelda's, she saw the front door was open. She paused, then called Drew. The call went straight to voice mail. So maybe Sam and him were talking. She sent him a quick text about the open door, then started to walk past.

The image of Madame Zelda on the floor made her stop. "This may not be smart," she said as she amended her text with the words, *I'm checking it out now.*

# Chapter 17

Rarity forced herself to climb the stairs to the small porch where Madame Zelda had a bench for people to wait. She poked her head into the shop. She didn't see anyone. She stepped in and grabbed a carved walking stick from a display near the door. If she hit someone with it, she'd buy the stick. Otherwise, she'd just put it back where she found it.

Three deep breaths to try to slow her heart rate. It wasn't working. "Hello? Madame Zelda? Heather? Anyone here?"

No answer. No rustling, no moving. Just nothing.

She stepped farther into the shop. No one rushed to attack her or even welcome her. She let the walking stick drop a bit as she kept walking around. Finally, she checked the reading room. It was like the rest of the shop, empty.

She was about to leave when a ringing phone made her jump. It took a few seconds for her to realize it was her cell. She answered, "Hello?"

"What in the heck are you doing?" From the pitch of his voice and the volume, Rarity guessed Drew thought she'd done the wrong thing.

"Madame Zelda's shop is completely empty. The door was wide open but no one is here." She wondered if there were back storage rooms. Maybe she should check those too.

"That's because Heather just ran Gay to the hospital. She started talking in voices and Heather couldn't get her to come back to reality. The doctor thinks she might have a brain injury from the attack." He sighed. "But let's get back to you. Why are you going into a shop that's not yours? You told me you were going to the bookstore. I need to know where you are when there's a situation like this."

"I thought something might be wrong. Again. Remember I found her in the first place. I was trying to help."

"Sure you were," Drew snorted. "Look, just get out of there. Lock the door behind you and go back to your shop. At least until we find this idiot. Tell me you're parked close."

"I'm on the corner of Highland and Main." Rarity knew she was going to get a lecture since he would be freaked out when she told him. "And I'm locking the door now. You'd think I'd get a good neighbor award, not the third degree."

"They don't give good neighbor awards to dead people," Drew reminded her. "Just keep talking to me until you're in your store. Then give your phone to my dad."

"What, are you sending him over to watch Sam?"

"Do you disapprove? I can't be there because I'm running the search for this guy, who isn't at the motel now. You'll be safe with Shirley and Katie there." He paused. "Rarity, I can't risk her being alone."

"It's okay. I get it." Rarity opened the bookstore door and a family walked out with a bag that appeared to be filled with books. "Have a great day."

"Wait, hand me over to Dad," Drew said.

"I wasn't talking to you. A customer just left the store." When she got inside, the store was busy. There must have been ten or more people wandering around. Shirley was at the register, checking someone out. And she saw Katie over by the kids' section, talking to a girl and her parent. Jonathon was at his table, writing. He'd looked up when the door opened but then went back to writing when he saw it was her.

She walked over and handed him her phone. "It's Drew. He needs a favor."

Jonathon frowned but he hit some keys, then closed the laptop. "Thanks."

She walked over and joined Shirley at the counter. She tucked her tote under the counter, then picked up the books that Shirley had already rung up and slipped them into a bag. She held up *One Step Too Far*. "This is a great book. I couldn't put it down. The author has more in this series if you like the main character."

"Oh, Lisa Gardner's an auto-buy author for me." The woman handed Shirley a credit card. "You should see if you could get her in for a signing on her next book."

"That would be awesome. I'll see what I can do." Rarity didn't think the author would choose a small shop like hers, but she'd ask the publisher. She handed over the bag. "Thanks for coming in today."

"No problem. We saw the article in the *Sedona Star* and wanted to support your store more. Especially after you sponsored those girls in their charity project. It's not often you see kids helping other kids." She waved and headed to the door.

"That was unexpected." Rarity turned to Shirley. "Have you been busy since I left?"

"Yes. And a lot of people have referenced that article. We're having an amazing day." Shirley smiled at a woman who was waiting to check out. "Are you ready?"

Jonathon handed her back her phone. "Call me if there's a problem. I'm heading to Sam's."

"I think we're good. Lots of customers make us a bad target," she said quietly as she followed him to the door. "Just make sure she's safe."

He chuckled. "The last time I showed up she yelled at me for leaving you alone. You two girls are good friends."

"She's my best friend." Rarity gave Jonathon a hug. "I'll see you soon."

The rush of customers lasted until closing time. Before she chased everyone out, Rarity checked out the bathrooms and storage area to make sure they were empty. Then she checked the lock on the back door. It was unlocked. She relocked it.

When she got back to the front, Shirley was helping the last customer and Katie stood by the door, letting people out and relocking it as she waited for the next customer to leave.

When Shirley gave the credit card and receipt to the last customer in the store, she blew out a sigh of relief. "My dogs are barking. I don't think I've sold that many books in one day in all the time I've worked here. We should do more charity events to get people in."

Katie came over and sat on one of the stools. "It was a really busy day."

"Who took the trash out?" Rarity asked the two.

Shirley and Katie looked at each other. "It wasn't me," Katie said.

Shirley just shook her head. "'Not I, said the cat.'"

Rarity frowned, then went to stand near the entrance to the back room. She could see both doors.

"Why?" Shirley came to stand next to her to see what she was looking at.

"The back door was unlocked when I went to make sure the place was clear." She stood straighter as she watched a man stroll up to the back door. He checked his watch, then went to open the door. When he found it was locked, he looked up and into Rarity's face. It was the man from yesterday. The one Drew was looking for.

"Shirley, use my phone and call Drew. Tell him Johnny Simmons is outside the shop in the alley." Rarity didn't turn her head. She kept watching the door.

Johnny slammed his shoulder against the door frame, but it held. Archer had rebuilt all the doorways last summer, just to make sure no one could easily break in. Rarity had thought it was overkill. Now she wasn't so sure.

"Katie, Shirley, go stand by the front door. If I tell you to run, open it and run to Sam's shop." Rarity didn't think he could break down the door, but he could bust a window and crawl in if he was desperate enough.

"Drew says a car is on the way and to stay on the line," Shirley called over from the front door.

Rarity saw Johnny walking away from the door. "It might be over."

She took a breath but then watched in horror as he picked up a bench from behind Sam's shop and rammed it into the glass window, shattering it. An alarm began blaring.

"Get out of here, go. I'm right behind you." Rarity paused before she left, and saw the bench catch on the door handle. She'd been given a little bit of time. Instead of running to the door, she stepped behind the counter and grabbed the fire extinguisher. She'd tested it last week. Then she put the bat on the counter. She had a plan. First, she'd spray his face, then take out his knees with the bat. And then she'd run for the door. He wasn't getting away before Drew got here to arrest him. Her tote was already tucked over her shoulder.

If Drew's guys weren't quick enough, he'd get away. She wasn't going to be looking over her shoulder for the next week or month or even longer, waiting for him to come back. She heard the bench rip out of the door and the door creak open.

"Ouch," someone yelled from the back.

*I hope you cut yourself on the glass.* She steadied herself with the fire extinguisher. What seemed like an eternity passed, then someone came around the doorway. She saw the blue uniform seconds before she emptied the fire extinguisher in the man's face. Instead, she aimed the nozzle down and away from the Sedona Police officer and to the floor. She moved her finger from the trigger.

"I was coming in to let you know we have Mr. Simmons in custody. But I think"—the officer took the fire extinguisher from Rarity's shaking hands—"you might have had everything under control without us."

\* \* \* \*

Archer showed up a few minutes after they took Johnny Simmons away in the police car. He enveloped her in a hug as she told him what had happened. He took one look at the shattered window and left again. Thirty minutes later, he'd brought wood to board up the door. "We'll need to replace the door tomorrow and get new locks set up."

Rarity stood at the counter, closing up the register and tucking receipts away for reconciling later. She didn't look up when Archer came back to the front of the shop. She'd sent both Shirley and Katie home after they helped her clean up the mess from the fire extinquisher. Jonathon was still at his usual table. Pretending to write, but she could feel him watching her.

"Rarity, did you hear me?" Archer asked, concern lacing his question.

She nodded again. "We'll replace the door on Sunday. I'm about ready to close up."

"Rarity, are you okay?" Jonathon had closed the laptop and walked over and now stood next to Archer. "What you did, that must have been frightening."

"I wanted to make sure he didn't get away again. I couldn't take worrying." Rarity looked down at Killer's bed, then remembered she'd taken him home. "I feel numb."

"It's probably shock," Archer said as he turned to Jonathon. "I was so intent on fixing the door, I didn't realize. Should we take her to the hospital?"

"No!" Rarity turned sharply and shook her head. "I'm fine. I need to get home and check on Killer. He's been alone for too long. And thank you for fixing my door. I would have worried about the shop tonight."

Archer and Jonathon exchanged glances.

"I'm not crazy. I'm not hurt. I just need to cuddle with my dog and maybe swim. And eat pizza." Rarity realized she was starving.

"Okay, then let's go home." Archer picked up her tote.

She handed him the murder book that had been under the counter. "Put that inside and I'll check the back door lock."

"I've already done that," Archer said, but then moved out of her way as Rarity stared him down. "I'll wait out here."

Rarity stepped into the back room. The glass had been cleaned up and the only evidence that Johnny Simmons had even been there was the board covering the window of the back door. She went and turned the lock, unlocking and then relocking. She wasn't going to let this upset her. Not now. She'd won. Simmons was in jail. So why did she still feel scared?

She'd worry about that tomorrow. Right now, she just needed to get home.

As she locked up the bookstore, she turned to Archer. "My car is down the street. You can meet me at the house."

"Why don't you ride with me?" Archer nodded to his Jeep out front of the bookstore.

Rarity shook her head. "I don't want to leave my car sitting out here all night. Simmons may not be the only criminal in the area. Especially at night."

Jonathon held out his hand. "Give me the keys and tell me where you parked it. I'll drive it to your house, then walk to Drew's."

For a minute, Rarity thought about rejecting his offer. She hated feeling weak. But then a wave of bone-weariness fell over her. She was crashing from the high-adrenaline fight she'd planned for earlier. She handed him the keys, after checking the bookstore lock one last time. "It's near the corner of Highland, just that way."

Jonathon smiled. "I actually know the street. I'll probably beat you home."

"There's a garage door opener on the visor. Just park it in the garage." Rarity leaned into Archer as they made their way to the Jeep. "I'm so tired. I feel like I could sleep for a week."

"From what Drew said, you were all Batgirl on the guy. Why didn't you just go to Sam's with the others?" He opened the door for her and helped her inside. Then he ran around to get in the driver's seat.

"I wanted to make sure they were safe and that the cops had time to arrest him. If I'd run, he might have just followed me." Rarity thought about her plan. "Maybe it wouldn't have worked, but it would have delayed him from escaping."

"And you might have gotten hurt, or worse." Archer started the Jeep and made a U-turn to head toward Rarity's street. "I was worried about you when Drew called me."

"I was really mad about what he did to Madame Zelda. She's back in the hospital because of this guy. Maybe it wasn't my smartest move, but I think the plan could have worked." Rarity leaned against the back of the seat, hoping she wouldn't fall asleep during the short ride home. "He was a bad man."

Archer turned on his blinker. "There seems to be a few of them around, lately."

"But there are also a lot of good ones, like you and Drew." Rarity pointed to her car, which was in front of them on the street. "And Jonathon. He looks like he's driving a clown car. I didn't realize how small my car was until now."

"Why do you think I always offer to take the Jeep if we're going somewhere? That car makes my legs cramp if I drive it for any amount of time." He reached over and took her hand. "I'm proud of you. Even though I was scared and worried, I'm proud that you thought of saving your friends first. Just don't pull anything like that again, okay?"

Rarity smiled and squeezed his hand. "No promises."

When they got home, she collapsed on the couch. Any idea of swimming went right out of her head when Killer, sensing her unease, jumped on her lap. In fact, she must have fallen asleep right there because the next thing she knew, was the doorbell ringing and Archer bringing a large supreme pizza to the coffee table.

She stretched her arms and Killer got down to sit and stare at the food. "That smells like heaven."

"I'm glad you think so." Archer grabbed plates and napkins he'd set out on the counter. He also brought over two cans of sparkling water. "We'll start with this."

Rarity's stomach growled. "Please tell me that Drew still has that guy locked up."

"According to Drew, between these attacks and the ones he committed in other states, he'll be held without bond while all the trials are happening. So yes, he's still in jail." Archer sat down and turned down the volume on the television, which was showing a college football game. "I can change the channel if you want to watch a movie or something."

"I want to eat. Then maybe sit in the hot tub and go to bed early. I'm still worn out." Rarity picked up a slice of pizza and took a bite. The warm pizza sauce and the cheese filled her mouth and tastebuds. She quickly finished a slice and went in for a second.

"Drew said he brought that vortex author in for questioning, but he has an alibi. He didn't want to give it, but apparently he was sleeping with a married Sedona resident whose husband was out of town that weekend."

"I bet her marriage is going to be in trouble." Rarity finished her second slice and picked up her soda can. She drank most of it. "You would think I'd been stranded on a desert island for years the way I'm attacking this food."

"Being in a traumatic situation can affect our body and our mind," Archer reminded her. He set down his pizza on the plate and pulled her closer. "I'm a little freaked out and I wasn't even there. I'm so glad you're okay. I know I'll probably say this over and over, but I don't care."

She smiled and wrapped her arms around him. "I don't care either."

They stayed that way until Killer started jumping on two feet on the coffee table, trying to get to the pizza. She swatted him down and gave him a stare. "You have food in your dish. You don't need pizza. It's not good for you."

The look on her dog's face told her everything. He thought she was wrong.

# Chapter 18

Sunday morning, Rarity awoke to a ringing doorbell. She glanced at the clock on her side table; somehow it was already nine. She dragged herself out of bed and went to let Killer out into the backyard. Then she answered the door.

Shirley stood there with a Crock-Pot in her arms. "Oh, goodness, I didn't think you'd still be asleep. Everyone's going to be here at nine thirty. Maybe you should go get dressed."

Rarity ignored Shirley's directions, but she did open the door so Shirley could come inside. She went over and started a pot of coffee. "Why are you here? Did I forget about a meeting?"

"Oh, no, dear. We just decided to come over and get the bookstore right before tomorrow. No need for you to go to work tomorrow and be reminded of that horrible man." She put the Crock-Pot on the counter and plugged it in. "I made cheesy potatoes for lunch, but I also have banana bread and coffee cake in the car. Terrance will be bringing it in any minute. Now, go get a shower and get dressed. I'll take care of things out here."

"I still don't understand—" But Rarity didn't get to finish her question. Shirley grabbed her by the arm and led her to her bedroom.

"Jump into the shower and I'll set a cup of coffee right here with a treat before you get out. We'll get some coffee and sugar in you and you'll be fine as rain." Shirley pushed her inside and closed the door. "I'll let Killer inside too."

"I think it's 'right as rain,' not 'fine as rain,'" Rarity mumbled as she went to the adjoining bathroom to turn on the shower.

As promised, there was a cup of coffee and a warm, thick slice of banana bread sitting on a tray on her dresser when she came out of the shower. She could hear voices in her living area. More than just Shirley and Terrance, but she couldn't separate them out. If she had to guess, as she pulled her jeans on, it was the Tuesday night group with Drew, Archer, and Terrance as additions.

She finished the banana bread before she finished dressing and she looked longingly at her swimsuit hanging over the tub. She'd have to put off her swim until later when everyone was gone. And who knew when that would be? When the group decided they were needed, they didn't walk away from a fight. After finishing her hair, she grabbed her coffee and took a sip, staring at the woman in the mirror.

A full night's sleep hadn't taken the dark circles away. It might take a few days to recover from yesterday's activities. But she didn't regret what she'd done. "I am invincible," Rarity told the woman in the mirror.

She didn't look convinced.

She headed out to see what her group of friends was planning for her one day off.

The living room was full. Archer was chatting with Dane O'Conner, Malia's boyfriend. Terrance was talking to an older man she'd seen around the neighborhood but didn't know. The Tuesday night club was all here as were Drew and his father. Archer saw her first.

"Rarity, now don't freak out, but we're going over to replace that back door. I've got some pictures and I want you to choose the door you want."

She sat at the table while Archer went through the choices. Finally, she looked up at him. "I don't care as long as it doesn't have a window big enough for someone to crawl through. And is the cheapest option. Or at least affordable. My capital outlay fund is a little low. And I'm not sure what my insurance will cover."

"Don't worry about the cost. When people found out what you did, we had enough in donations to repair the door and upgrade the security system in the alley for yours and Sam's and Madame Zelda's shops." Drew came over with the pot of coffee. It was almost empty. "Do you want more before I make a second pot?"

"Please." She let him fill up her cup. "Seriously, people donated to repair my door?"

"Someone wanted to give you a shotgun to replace the baseball bat, but I turned it down for you. I know how you feel about guns." Drew smiled and went to make coffee.

Sam pushed a tray of cookies toward her. "While the guys are over fixing your shop, the sleuthing club is going to meet here. We figured we could take your mind off what happened yesterday by thinking about an actual murder."

Jonathon held up his cup. "I'm staying here at the house. My cover story is I'm protecting you all, but really, I just don't like building things or working with my hands."

"Isn't that the truth." Drew came back and put an arm around his father. "Isn't Mom still waiting for that shed you promised when the two of you bought that house?"

"I'm waiting for you to visit so you can help. I'll get it crooked or it would leak and your mom would never let me live it down." Jonathon looked at his watch. "Speaking of, isn't it time for you guys to get started?"

After the guys left, Rarity went over to her tote and took out the murder book. "I went to the gallery yesterday, and Eleanor's been doing some hiring. She has a marketing director as well as a receptionist now. So I take it she's staying on as general manager?"

"Taking over Jackson's job as general manager, I'd say." Holly had a large notebook. "She had the title of administrative assistant before he died. I guess she sold the family the line that she was the one who did all the work. Jackson had been a figurehead."

"She got a promotion when her boss got whacked." Jonathon looked around the room. "Seems like motive to me."

"And she has a new boyfriend who is an artist. Daniel Cleary." Rarity pointed to the painting on the wall. "According to Mike from Framed in Arizona, the value of his paintings has just gone up after being invited to do a show at the Moments in Time gallery. He offered to buy that one from me."

"What does that have to do with Jackson's death?" Malia broke a decorated sugar cookie open and ate the top half of the leaf.

"If I'm not mistaken, I thought that Eleanor had a crush on Jackson." Rarity glanced at Shirley and Jonathon. Then to Sam. "You three were there Friday night. Didn't it seem that way?"

Sam nodded. "I watched her watching him all night. I swear they were either sleeping together or had in the past. She was obsessed."

"So Eleanor and maybe Daniel are still on the suspect list." Holly glanced around the room. "Anyone else? We know Archer's off Drew's suspect list because of that thing with Calliope."

"Don't remind me." Rarity smiled in spite of herself. "So what about David Valles? We know that he was fighting with Jackson before the open house. And he was furious about him putting up a fake vortex circle. Is that enough to be a killer?"

"He was sleeping with that woman," Jonathon reminded her. "He has an alibi."

"And sometimes alibis lie," Rarity shot back. "Something's weird about David."

Malia nodded. "Maybe. I heard him talking one day at the Garnet. He said he was making seven figures off that book. He didn't want anyone to mess with his legitimate vortex sites. It would dilute his branding."

"Do you know him or how to get in touch with him? I'd love to talk to him about that and what he thinks about Jackson's death. Or even get a list of others in Sedona who believe in the vortexes." Rarity sipped her coffee. She was feeling better, more in control this morning.

"He's giving a talk tonight in Flagstaff." Malia glanced at her schedule. "I was planning on cleaning the apartment, but I could drive you over there."

"Let's make it a girls' night." Holly held up her hand. "I've got the night off from the city water bureau. They're switching systems on Monday, so I have to be there during the day to make sure everything goes as planned."

Malia grinned. "Sounds like a fun trip. Maybe we can grab dinner before or after the talk? Rarity, I mentioned I knew you and he was all about me bringing you to an event. He wants to do a book signing at the store."

"Well, that should give us our opening to chat with him." Rarity glanced around the circle. "Do the rest of you want to come too?"

Sam shook her head. "I'm beat. And I have laundry still. I didn't get it all done the other night."

Jonathon shook his head. "Tonight's pizza and FaceTime with my woman. She insists on seeing me at least once a week when I'm traveling. I think she wants to make sure I'm eating and not wasting away without her."

Shirley flushed pink as she declined. "I have dinner plans. So we just have the two suspects?"

Rarity noticed the change in subject and assumed dinner was with Terrance, but she didn't push. "Does Drew know anything about Jackson's finances? Have we confirmed that the family was bankrolling the gallery? He sent me a list of the paintings that the killer took. We could look at that."

"According to their lawyer, yes, the family gave him the money. Drew asked about any financial troubles and the guy just laughed. He said these people could build an entire city out here around the gallery and not blink an eye. Apparently, the family has old money," Sam reported, then when everyone looked at her, she shrugged. "What? It gave us something to talk about besides us last night when he took me home from the shop."

"Drew is pulling phone records from the gallery. Maybe that will show something." Jonathon glanced at his phone as it beeped. "Ask and it will be provided. Drew just asked if I'd help him check out the numbers tonight."

Rarity thought back to opening night at the gallery. It seemed so long ago. "Are we still meeting Tuesday night?"

"I think we should. Someone needs to talk to this David Valles. I don't think we'll actually get him alone tonight. Maybe someone can take a trip out to the gallery Monday morning and chat with Eleanor about all the changes." Jonathon looked around the room.

Sam held up a hand. "I'll go, but Rarity, will you go with me? I feel like I'm not participating enough. My sleuthing card is going to be suspended."

"Maybe we can look at the vortex area as well." Rarity planned out the trip as she talked. "And get pictures for David? That should make him think we're on his side. Hopefully, we can stop by his office early on Monday?"

"My shop's closed on Monday. Do you think you could get someone to cover you that afternoon or close the shop?"

Shirley interrupted. "No need to close the bookstore. I'll cover you on Monday."

"It's settled then," Sam said before Rarity could speak. "I'll come get you Monday morning at about ten. We'll visit the gallery, then head over to the college where Valles has an office. He teaches Arizona history."

Malia spoke up. "He has office hours every Monday from one to four. But he's gone at four sharp. And he only has office hours twice a week."

Everyone turned to look at her, but it was Rarity who spoke. "I take it you were in one of his classes?"

"Two actually. He makes history relevant." Malia blushed as Holly stared at her. "And he talks a lot about vortexes, so if you read his book, you can ace his tests."

"So an easy A is what you're saying." Jonathon shook his head. "You realize you're paying by the credit hour to actually learn something."

Malia laughed. "Yes, Dad. I realize I might be shortchanging my knowledge of Arizona history, which I'm not going to use anytime or anywhere unless I go to trivia night."

"And with that discussion, I think we should end this meeting, as we all have our assignments." Rarity glanced at the clock. "Who's going to the vortex talk with me again?"

Malia and Holly made plans to pick up Rarity at five so they could grab dinner before the talk, and the rest of the group left. When the house was empty except for her and Killer, Rarity collapsed on the couch and Killer jumped up to curl on her lap. "Sorry, buddy, I'm going out tonight and you have to stay home."

The look the little dog gave her almost broke her heart.

"But we have hours to cuddle and watch our favorite shows." Rarity turned on the home network and found a remodel show they both liked. Sundays were supposed to be a day of rest, right?

\* \* \* \*

When she heard the knock on the door, Rarity was already dressed in capris and a fancy tank top. She grabbed a sweater to go over the top just in case the venue or the restaurant was enclosed. It could be close to a hundred degrees outside, but if the air was set low inside, Rarity felt like she was on a Colorado mountaintop covered in snow. She grabbed her bag, into which she'd tucked a pen and small notebook to write down any questions that could be useful tomorrow when she and Sam interviewed Mr. Valles. It was a long shot that he would have killed Jackson over lying about a vortex, but weirder things had happened.

Malia was at the door and Holly had stayed in her new electric car. Rarity checked the back door and Killer's food and water dish. He was in his bed, his back turned toward her in protest for her leaving him alone. She picked him up, gave the Yorkie a kiss on the head, and then tucked his favorite toy, Lamb Chop, next to him on the bed. He ignored it.

Malia laughed as Rarity came out the door. "He's mad at you."

"I think I've created a monster," Rarity said as she locked the door. "Terrance and Shirley are coming by after dinner to let him out. And he'll probably talk them into staying around or taking him back to Terrance's to wait for me. I feel like I have a child instead of a pet."

"Killer is your child," Malia said as they hurried to the car. "You can ride shotgun."

Rarity climbed into the front seat and noticed how quiet the car was. "Are you sure you have enough power to get us there?"

"The battery will recharge as we drive, don't worry about it." Holly put the vehicle in gear and backed out of the driveway. "The technology on this new model is amazing. You should get one."

"My Mini Cooper is as energy efficient as I can get. I rarely drive anyway. I'd rather have a car that I understand how it works." Rarity glanced at her watch. "Do we have time to eat before the event?"

"As long as the car doesn't die and we have to hitchhike into town." Holly stared forward toward the corner where they'd get on the highway.

"Holly!" Rarity gasped as she tried to see where the battery charge indicator was located. Was it full, like a gas tank? She couldn't tell from where she was sitting.

Malia broke out laughing and Holly joined in. Holly glanced over at Rarity. "Sorry, we just wanted to see your face. We're fine with power, I promise."

"I hate both of you right now." Rarity took a breath and tried to relax in her seat. "So let's talk about Valles. Do either of you really think he could have done something like this?"

"Killing Jackson?" Malia leaned toward the front. "Valles was under investigation for attacking a hiker who had gotten lost and walked through a vortex where they'd been working on setting up a visitor center. The guy was a little drunk and said some things about crazies in the desert. I guess Valles was offended."

"How long ago was that?" Rarity pulled out her notebook and started writing.

"Last year?" Malia looked at Holly who shook her head.

"Two years ago in October. Jackson came into town the next month and paid him to evaluate sites for vortex activity just before Christmas, then bought the land for Red Rock and the art gallery that next January. The building went up quickly." Holly turned down the radio. "Everyone was glad for the work. Red Rock was a big addition to the area."

"And Jackson's family bankrolled all of it?" Rarity wondered just how much money this family had.

"Yes. Although there was some talk around town about a few dealings with some Vegas types, I think that was just Jackson's gambling habit." Malia sighed and looked out the window. "Jackson has, I mean, had a bit of a reputation. I'm surprised you didn't hear any of the rumors about him."

"Running a bookstore doesn't get you around the party crowd. I get most of my information on that side of life from the two of you." Rarity looked at what she'd written down. "Did either of you hear of Jackson dating Eleanor?"

"The gallery manager?" Holly shook her head. "She's not his type. She has a brain and actually wants to work. The women Jackson dated, well, most of them were looking for a sugar daddy and thought they'd found him as soon as he showed interest. Until he dumped them."

Malia added, "A girl at school left town because she was so upset when they broke up. She'd stopped going to class when they got together so she was too far behind to salvage the semester. If she'd even wanted to."

"I swear I saw something between Jackson and Eleanor, but maybe it was one-sided." Rarity saw a mileage sign for Flagstaff. "We haven't even talked about David Valles and we're almost in town."

"We can talk about him at dinner. There's not a lot out there about the guy. He keeps his social media profile pretty clean. I think it's because of his adjunct professor position. He likes being attached to the university. It gives him a constant supply of people to convert over to believing in vortexes. He has a nonprofit that he set up. He's on the board and someone else runs the website and the merchandising division." Holly snapped her fingers. "How about that Vietnamese place over on Clark? The food there is amazing."

As they discussed where to go to dinner, Rarity kept thinking about the economics of running a nonprofit organization with merchandising. Maybe they had more questions for David Valles than she'd expected.

# Chapter 19

The entrance to the talk reminded Rarity more of a carnival or state fair than a serious lecture. When they entered the large stadium, the halls were filled with people and stalls selling all kinds of natural healing products. Rarity found tinctures that promised to cure anything from diabetes to cancer. Weight loss products were sold in several booths along with energy boosters. Several booths sold books and cookbooks that focused on natural energies, not just the local vortexes. And people were lined up at all of the booths. Rarity paused at a crystal shop, then leaned over to Holly. "Sam's stuff is a lot higher quality."

"Sam says they source their stuff from another country. She applied to be one of his vendors but the entrance fee was huge." Holly shook her head. "We should have brought her cards and given them out."

The last booth appeared to be selling a time-share opportunity. Rarity picked up one of the flyers. The property was Red Rock. She turned over the flyer to see the company name. Sanders Incorporated out of New York. She handed a flyer to Holly and Malia. "This is Jackson's family, isn't it?"

Holly nodded. "The building permits for Red Rock and the art gallery were all filed by Sanders Incorporated. So now we find out that they're selling time-shares. At David Valles's talk? I wonder if the county commissioners know about this?"

"I thought Red Rock was built as housing for the gallery's employees?" Malia flipped through the flyer. "This place is huge. It has three pools, tennis courts, and a golf course."

"A lot bigger than what the gallery needs for staff housing," Rarity observed. Then she pointed to one of the selling points. "Red Rock has a newly discovered vortex and on-site spa as well. I wonder who certified it?"

As they made their way to their seats for the actual talk, Rarity's thoughts were circling. If David Valles had certified a vortex for both the gallery and Red Rock purely for money, he wouldn't have been the one to kill Jackson. Was David mad because of the vortex or something else? The more she found out about Jackson Sanders, the more she questioned if there was anyone who didn't want to kill him.

The lights dimmed and a woman walked on stage. She had a microphone in her hand. "Ladies and gentlemen, I'm Heidi Callen with Valles Investigations. I organize these get-togethers, so if you have suggestions, come see me. I'm also here to get this party started." Heidi waited for the cheers to stop. "David will be taking the stage in just a few minutes, but first, we wanted to give our newest sponsor some time to tell you about a new, exciting partnership we've developed with Sanders Incorporated. Being in the Red Rock community is a life-changing experience. You may be at the spa for only a week, but your life will be changed in ways you never expected. Here's the head of development, Calliope Todd, to tell you about Red Rock and the exclusive, limited-time offer we have for you tonight to become a founding Red Rock owner."

Rarity stared at the stage. She could feel Holly's and Malia's eyes on her. Calliope was working for this time-share company. Was that why she'd been at the gallery Monday night? The world was just getting curiouser and curiouser. She pulled out her phone and texted Archer.

*Do you know where Calliope is working now?*

The response came quickly. *Some real estate thing. She tried to get me to invest Friday night. I have a folder at the apartment. That's why she stopped by, and I made her stay over because she'd been drinking. Why?*

*I'll call you later.*

Rarity snapped a picture of Calliope on stage in front of the screen showing the Red Rock time-share to show Archer later.

Holly leaned closer. "Did you know about this?"

"Not a clue. I guess Archer did though. He just told me she tried to sell him on the project." Rarity was texting Drew the information as well.

A woman from the row of seats in front of them turned and glared.

"Sorry," Rarity told her. Then she turned to Holly. "Things are getting interesting."

As Calliope finished her sales talk about the time-shares, she mentioned the healing powers of the vortex. "Now, I'm not going to tell you it heals cancer or broken bones." She laughed at the foolishness and some of the audience laughed with her. "But I do remember that one of our presidents believed in the power of certain hot springs to help with his rheumatoid arthritis. Maybe we've forgotten about the fundamentals as modern medicine has decided to cure everything with a scalpel or a bottle of pills. I'm not an expert on vortexes, but the man you came to see tonight is. David Valles knows more about this area than anyone I know, and I'm a Flagstaff native. Here to introduce David is the manager of the new Moments in Time art gallery, which is just a golf cart ride away from Red Rock—Eleanor Blanchet."

Holly, Malia, and Rarity all locked gazes. As Eleanor walked on stage, Rarity muttered, "And the clown car has one more surprise."

\* \* \* \*

Holly parked the car in front of Desert Grounds Coffee on the outskirts of Flagstaff. "I'm getting some coffee. I need to process what just happened."

Rarity reached for the door handle. "I'm in. I won't be able to sleep tonight anyway. I might as well blame it on the caffeine."

"That was weird, right? It's not just me?" Malia asked as she got out of the back seat.

"Let's order first, then we can talk." Rarity patted her purse. "Thank goodness I brought a notebook. We've got a lot to report to the group on Tuesday night."

"Connections." Holly shook her head. "So many connections."

Rarity laughed as she held the door open for her friends. "Too bad no one wore a shirt saying 'I killed Jackson.'"

"No, but there was that lovely montage of pictures at the end in his memory. Jackson had to be part of this whole thing. He brings everyone together," Malia pointed out. Then she aimed her attention at the dessert case. "I'm getting a slice of cheesecake to go with my coffee."

They all got something for dessert with their coffee. Then they found a booth in the corner out of the main flow of traffic.

"So where should we start?" Rarity's head was still spinning.

"Calliope. She's working for the time-share division." Holly sipped her coffee. "She was with Jackson on Monday night per your statement."

She looked at Rarity, who nodded. "And she was pretty close with him. I know she's aiming her Cupid's bow at Archer, but maybe Jackson was a hot stand-in until she could get you out of the way."

Rarity was writing and paused to look at her friend. "I'm not the one who's dead. Jackson is. I believe if Calliope wanted someone dead, that I'd be first on her list."

"True, but I like her on the suspect list just because she's a piece of work." Holly grinned at Rarity. "Anything else we need to add?"

"Calliope seemed to know both Eleanor and Heidi," Malia said after taking a bite of her cheesecake.

"Maybe." Rarity wondered if Calliope was just there for the money. Sales could be a hard life to make a reliable living with. Of course, you could be rolling in the dough. Or living off savings. Living on commissions was a fickle master. "I'll write it down. I don't want to weed out any suspect until we do it together as a group."

"Maybe I should go check out the time-share?" Holly offered.

Rarity shook her head. "You're the wrong demographic. If it was an apartment, maybe. But Shirley or Jonathon would be better to pose as potential buyers. Jonathon, definitely. He's looking for something that he can use when visiting Drew without the hassle of keeping up a place here."

Malia pulled out the flyer. "This says Diamond members get three weeks use of this or any time-share in the Sanders system of communities."

"I'm not sure what that's going to run him pricewise, but it's going to be substantial. We'll warn him that Edith has to have some inheritance or some income more than his police retirement to make him a prized buyer." Rarity wondered if he could lie and tell them he'd sold a book and wanted to surprise his wife. She'd bring up that possible cover story when Malia and Holly weren't around since she didn't think he'd told everyone about his writing yet. "I'll talk to him Tuesday if not before."

"And Eleanor, she's always in the most interesting places. She has a new boyfriend and she's working with Valles recommending these time-shares." Holly pointed to Rarity's page. "I think she's number one on the suspect list just because her hands are in so many pies."

"Don't forget she took over Jackson's role at the gallery. The woman is everywhere." Malia ate the last bite of her cheesecake, licking the fork.

"I agree. I think there's more to learn about Eleanor. Sam and I will see what we can find out tomorrow." Rarity took a bite of her apple cranberry pie, thinking as she savored the cinnamon goodness. "I started trying to research her a few days ago but got sidetracked. Maybe we should look into what she did in New York too. Archer thought she'd worked with Jackson's dad. She seems really adaptable to any situation."

Holly finished her crème brûlée. "I don't know. They make this look so easy on television. Why can't we just have a bright red arrow drop out of the sky and point to our killer? It would make life so much easier."

"The fun is in the investigation." Rarity sipped her coffee. "If the clues are too easy, the puzzle isn't any fun."

"I don't really agree," Holly said as she checked her watch. "I've got to be at work at seven tomorrow, so I need to get some sleep. Are you guys ready to head back to Sedona?"

"Drop me off at the Garnet. I'm meeting Dane there at ten thirty." Malia stood and gathered their plates, setting them in a tub near the wall.

"Dane, huh?" Rarity tried not to look interested.

Malia sighed. "It's no big deal. We're just dating, okay? Nothing serious."

"Yet," Holly added to Malia's sentence. When Malia looked puzzled, she repeated herself. "Nothing serious, yet."

The pink showing on Malia's cheeks was cute, Rarity thought as she walked out to Holly's car in the cooling air.

Malia opened the back door of Holly's car. "Whatever."

Holly and Rarity locked gazes over the car and giggled. Whatever it was between Malia and Dane wasn't simple and it probably was more serious than Malia was ready to admit. Rarity was happy for her friend, and she hoped Dane was good enough for the brilliant but shy Malia.

When Rarity got home, Killer was in his bed and there was a note on the counter from Shirley. Rarity read it aloud. "I had to head home but Killer's been walked, twice. And he's had three treats so don't let him tell you he's starving. I'll talk to you tomorrow. I'll be there to open the store at noon. Let me know if that plan has changed."

Killer walked over to his empty food dish, then turned and stared at her.

"Nope. You've been fed and treated, so it's time to go to bed. Mama has a lot of playacting to do tomorrow to try to find out who killed Jackson." Rarity figured he didn't understand half of what she told him, but there were words he recognized, like food, water, walk, and swim. She'd just keep talking and see what else he picked up.

* * * *

The next morning, Sam arrived at the house after Rarity had gotten in a swim. She was sitting at the table with her second cup of coffee and a warmed-up cinnamon roll when Killer barked at the door to announce Sam's presence.

Sam held up a bottle of orange juice. "I didn't come empty-handed."

"I have day-old cinnamon rolls over by the microwave." Rarity stood to grab two glasses as Sam set the juice bottle on the table. "And coffee, of course."

Sam got a roll and sat down next to Rarity. "So how was your lecture last night?"

"Illuminating. You really need to hitch your crystal business to this guy. The stuff they sold at the stadium was junk compared to yours." Rarity put her pen down and told Sam about the rest of the night.

"The price of entry is too high." Sam finished off her orange juice before she spoke. "So Calliope works for this guy and somehow Eleanor is attached too?"

"That's the meat of it, yes. Red Rock is there as an employee benefit, but they're selling the place as a time-share too." Rarity thought about this last statement. "Someone who approved the building plans had to know about this, right? They were putting in way too many townhouses for just the employees of a gallery. Maybe Holly can get a copy of the original plans they used to get permits. This might have been the plan all along. This might just be a red fish."

"You mean a red herring." Sam finished her roll.

Rarity frowned and looked up from her notes. "That's what I said."

"You said, fish…" Sam sighed and took her plate to the sink. "Never mind. Let's get ready and go talk to Eleanor. I talked to that marketing chick, Jade Williams. She said Eleanor is planning on being in the gallery today at ten."

"How did you get her to tell you that?" Rarity felt amazed at Sam's ability to snoop.

Sam smiled as she lifted her coffee cup. "She thought I wanted to show my jewelry at the gallery. She says it's beautiful and they'd love to showcase it, for a twenty-five percent cut. I argued for ten. I'm sure we'll end up somewhere around fifteen percent, which is standard. Jade tried to push that the clientele they bring to the table are more likely to buy. I told her I'd only negotiate with the person who could make the final decision. That wasn't Jade."

"Remind me never to negotiate with you." Rarity stood and took Killer outside. When they came back in, she locked the back door and took off his lead. The dog got the hint and ran to his bed. "He's going to hate me when this is over. I've been gone too much lately."

"He'll forgive you. As long as Archer doesn't go to jail for something he didn't do." Sam tossed her keys. "We can take my Jeep. It has more legroom."

"Are you taking some jewelry samples?" Rarity followed her friend outside and made sure the front door was locked too. "I'd hate for you to lose out on possible shelf space."

"I'm already packed. As long as Eleanor's not heading to jail for killing Jackson, I intend to leave the gallery with a signed commission contract. Maybe even if she is." Sam remotely unlocked the doors and grinned at her. "I love killing two birds with one stone. Especially when there's money on the table."

# Chapter 20

Jade wasn't at the reception desk when Rarity and Sam walked into the gallery. Instead, a young woman in a professional dress stood as soon as they walked in the door and greeted them. "Good morning, I'm Allie Meeker. I'd like to welcome you to Moments in Time, Sedona's newest art gallery for those with discriminating tastes. How can I help you today?"

Rarity felt underdressed, even though she'd stepped up her normal workday outfit of capris with a nice top. But as a bookseller, she needed to look approachable, not rich. She was about to respond when Sam stepped forward. "Good morning, Allie. I'm Samantha Aarons, owner of Sedona Crystals. I'm here to speak with Eleanor Blanchet. Jade was supposed to tell her I would be coming by."

"Oh, yes, Ms. Aarons, you're on Ms. Blanchet's list for today. Let me call her and tell her you've arrived." Allie shot Rarity a look but when she didn't say anything, she went to call Eleanor.

"We'll be over here taking in the collection. When you have a minute, please bring us some water." Sam took Rarity's arm and led her away from the entrance. "I wanted to show you this painting. It's by a local artist."

When they were out of earshot, Sam nodded toward a collection from Daniel Cleary. "It looks like Eleanor's new boyfriend is doing well here at the gallery. Several of these are already sold and from the price tags, the one you own has just gone up in value. You should sell it now, while he's hot."

"I bought that painting because I liked it and it would fit into the house. I didn't buy it as an investment." Rarity stepped closer to one that she'd considered purchasing at Art in the Park. The price had gone up ten times or more since she'd last seen it. "Although maybe I should consider selling."

"Isn't Daniel's work something special?" Eleanor asked as she walked over to where Rarity and Sam were standing. "I discovered him a few weeks ago in Flagstaff. Rarity, I think I remember you purchasing one of his creations. I'd be glad to make an offer on it to add to the gallery's collection. Just let me know. It's so nice to see you again. And Samantha, I loved the sample of your work that you left with Jade. I hope you're considering our commission offer."

Rarity leaned in when Eleanor gave her an air-kiss. Then Allie pressed a glass of water in her hand. "Eleanor. I'm glad to see you again. I hoped that the family would keep you on here at the gallery."

Allie's eyes widened as she gave Sam her water. Then she scurried off, calling back to us, "Let me know if you need anything."

Anger flashed in Eleanor's eyes. "There was never any doubt. I guess I was just feeling vulnerable the day I saw you at the art show. Did you just come by to support Samantha? Or are you here snooping? I hear that bookstore of yours has a sleuthing club. Don't you find it boring since nothing ever happens here in Sedona?"

"Oh, plenty happens." Rarity smiled, trying not to let Eleanor rattle her. Which clearly was her purpose. "I did want to know if I could see the vortex. Everyone has been raving about it and I didn't take the time to experience it during the open house."

Eleanor searched Rarity's face with her gaze, but when she saw no subterfuge in her appearance, she shrugged. "Go ahead. It's through the red door. Samantha, can we go to my office to discuss the details?"

"Sounds perfect." Sam met Rarity's gaze.

Rarity smiled. "I'll meet you out here when you're done. Don't forget, we're meeting Drew and Archer for lunch."

Sam nodded like Rarity hadn't just made that part up. At least now Eleanor knew they were expected somewhere by a police detective. Rarity didn't think Eleanor would kill them and bury them in the desert with Sam's car, but weirder things had happened. Besides, Eleanor was still on the suspect list for Jackson's killing.

Rarity watched as the women went down a hallway to Eleanor's office. Then she walked toward the doorway. Allie brought a pitcher of water over to a table by the door.

"Just in case you need more when you come back inside. The vortex seems to make people very thirsty." Allie glanced out the window at the rock circles that indicated the location of the energy spike. Her voice was filled with reverence for the site. "I try to visit the vortex every day at three during my second break. It's like a shot of espresso that gets me through the rest of the afternoon."

"Do you live at Red Rock? I hear there's a vortex there as well." At least that was what the time-share people had been saying last night. Rarity didn't mention the source of her intel.

"It's next to the pool. Our monthly community newsletter says that they're building a spa next to the pool that will highlight the vortex and help us use its power for our healing and health. It's all very exciting. I can't believe I get to live there, just because I work at the gallery. My townhouse is twice the size of my last apartment," Allie gushed.

"I don't remember a red door here when I attended the open house. Is this new?" Rarity touched the wood door and tried to picture the area from that Friday.

"Oh, yes. The original door was glass, but it was broken when they found Mr. Sanders, so Ms. Blanchet had it replaced with this one. It was hand-carved by a local craftsman."

The phone rang and Allie excused herself. Rarity took a picture of the door. Neither Archer, Drew, nor Jonathon had said anything about a glass door being broken. Maybe the damage hadn't been extensive, but Eleanor had wanted the door to be perfect. And even a small chip in glass tended to expand over time. Especially in the desert.

Rarity stepped out into the courtyard and felt the heat of the day hit her. She breathed in, expecting hot air to fill her lungs, but instead, the air felt cooler than it should. She looked around and found a mister hung over the top of the vortex. Probably to keep visitors cool while they filled up with the energy from the spot.

But according to David, there was no vortex here. At least, that's what he'd said up until last night. In his talk last night, he'd listed both the gallery and the one at Red Rock as being certified by his time-tested process. Rarity wondered if the payment for the certification had finally happened. She wondered if there was any way Drew could check David's financials and see how much the speaker was being paid to certify a vortex. And, more telling, if he'd gotten a check from the gallery or Red Rock in the last week. The payment might have come directly from the family's coffers, though.

Rarity walked around the rock circle that enclosed the vortex. Then she stepped inside.

She closed her eyes and waited for the rush of energy Allie described. She opened her mind, her heart, her breathing to the possibility. She'd felt a vortex before. She knew how it could overwhelm your senses. She took another breath. Then another. Finally, she opened her eyes.

Nothing.

If this was a vortex, she wasn't feeling its power. David's declaration on Monday that Jackson was trying to fool everyone seemed more likely, even though he'd changed his mind now.

As she stepped over the rocks, she saw a red spot. She knelt beside it and saw a drop of blood, dried in the sun on the side of a rock. They'd cleaned up the area so you couldn't tell a person had been killed here, but they'd missed a spot. A spot that reminded Rarity that for all his faults, Jackson had been a human being and hadn't deserved to die. She stood and listened for a minute. "Jackson, I swear, I'm going to find out who did this."

An owl hooted in the distance. That and the sound of the mist coming out of the tubing was the only thing that answered her.

Rarity went back inside.

Allie had been right, she was thirsty when she came in, but she blamed the high desert heat more than the power of the vortex. Especially since she already thought it was a hoax. A way to bring people into the gallery so they could sell overpriced art. And soon, Sam's jewelry. Daniel Cleary probably didn't think that his art was overpriced. Rarity guessed that art value was more about what a person could pay than the actual value of an item. Like a book. She was glad she dealt in items with prices already set by the marketplace. Although a rare book could be more like a piece of art, she corrected herself. She just didn't deal in rare books.

When Sam came out of the office, she was grinning like the Cheshire cat. She paused where Rarity was now sitting, checking her email on her phone. "I'll be ready to leave in a moment. I need to bring in my inventory."

Rarity watched as Sam hurried out to the car and brought in a box. Then she and Allie cataloged it and wrote down sale prices for each item. Sam took a picture of both the handwritten listing with prices and the box of jewelry, documenting what she'd left and what they'd agreed to sell the items for.

Rarity wandered around the shop, pausing before a painting. It seemed familiar. She took a picture of it.

"Cameras are not allowed in the gallery," Eleanor growled next to her. "Please delete the photo."

Rarity spun around and saw Eleanor standing next to her. The woman's hands were curled into tight fists. "I'm sorry. I didn't know that. You should have signs."

"If you'd ever been in a real gallery before, you'd know that." Eleanor grabbed her phone and deleted the pictures of the painting. She shoved the phone back into Rarity's hand. "Of course, you do your art shopping in the park. I guess I can't expect someone from Sedona to have an inkling about art. It's not like you went to college."

"You were at Art in the Park as well," Rarity reminded her. She didn't like this snobby version of Eleanor. In fact, Rarity didn't like any version of Eleanor. "And I do have a college degree in marketing."

"Business degree, it figures." Eleanor rolled her eyes and spun back around.

Rarity watched as the woman headed to her office. She took a breath to calm herself. Seeing Eleanor this angry was shocking. Sam touched her arm and Rarity jumped.

"Sorry, are you ready to go?" Sam was beaming. "I'm so glad I took the chance to show Eleanor and Jade my jewelry. If what I left sells, we're talking about doing an exclusive collection for the gallery."

"So you got a good agreement?" Rarity asked as they walked to the car. Being outside had calmed her and she wondered if she'd overreacted to Eleanor's actions.

"Great one. If she sells just what's there, my share will pay rent on my shop for a full quarter. I really hope this gallery stays in business. And it's made me realize I need to get my work out there in other shops as well. Maybe in Flagstaff or Cottonwood, or maybe in Phoenix." Sam bounced as she unlocked the car.

"Well, it sounds like this was a productive visit." Rarity clicked her seat belt. "I took pictures of their supposed vortex. I didn't feel anything there. Oh, and of a door. They replaced the glass door that was there the night Jackson was killed."

"Sorry if the investigation got sidetracked by my business venture. But I did ask Eleanor about her being at the lecture last night. She dismissed it as a way to get the gallery's name out there. A marketing ploy that Jade set up for her. She laughed about David and Jackson's relationship. She said Jackson had done a number on David, but now Jackson was the one winning. Or would be if he was alive." Sam turned the car on the access road and started driving to the highway. "Are we still going to the university or are we really meeting the guys for lunch?"

"That was just an insurance policy to make sure Eleanor didn't kill you in her office and send Allie after me." Rarity laughed at the look Sam gave her. "What? You didn't think it was a little coincidental that Eleanor wanted to sell your jewelry in the gallery? Not that you don't deserve this attention, you do. I was just making sure we weren't going to be coyote food."

"You have a twisted mind, my sister." Sam turned the car toward Flagstaff and the university. "But now that you brought up lunch, you're buying."

"You just made this big deal," Rarity reminded her.

"It's not a big deal until the items sell. The first lesson of running your own shop. Don't count your sales until they happen. Or the check clears." Sam turned up the radio. "I love this song."

They ate lunch before heading to the university and caught up on their lives. Even though their shops were next to each other, sometimes Rarity didn't see Sam except at the book club meeting for weeks. And they were just getting back on normal terms after the blowup around Sam's brother, Marcus, and his visit to Sedona. Rarity didn't begrudge Sam's newfound closeness with her brother, but sometimes she wished for the old days when she and Sam were inseparable. Life happened, she guessed.

As they were walking to the building where David Valles had an office, Rarity was struck by how young everyone on campus looked. She glanced over at Sam and realized she was thinking the same thing. "We aren't old, right?"

"Not in the least. These are all just child prodigies who came to college at fourteen." Sam grinned and hooked Rarity's arm in hers. "Besides, I wouldn't give up the last ten years for anything."

"Me neither." Rarity thought about how certain of life she'd been in college. She was going into corporate marketing. She'd be a vice president by the age of thirty and have her own house or better yet, a condo in the city, where she had a grand piano for when she decided to take lessons and her own rooftop pool. That life had been sideswiped by her cancer diagnosis. But the pieces were still here in Sedona. She had a house and a pool. She might not make seven figures in the bookselling business, but she made enough to have a good life.

And she had friends, and Archer, and Killer. Things that weren't even on her mind when she was planning for her world domination in the marketing field. And most of all, she was happy. Most days. Most moments. Like right now, hanging out with her best friend. A day of hooky from the shop and yet the world hadn't ended because she took off a day from work.

A young girl was standing by David's desk when they finally found his office. It was in the back and appeared to be about the size of a janitor's closet. No other instructors' offices were in this hall. And the light just over his doorway was down to one bulb, so the place looked as gloomy as it felt.

The girl didn't seem to mind. He was signing her copy of his book and she was in heaven. She took a selfie with him and bounced when she checked the picture a second later. "It's wonderful, Professor Valles. Thank you so much. Maybe we can chat about a vortex I think I've found out near the dorms. My roommate left school so I'm alone in my room but I got pictures."

Sam rolled her eyes at Rarity as they stood and listened to the young woman try to seduce her professor. A possible vortex and a roll in the hay? How could he turn that down? But when he heard them at the door, the look on his face was priceless. He looked relieved that someone had come to rescue him. Rarity's impression of David Valles shot up a few points.

"I'm sorry, Tina. It looks like I'm needed elsewhere." He stood and walked over to them. "How may I help you today?"

Tina picked up her book and pushed past Rarity into the hallway. When a door slammed at the far end of the hall, David breathed out a sigh.

"I really need a new office with more people around me. Thanks for the save." He looked between Sam and Rarity. "You two aren't in my class, but I feel like I've seen you before. Were you at the lecture last night?"

"I was," Rarity spoke up. "Sam and I are from Sedona. We're trying to figure out what's going on with the gallery vortex and the Red Rock vortex. Before last night, I thought I'd heard that you said they were fake. That Jackson Sanders made up the vortexes to bring people into his gallery."

David's face hardened and he went back to his desk. "I shouldn't be talking with you."

"Why? Is there something going on? Something that got Jackson killed?" Rarity figured David was a few seconds away from asking them to leave, and even though he had a crappy office at the university, it was still protected by campus security. Rarity didn't want to go to jail today. Or tomorrow.

To her surprise, he nodded to the chairs instead. "Sit down. There are some real-world truths you need to hear before I tell you to leave."

Sam and Rarity sat in the indicated chairs. Rarity leaned forward. "Why did you support the certification of the vortexes?"

"It was already a done deal. Jackson had paid the county commissioners for the certification and my denials weren't going to do anything but make me look like a loon. So when they came to me with a proposal and a check,

I took the check." He straightened out the papers on his desk. "Not my finest hour. I'm fighting for people to believe in the power of vortexes and yet I let two be certified that were fakes."

"You fought with Jackson Monday night at the gallery about this. About him setting up a fake vortex," Rarity reminded him. She'd figured he was the man she'd heard fighting with Jackson. She ran with it. "When did you change your mind and decide to work with Eleanor and Calliope?"

He didn't look at Rarity as he spoke. "The next day, Jackson came by my office here with a check and a form for me to sign. He said he'd never ask for this again, but he needed this one favor. He needed certification, as he'd already told his family it was a go. He didn't want to disappoint them or jeopardize the money they'd already invested. Everything would be gone. And I'd still be fighting for people to believe me."

Finally, he looked up. "I've never done anything remotely like that before. Now, I'm locked in this agreement with the devil. You saw the dance last night."

# Chapter 21

Sam dropped Rarity off at the shop when they got back into town. "I'm going to put the contract away in my safe, then get ready to open tomorrow. I think I'll do some research on new sales possibilities for a while. Do you want me to drive you home at five?"

"Archer's coming over and we're making dinner, so no. I'll be fine." Rarity paused before she closed the car door. "Thanks for today. I've missed hanging out."

Sam nodded. "Me too. It's been too long since we've just spent a day together. Maybe next week we can run into Cottonwood if I find another consignment shop. I'll even buy lunch."

"So now I'm your marketing guru?" Rarity laughed but nodded. "I'll see if Shirley can cover me again next week."

"You're my lucky charm," Sam corrected as she drove off to park the car in front of her shop. She'd carved out a bit of the front area for her own parking space since her building sat back on the lot and away from the sidewalk.

Rarity went into the shop and was surprised to find several people walking around shopping. Shirley was at the register. "This is busy for a Monday. You should have called me. I would have come back sooner."

"Oh, these are friends from church. I mentioned yesterday that I'd be all by myself today and everyone came to keep me company. I've sold a lot of books." She handed a credit card and receipt back to the woman who was at the counter.

"I didn't even think I needed a book, but Shirley proved me wrong." The woman laughed as she took the bag. "You have an amazing salesperson there."

"You know you're going to love making those bread recipes," Shirley responded. "Mary, this is my boss, Rarity Cole. Mary is head of my women's group at church."

"Shirley lets me think I'm in charge," Mary said as she shook Rarity's hand.

Rarity laughed and nodded. "It's the same here. She lets me think I'm the boss. Thanks for coming in, and I hope to see you again."

As they worked together to help the rest of the people in the store, Rarity thought about what she and Sam had found out. She didn't think David had killed Jackson because he was already stuck supporting the fake vortexes—even with Jackson dead, since he'd signed the paperwork. Eleanor, she still didn't have a feel for. She ran that gallery like it was her own. But she'd done the same job when Jackson was alive. He'd just gotten all the credit for her work. Daniel was a new artist at the gallery. Had Jackson and Eleanor fought about adding Daniel to their stable of artists?

There were a lot of maybes floating around. She hoped tomorrow night when they talked about what everyone had found out that they'd be able to point Drew toward the actual killer. She could tell that Jonathon wanted to go home, but he wouldn't leave until someone was behind bars for the killing.

Archer came in exactly at five and Shirley left quickly, explaining that she and Terrance were going into Flagstaff for an exhibit and dinner. Rarity hoped her friend wasn't going to get hurt in this relationship. She knew Terrance was falling in love, but Shirley wasn't free to do anything about it. And Rarity didn't think Shirley would take a drastic step. She'd see it as a betrayal.

Archer locked the front door and turned over the sign. Then he went to the back and locked the door in the break room. He stood by her as she was finishing her closing tasks at the register. They had a routine.

"So why were you interested in where Calliope was working? Did you find out something?" Archer took her tote as they walked out the front door and waited as she relocked the door.

"She's working for the Sanders family. They are selling time-shares out at Red Rock during David Valles's lectures about vortexes in the area." She tucked her keys in her pocket and took Archer's arm. "And she's not the only one who is attached to David. Eleanor actually introduced him and called him a blessing for certifying the vortex at the gallery."

"I thought he said that one was fake." Now Archer slowed down to watch Rarity's face as she filled him in on what they'd found out today.

She bounced more questions off him. He didn't have any answers, but it felt good to have someone she could tell everything to.

He took her keys as they arrived at the house. "I'm at a loss with Jackson's death. I know he didn't put that arrow in his own back. If it was just the drug, I'd think he overdosed on something new. But it's a little hard to overdose when the delivery system is an arrow."

"I can't see David killing him. Eleanor, well, she's a possibility, but if she did it, she's a cool cucumber. She's acting like she's totally fine. She works in the same building where Jackson died and I know she had feelings for him. And she's dating someone else, just like that." Rarity felt like she was talking herself into Eleanor being the culprit just because she didn't like the woman. "Anyway, maybe we can just put this away and have a night to ourselves?"

"Not talk about murder and suspects?" Archer's eyes widened and he picked up Killer and put his leash on. "What would we have to talk about? I'm taking this guy out for a quick walk. You decide on what you want for dinner and I'll cook."

Rarity went to the freezer, pulled out two chicken breasts, and put them in the microwave to thaw. Then she went to her bedroom and changed into yoga pants and a tank. She put on slippers and brushed her hair. She heard the door open and soon after, Killer was jumping at her feet.

"Hey, buddy, sorry I didn't take you with me today, but you can go tomorrow even though it's Tuesday." She picked him up and cuddled him to her as she went out to the living room.

Drew stood in her living room, talking to Archer. She looked between the men. "What's happened?"

"Tell me about your visit to David Valles today." Drew pulled out his notebook.

"Okay, but I don't think there's anything there." She went to sit at the table with the men. "Why do you want to know?"

Archer took her hand. "Rarity, they think David tried to kill himself today. He's at Flagstaff South."

\* \* \* \*

After Rarity told Drew about their talk, he tucked his notebook into his pocket. "That's exactly what Sam told me a few minutes ago."

"What, did you think we'd lie to you?" Rarity asked.

He ran his hands through his hair. "No. Maybe. I was hoping there would be a reason behind this."

"I don't know. David was upset about Red Rock and the gallery pushing him into doing a fake certification of the vortexes, but that shouldn't have caused him to kill himself. Unless he knew more than he told us or he killed Jackson himself." Rarity took the cup of tea that Archer had made her and curved her hands around it for the warmth. "Thanks."

"No problem." Archer turned to Drew. "So what did he overdose on?"

"The toxicology is still being processed. I just got the report back on what Jackson was killed with and it was pentobarbital. It's used in assisted suicides." Drew nodded to Rarity's cup. "Any chance I can get one?"

"There's still hot water in the teapot." Archer pointed to the basket that held the different types of tea. "Grab one of those."

Drew pushed the basket toward Rarity. "Tell me there's one with caffeine. It's going to be a long night."

"Are you going into Flagstaff?" She handed him an Earl Grey packet.

"Yeah. I want to chat with David when he wakes up. I guess a student found him in his office. She's been hanging out at the hospital to see if he wakes up. She seems very attached." Drew took the cup of hot water from Archer and dropped the tea bag inside. He looked up at Rarity, then sat back. "You have a look on your face."

"What look?" she asked.

He smiled and dunked his tea bag. "The one where you don't want to tell me what's going on."

Rarity shrugged. "David has groupies. There was one there when we went to his office earlier. We're lucky this one showed up when she did."

"He talks about vortexes and teaches history. How can he have groupies?" Drew asked, confused.

"The man has a certain appeal," Rarity admitted.

"Oh, does he now. Tell me all about it," Archer challenged her.

"Hold on, guys, wait until I finish my tea before you start fighting. You know the kids hate that," Drew teased. He shook his head. "I feel bad that we're joking around about David when he's in the hospital, but his doctors assured me that he was found in time. They say he's lucky he's not in a coma."

Rarity sipped her tea. "Something doesn't make sense. David was in his office when they found him, right? Why would you try to kill yourself during your stated office hours? Especially when you knew that you had a lot of visitors during that time? Wouldn't he have been more successful planning it for when he was at home? Did he live with anyone?"

Drew checked his notebook. "No. He lived alone. You think this wasn't intentional."

"It's just suspicious." Rarity looked at Drew. He stood and pulled out his phone.

"I'm calling to make sure there's a guard on David's room. If someone tried to kill him, they might try again." He stepped away from the table to make the call.

"And Drew? If someone did this, the university has cameras everywhere. You just need to find out who visited him this afternoon after Sam and I left his office."

*  *  *  *

The Tuesday night book club was already buzzing by the time everyone arrived and they'd poured their coffee and got cookies. Killer was enjoying being part of the club since typically, Rarity kept him home on Tuesdays. She didn't like him being stuck at the bookstore for that long, but he didn't seem to mind. Currently, he was curled up next to Shirley as she talked to Holly about the blanket she was crocheting. Holly glanced as Rarity walked over to join them. She'd put a sign up for any stray customers who might arrive during the club meeting, but in the months that they'd been doing book club, she'd had only one walk-in customer during the club hours. Locals knew the group met and when, so they didn't disturb them. Small-town manners at work.

"Okay, it looks like we're all here. I think there's a lot we need to talk about. Rarity, do you want to go first?" Holly stood and walked over to the flip chart. Everyone else opened their notebooks.

Rarity went through the lecture they'd attended on Sunday, highlighting the fact that Calliope worked for the time-share company as well as Eleanor's participation. Malia and Holly joined in to fill in points they'd noticed. Then Rarity told the group about visiting the gallery and the door change. She turned to Jonathon. "Did Drew say anything about the door being damaged when they found Jackson?"

Jonathon shook his head. "No. Maybe the glass was damaged earlier?"

Sam raised her hand. "No, it wasn't. Drew and I went out to the vortex during the open house on that Friday night to talk about us. He pointed out the way the glass windows and the door made the area seem to be part of the gallery, not the outside. If there was a crack, we should have seen it. You know Drew, he notices everything, especially if it's not supposed to be that way."

Jonathon nodded. "I think the damage must have happened during the attack on Jackson, or afterward. I'll ask Drew if there's anything in the police report about damage to the door."

Holly wrote the word DOOR on the flip chart and put Jonathon's name by it. As the discussion leader, she was responsible for following up on ideas and questions they'd had during the discussion and assigning the questions or research to someone in the group. Then she used that list to lead the next discussion. They had a process, even if they weren't professional investigators like Drew and his staff.

"Okay, there's another stop we made—to visit David Valles. He's not happy that he got involved with the Sanders family of businesses. He felt forced into certifying vortexes for both Red Rock and the gallery. Now he feels like they're using him and his vortex knowledge and credibility to sell their products. At least the time-shares." Rarity told everyone what David had told her and Sam, then she glanced at Jonathon, who nodded. "Drew came to my house later and told me that David was in the hospital. Somehow, he overdosed. It's being looked at as a possible murder attempt."

"Because he talked to you?" Shirley dropped her hook and blanket onto her lap. "Rarity, I'm worried that you're getting a little too close to this murder. Maybe someone is going to attack you next."

Rarity went over and put her hand on Shirley's shoulder. "The problem with that is I don't know anything. I still haven't figured out why Jackson is dead. Or who did it. There's no reason to think that I'd be on anyone's worry list."

The room got quiet. Finally, Jonathon spoke up. "The problem with your theory, Rarity, is that the killer doesn't know what you know and don't know."

As they finished talking about what they knew, Holly made the new assignments for the week. Rarity didn't have anything on her list but when she complained, Jonathon shook his head. "You did a lot this last week. Let the rest of us poke around and see if we can stir up any new clues."

Archer had come into the bookstore a little earlier and was sitting in a chair reading. Killer was on his lap. Archer looked up and smiled at

Jonathon's comment. "And if you all think that you can keep her from sticking her nose in where it doesn't belong, you're delusional."

"I'd rather say optimistic," Holly agreed as she ended the meeting.

Rarity went over and gave Archer a hug. "Just for that, you're helping clean up."

He kissed her and stood, leaving Killer on the chair. "I was planning on helping anyway. Did you all solve the mystery yet?"

Shirley laughed as she cleared off the mostly empty treat table. "Not today. I think we have more questions than we did right after Jackson was killed."

"At least my guilt is off the table." He put the coffeepot on the trolley they used to move things from the break room to the area near the fireplace where all the events were held. When no one said anything, he looked around. "Right? You all know I didn't kill Jackson."

Malia folded a chair and put it on the storage stand. "Dude, you're so needy. I'm not sure how Rarity puts up with you."

"I'm cute," he shot back, putting his hands up on his face to make a frame.

Rarity put the empty lemonade bottles on the tray. "You tend to earn your keep. That's why I keep you around. Besides, Killer loves you."

With the treat table cleared, he went to help Malia with the chairs. "At least someone does."

Rarity laughed as she pushed the trolley toward the break room. "Whatever. I'm beginning to agree with Malia. You are needy."

She washed the coffeepot and set it up to brew tomorrow morning. Then she unlocked the back door and took the trash out to the dumpster in the alley. A coyote howled in the distance, sending chills down her spine. Even the animals were on edge.

Archer stood waiting for her at the door. "Everything okay?"

She nodded as she went inside. "I'm fine. Just getting the trash out."

He looked at her as she locked the door and then checked it again. The new door was sturdy but the other one had been pretty. Sometimes for safety reasons, you had to go with the less attractive alternative.

"Rarity, I'm sorry about not figuring out Calliope and her agenda earlier. I've been thinking about this a lot, and even Drew had told me she was trouble." He rinsed a washcloth in the sink but paused before going back to the treat table in the front of the shop. "I just never saw her as anything other than a friend."

She went over and kissed him. "I wasn't worried about it, much."

"Well, you don't have to worry about anything like that again. I've learned my lesson." Archer left the break room and headed to wash off the table.

As he left, Rarity shook her head. "No, you probably haven't, because you're too nice. You don't see the bad in people. And that's why I love you."

Jonathon poked his head into the break room. "Sorry, am I interrupting? There's no one in here, who were you talking to?"

"Just musing about something." Rarity smiled and walked over to turn off the lights. "What's up?"

"I'm heading out. Shirley, Malia, and Holly have all left, but I told Sam I'd walk her home. There's been some reports of coyotes here in town the last few days." Jonathon followed her to the register, where she locked it and tucked her key into her tote. "I'll see you in the morning?"

"Have you officially been assigned babysitting duties?" Rarity knew Drew worried about her and Sam. "Shirley will be here most of the day for Mommy and Me class if you have something else you need to do."

"Nope, I'm just anxious to get some work done on the book," Jonathon lied.

Rarity could see it in his face, but it was such a kind gesture, she forgave him immediately for the falsehood.

# Chapter 22

Rarity couldn't sleep that night, so finally, at about four in the morning, she got out of bed and put on a robe and slippers. Then she took out her murder book. She grabbed a piece of blank paper from the printer in her home office and drew a long line down the middle of the page. Then she turned it horizontally.

She needed to make a timeline. The Tuesday night group was right about one thing. They had no clue why Jackson was dead. Maybe making a timeline would take some people off the list of possible suspects. And dwindling that down allowed them to focus on who might be an actual suspect.

Rarity glanced at her notes. Holly had gotten a copy of the original building and business applications that had been filed with the city and the county. The gallery was just inside the city limits; Red Rock, on the other hand, was in the county. She put the dates that each paper was filed as the starting point on the line. The gallery was filed first, then a week later, the development plan for Red Rock. She was surprised to see the time-share had been part of the original plan. So why had it been such a shock to everyone she knew? Someone was using the good deed of housing the gallery employees as a cover for the time-share development.

Six months later, the gallery was ready to have its open house. That seemed fast for a building to be constructed, not to mention the townhouses for the employees. She added the date to her timeline and wrote a note about visiting with the local developer who had built both projects and now was in the time-share business. At the lecture the other night, she'd picked up a card for the time-share sales team. She wondered if she could get more information by posing as interested in buying a unit. Or a week, however they described it. She needed to talk to anyone but Calliope for this to work, as she didn't know what Archer had shared about Rarity's family or lack of one. Maybe a long-lost aunt had been asking Rarity to look into somewhere she could buy so she could visit without having to sleep in a house where there was a pet. Allergies?

It was still too early to make an appointment to visit the time-share office, so she finished sketching out the timeline. She pulled up Jackson on Facebook and in the New York social pages and put little notes throughout the time frame. If he was supposed to be keeping an eye on the building, he was doing all of it from his high-rise condo in the city.

Or someone else had been watching the progression for him. Like Eleanor.

Rarity thought about how Eleanor had gone from snotty to full-on witch in their last encounter. What was wrong with the woman? And why the comment about Rarity and her not going to college? A lot of people were hung up either in their high school or college glory years. But Eleanor seemed so cosmopolitan. Did it really go back to what happened to her as a young adult?

Just as she had with Jackson, she did a social media deep dive on Eleanor. That's where she found the first mention of Moments and Red Rock. Eleanor had moved to Flagstaff before the permits were filed. She must have been the boots-on-the-ground person for the development. She'd known all along about the time-share addition to Red Rock.

Rarity went to refill her coffee cup and found that the coffee was all gone. She glanced at the clock. She had time to swim before she got ready to go to the bookstore.

Once she was there, she'd call the sales office and see if she could get a tour to check out the place for her traveling aunt. She hoped she could keep the focus on that and off the Tuesday night sleuthing club. The club's habit of investigating murders was no secret in Sedona, but maybe she'd be lucky and get a salesperson from Flagstaff or one they'd brought in from New York.

A girl could hope.

Jonathon arrived just ten minutes after Rarity opened the bookstore. She smiled as he hurried inside, throwing his tote on his favorite table. It was then that she remembered they'd talked about him visiting the Red Rock time-shares. Maybe she didn't have to go.

"Good morning, Jonathon. Coffee's hot." She pointed her thumb toward the break room.

"Thank goodness, you're an angel." Jonathon disappeared and when he came out, he had a cup of coffee in one hand and one of Shirley's cookies from last night in the other. "Sorry, my alarm didn't go off."

"This isn't a job. You aren't required to be here at any specific time of day. And like I told you last night, I don't need a babysitter." Rarity finished setting up the register for the day, then took her own cup over to the table where Jonathon usually sat. "Hey, we didn't get a report last night, but did you go over to the time-share sales office?"

He shook his head. "I couldn't get away from Drew last week for some reason. He kept a close eye on me and my comings and goings. I think Edith has him watching me. It's a little frustrating."

"Really? I can't imagine how you feel." Rarity tried to make every word drip with sarcasm.

"Fine, I get your point, but you need to tell Drew to call me off. I'm not being your errand boy." He opened his notebook and glanced at where he'd left off yesterday. "This book is going to be finished in just a few more weeks at this rate. I should stay here and finish it before I tell Edith I'm done. She seems to think I can write anytime and anywhere, no matter how many times she interrupts my flow to ask what a tool is used for and where it should be stored."

"Do you want to go on a field trip with me this afternoon after lunch? Shirley can watch the store while we head off to the time-share sales office." Rarity glanced at her watch. "I'll wait and make sure Shirley's planning on staying all day, but if she is, we should be able to get out there and back before five and Archer shows up and rats us out to Drew."

"You know my son and your boyfriend too well," Jonathon responded. "It's a date. I need to be back at five anyway as I've got my writing group in Flagstaff tonight. We're having dinner before the meeting. They used to do it after the meeting, but I convinced them that old guys like me need to eat early."

"I'm sure if they wanted to go out afterward, they still would. This just lets more people be involved." She picked up her cup and stood. "Besides, you're not that old."

"I can get discounted meals if we eat before six," he countered.

Rarity laughed as Shirley came into the shop.

"Who's talking about the early bird special? I knew it couldn't be Rarity. I love eating early. That way I still have time to catch a show on television or work on one of my projects when I get home." Shirley tucked her tote under the counter. "Did you know Terrance didn't even know about them? He's been paying full price for meals for years that he didn't have to."

"It's different for men," Jonathon responded. "Edith had to convince me to take advantage of the discount too. I thought it made me an old codger to take the sixty-five-plus special. Now, I just realize it's more money I can spend on travel or one more outfit Edith can buy the grandbaby."

"There are some good things about getting older." Shirley opened a notebook that she'd decoupaged with the words Mommy and Me. "Like I don't have to worry about getting pregnant ever again."

No one said anything, and as Shirley looked up from her planning book, her face was beet red. "I mean, I'm not having sex, but if I was—"

"Shirley, stop." Rarity laughed as she put her hands over her ears. "I don't really want to know."

"But I need to clarify what I said. Terrance and I are just friends. I just meant since I am older, if I was having sex, there would be no chance of getting pregnant," Shirley tried to explain.

"Shirley, I think you might have caused Rarity to be at a loss for words." Jonathon grinned and pointed to his laptop. "After that stimulating conversation, I'm going to work."

"Me too. Those books aren't going to shelve themselves," Rarity said as she went to the back room to grab a box that had been delivered.

After a few minutes, Rarity came back out of the back room with the box on the trolley. "Hey, Shirley? Are you planning on staying all day? Jonathon and I have an errand to run."

"I'd be glad to stay." Shirley didn't look at her. She'd totally embarrassed herself, Rarity realized.

"Shirley, don't worry about what you said, it was a slip of the tongue." Rarity tried to make her feel better.

"I'm mortified." Shirley nodded toward the book club area. "I need to set up."

\* \* \* \*

Shirley finally started talking with them after lunch, but of course, that was exactly when Rarity and Jonathon needed to leave. Rarity gave her a hug as they headed out the door. "Is it okay for me to leave Killer?"

"We'll be fine together," Shirley answered, waving them out the door. "Killer doesn't mind when I say something stupid."

As they got into Jonathon's truck, Rarity looked back at the shop. "She's really kicking herself for finding joy in hanging out with Terrance."

"She's in a hard place. George isn't dead, but he isn't here, either. And it's not like he's coming back. Shirley needs to make peace with that fact before she can go on and have a new life. She's stuck in the old one, which isn't working anymore." Jonathon pulled the truck out onto the highway and made a U-turn in the middle of the quiet street. "I don't know what I'd do if I found myself in that situation. I'd probably come live with Drew again and ruin any chance at him having a full life."

Rarity laughed at the image. "I think Drew can handle himself. Besides, he likes having you around."

Jonathon accelerated the truck. "I'm thinking you're overestimating my charm, even on my own child."

They talked about the weather and the happenings around Sedona. Then Jonathon told her about his writing group. "The problem is, I like these people a lot more than the people who are in the one at home. I should just quit this one, but I'm up here too much to walk away from the group. I need the encouragement as well as the constructive criticism."

"Torn between two groups. It's kind of the theme of the day." Rarity saw the road sign with Red Rock listed as only five miles away. "We're getting close."

"We should make sure of our story. I'm looking for someplace where I can stay when I come up to visit my son." He glanced over at Rarity. "I probably shouldn't mention that Drew is a police detective, right?"

"Not unless it comes up. I think if we don't run into Calliope, that might not come up." Rarity scanned the desert in front of her; still no buildings. They were almost there when the road dropped down a hill and she saw the developed area. Building was still going on to the left and back side of the valley. But in front of them was a small town. There was a grocery store, a clothing store, and a gas station. They even had a coffee shop with a drive-through. Rarity hoped no one would get the bright idea to open a bookstore here. She'd lose everyone who worked here and all the time-share visitors as customers. "We're here."

A large sign directed them to a building near where the construction was still going on. Jonathon pointed toward it. "Time-share sales office, that way. It's time to brush up on my senior drama club acting skills. I can make a really excellent soldier. And a tree. I was a tree in my elementary program."

"Don't worry about it. Just pretend like you really want to buy it. Or Edith wants it and you're here to blow holes in her plans. Edith sent me to keep you from ruining her chance of getting the real story about cost and availability." Rarity could see the pool from where they'd parked as they walked toward the building.

"That sounds like Edith. She always thinks I'm hiding something from her." Jonathon winked at her as he held open the door. "Let's do this."

The smell of home-baked cookies filled the room, and there was a large pitcher of fruit-infused water on a table with glasses and the cookies. Rarity picked one up with a napkin. It was still warm.

"Please, have a treat and a glass of water to refresh yourselves. I know it was a long drive out here from Flagstaff or Sedona, so why don't you compose yourselves while I see who is available to help you today." A woman in a soft dress stood from her desk and, after indicating they should sit, disappeared into a doorway behind her.

"This is really nice," Rarity said.

Jonathon nodded, then leaned forward to pour some water. It blocked her view of the room for a second. He whispered, "There are cameras and probably mikes everywhere. The play has begun."

Rarity took the glass of water and nodded. "Thank you. This is just what I needed. I drink way too much coffee in the morning. I'm sure I'm dehydrated by the time lunch arrives."

"We all need more water, especially since we live in the desert." Jonathon poured himself a glass, then sat back.

They didn't have to wait long. The receptionist seemed to know exactly when they would be done with their cookies. She arrived back in the room with a young man in tow. He looked like he was about six foot and had stepped out of a GQ photo shoot. He stepped forward. "Thanks, Gigi. Welcome, friends. I'm Nash Howard. How can I help you today?"

"Hi, Nash. I'm Jonathon Anderson and this is my friend, Rarity Cole. Rarity lives in Sedona and runs the local bookstore. I'm looking for a place where I can stay when I come up here to visit my son." He held his hand out to greet Nash.

"Lovely. I'm sure we can work something out regarding the number of weeks you need available. Of course, we're attached to many other properties, so if your son moves, you're not stuck in Sedona for the rest of your contract."

"That would be unfortunate." Rarity smiled at Jonathon. "But I guess you would just have to visit me then."

The tour lasted over an hour and as they finished up, Nash turned the golf cart they'd been riding in and parked in front of a large building with

Roman columns in the front. "This is our future spa building. Right now, it holds an indoor and outdoor Olympic-size pool, several hot springs–fed private soaking pools, and a workout facility. We offer classes throughout the day that are free to residents, of course, and we have one special feature. Please come this way."

Rarity and Jonathon followed him to what appeared to be an outdoor meditation spot. There were plenty of places to sit and rest as well as a large open area in the middle. The vortex was circled with river stones.

"This is the reason we chose this site in Sedona. The company searched for months with the area's leading vortex hunter, and even though buying this property was more expensive than other sites we considered, the on-site vortex made it priceless." Nash turned to us. "Vortexes have a lot of power. I come here on my lunch break every day just to soak up the energy. I've lost ten pounds since I've been working here without even trying."

Rarity thought his weight loss, if even true, might have been due to the fact that he walked through the complex and the townhouses several times a day. She thought that her step counter should be close to hitting her daily goal after the tour. But she kept that information to herself. Instead, she asked about Jackson. "Was this the vortex where that guy was killed who owned the gallery? Your company is owned by the same people, right?"

"I have no idea." Nash didn't blink an eye. He smiled and said, "I'm sorry, that's all the time we have for the tour today. Please look over the information provided in your folder. Your car is in the lot on the right if you exit through the pathway at the end of the vortex. Take as much time here in the meditation room as you want."

Then he hurried back through the door and into the building. Rarity heard the door lock behind him. She turned to Jonathon. "Did I say something wrong?"

Jonathon laughed as he grabbed two bottles of water from the refrigerator near the wall. He handed one to Rarity and sat down on one of the couches. He stared at the vortex. "Why do these things keep coming up in this investigation?"

"Location?" Rarity took the bottle of water and opened it, taking a large drink. Then she sat next to Jonathon. The meditation room was more of a patio than a room, but it was lovely, even if she knew the vortex had no true power. "Do you believe in vortexes?"

Jonathon nodded. "Archer took us to one last year. I swear I could feel the energy flowing out of it. It was rejuvenating. Edith felt it too. Even this old cop, who has based his life on things I can prove, had to admit it was something I had to take on faith and feeling. The energy was there. I felt it. This one is pretty, but there's no power. No life."

Rarity stood and walked over to the vortex circle. She walked around it, then walked into the circle, right up to the middle where the rocks crossed. She met Jonathon's gaze. "Nothing. But still, it feels like a clue."

# Chapter 23

Rarity sat quietly as Jonathon drove them back to Sedona. She watched as the desert landscape flew past them on the highway. She kept replaying Nash's description of how Red Rock was developed.

"You're chasing a cat," Jonathon said.

"What? I don't understand." Rarity turned toward him, giving up her careful watching of scenery that hadn't changed for the last ten miles. "Maybe I didn't hear you right. I'm a little lost in thought."

"That was my point. We used to call it chasing cats when Drew and his sister were little. It meant that you were lost in your own world. Care to let me in?" Jonathon didn't look at her, he was staring straight ahead at the road.

"Nash said that the company looked at several spots before choosing that one for Red Rock. Was he lying or just spouting the company line? We both know that Jackson declared the vortexes to be where they are now, and David had to agree. But why did he have to agree? Why couldn't he just tell everyone that Jackson was lying? That's the part I don't understand." Rarity started to form a theory. "I wonder where Eleanor went to college?"

"Jackson had to have something on him for David to back off like that. And now, in for a penny, my mom used to say. He either admits he went along with the fib or keeps lying," Jonathon mused. "College seems a long time ago for these people."

"How far back has Drew gone on Jackson and David? Did they go to school together? Archer told me he went to school with Jackson. Maybe he knew David too." Rarity grabbed her phone and started texting.

"What are you doing?" Jonathon had a bemused tone to his voice.

"Archer's coming over for dinner tonight. I'm asking him to bring any old yearbooks with him." Rarity tucked her phone away. "We're going to take a trip down memory lane."

"It might be a short trip. Edith and I kept Drew's box of stuff from college until he bought a house. Archer's parents might have all his stuff in storage," Jonathon warned as he turned onto Main Street, which would take them to the bookstore.

"I think his mom sent him his stuff when she moved last year. He might have it stored with the business records in his building, but I think it's at least in town." Rarity grinned. "We might be eating takeout and digging through Archer's storage area tonight. I hope Killer doesn't get lost or into something."

"You sound cheerful about the prospect. I've got a stack of boxes in the garage that Edith wants me to go through, but I keep putting it off." Jonathon parked the truck in front of the store. He started to get out.

"You don't have to walk me to the door," Rarity teased as they walked up to the front door.

"Tell that to my son and Archer. If I just dropped you off and there was a problem at the bookstore, I'd never hear the end of it." He glanced at his watch. "Besides, I have some time before I have to leave for Flagstaff. I'll use it to refresh my reading stack. I'll probably finish the last book I brought tonight when I get home. Then what will I do? My son only likes spy novels."

By the time Jonathon had picked out a few books, Archer was there to walk Rarity home. She'd sent Shirley home as soon as she'd come back from her field trip with Jonathon. She didn't want her friend to work all the time. Especially now that she and Terrance were spending time together. Shirley needed a life just for her, and her friendship with Terrance gave her that.

As she locked up the store, she noticed Archer was carrying a box he'd brought into the bookstore with him. "What's that?"

"You asked for the yearbooks, so I brought all that I have. I'm missing my senior yearbook, but if we're looking to see if Jackson and David were at the same school together during this time, I think we'll find it if it's there." Archer came out of the break room. "The coffeepot's set up and I took out the trash and double-checked the lock on that door. Although it's solid. I'm happy we went with a more secure door. It's not customer-facing, so it didn't have to be pretty or fit into the decor."

Rarity pulled out her phone. She wished she had the picture that Eleanor had deleted. "Speaking of doors, come look at this. Didn't the door to the vortex used to be glass?"

"It was the last time I was there. I remember thinking about how the gallery mimicked the desert on that Friday night for their open house. The glass was dark and reflected the partygoers inside the gallery. I was impressed at the way they'd designed the room to make the gallery almost a capsule in the middle of a wasteland." He ran his hand through his hair. "I'm sounding poetic, but that's how it made me feel. I was more affected by the darkness in the glass all around us than by any of the paintings. I'm sure that's what the designers had in mind."

"You are a man of many talents and surprises. I didn't see or feel any of that. I wasn't drawn to the vortex, but now I know it was because there was no energy there. The energy was all inside the gallery." Rarity remembered Drew had sent her an email about the stolen paintings. That's what was bothering her. The one she'd seen had been on that list, she was certain. "I think I just found something else."

Archer was standing near the register. "What are you talking about?"

She pointed to the picture Drew had included in the email. "This painting is back at the gallery. I saw it today. I took a picture, but Eleanor deleted it. She was really upset that I'd even attempted to take a photo."

"Well, if she saw you, it's probably not up now." Archer handed her back her phone. "She's not that stupid."

"True. And even if she is lying about what was missing, it doesn't mean she killed Jackson." Rarity grabbed her bag and turned to Archer, who now was standing by the break room door. "Turn off that light and let's go home."

"Now you have me thinking." He held up one finger but did turn off the light before he headed to the bench where he'd put the box. "Hold on a second. Back when I was in school, there was an art installation on campus. It gave me the same feeling as I had on Friday night. I haven't thought about this for years."

She watched as he flipped through the yearbooks. One after another. Finally, he stood and brought one of the books over to the counter where Rarity had stayed. Archer's movements had woken Killer, scaring him. He barked before circling three times and lying back down. Rarity wondered if her dog had caught her OCD nature from her. Or if all dogs were used to comfort and routine.

Archer pointed to a picture in the yearbook, and she tried to focus. She was dead tired and needed to turn in early tonight. Even if Archer decided to watch a movie, she knew she'd be asleep before the opening credits finished running.

"That's the art installation. Jackson headed the group that won the contest." He pointed to the people standing around the windows circling an area of the quad like a glass Stonehenge. "I felt the same pull of the unknown with this installation that I did at the gallery."

Rarity blinked. She knew she was tired, but as she focused she saw Jackson, David, and two women. "That's not Eleanor and Calliope, is it?"

Archer shook his head. "It can't be." He pulled the book closer to read the description. It was them. "Son of a gun. Now we know where everyone met. No wonder I looked like a proper fall guy. Everyone knew me in college."

"We should go and confront Eleanor." Rarity felt the weariness leave her body. "Jackson must have turned her down again. She was so angry that Friday night."

"Rarity, we can't just run over and show her a picture from an old yearbook and accuse her of killing Jackson. It's not a smoking gun." Archer pushed the book away.

"He was shot with an arrow." Rarity pulled it closer and went to the index in the back and wrote down a bunch of page numbers. She flipped through the pages until she found what she'd expected. "Look, Eleanor was in the archery club."

"Still, it's circumstantial." Archer looked at the page with Eleanor in a group of twenty, holding a bow in front of her. "Now, tell me you found an empty package with a bottle of the drug used to kill Jackson addressed to Eleanor, and we have something concrete."

"We could go check the dumpster behind the gallery?" Rarity suggested, but she knew the answer before Archer even shook his head.

"I'm sure that's been dumped in the last week." Archer squeezed her hand. "I know you want to solve the murder, but maybe we should leave this to Drew."

"Now that's a great idea. I need to tell him about the painting showing up, too. She might have taken it down, but I bet if he went to look, it might freak her into doing something stupid." She took a picture of the two pages and texted it to Drew. "At least this will give him a connection between the four. And if he starts pressing on David, I think we might find out some interesting information. Or maybe we can go visit David in the hospital tomorrow?"

"You don't really think that either Eleanor or Calliope killed Jackson. What would be the reason?" Archer put the yearbook back into the box.

Rarity thought about Archer's question as she put the leash on Killer and grabbed her tote. She turned off the lights and followed Archer out the door. "You were in the hot seat because Jackson broke your sister's heart. What if he did the same thing to one of those two? Or both?"

"Then what did they have on David to make him lie for Jackson?" Archer adjusted the box and took Killer's leash as they started walking back to Rarity's house.

"That's another good question. We might not find all the answers in that box of yours, but I bet we find some clues." She felt a rebounding of energy. "Let's go home and order takeout so we can focus on the yearbooks. I feel like we're really close to finding out who killed Jackson, if not why."

"You should have gone into criminal justice. You really like this investigation thing." Archer kissed the top of her head as they turned the corner to her street.

"You keep telling me what I shouldn't be doing. Like going to visit Eleanor or dumpster diving. Why would you encourage me now?" She laughed as they crossed the street. "I'm kidding. I do like playing with investigations, but if it was my job? I think I'd be depressed. I hate the fact that people would hurt other people for any reason. I think that's why I like finding out who did it. That way, I can blame them and not our society as a whole. I would hate to think that we are all capable of this type of violence."

Archer was quiet for a minute. As they walked up to Rarity's house, he put an arm around her. "I think the only place that good always wins over evil is in the books you read."

She pulled out her keys and before unlocking the door, she kissed him. "I don't think that's true. But I think that if we don't take part in our community and try to stop people who do evil, then it could be true. It's up to each and every one of us to make sure life is fair to everyone, even the dead."

"You're amazing, Ms. Cole." As they went inside and shut the door, he pulled her close to him. "I don't think I tell you that enough."

It took a couple of hours, but they found a page that the yearbook editor had called Hot and Quits. It listed romantically linked couples when they were first spotted together and when the passion cooled. Sometimes there were photos. Jackson had his own column. As Rarity read the rules, she realized they'd tried to weed out random hookups. It also listed the fraternity or sorority of each person in parentheses behind each name. She scanned Jackson's list, then found that same page for all three years that Archer had found yearbooks.

She arranged them by year and Jackson's list kept growing longer. "How did he even have time to go to class if he was seeing all these people?"

"He had a really good memory and was a fast reader. And his charm didn't just work on the ladies. Professors liked him too." Archer studied the Hot and Quits list. "He's not mentioned as seeing either Eleanor or Calliope in this one."

"Hey, you're not in any of the books. Did you take a vow of celibacy?" Rarity grabbed the book Archer had just set down. "Nope, not here either."

He smiled and Rarity's heart fluttered just a bit. The boy was good at flirting. And smiling. And kissing. He really should be listed.

"I wasn't in a fraternity. I didn't have the money to play with the cool kids." He glanced at the first book. "And when Jackson found out who my sister was, he blackballed me from even being part of a rush. Not that I wanted to be in their club anyway."

"You saying that this Hot and Quits list was only for the Greek houses? So even if Eleanor or Calliope dated him, if they weren't in a sorority, it wouldn't be listed?" Rarity was beginning to think they were on a wild goose chase.

"Usually. But there were exceptions. Especially if the other member of the couple was Jackson. Or, I guess, any guy who was a hot prospect for sorority chicks. If Jackson dated someone, it would be listed."

Archer sounded so sure about it. She wondered how his college experience had been. Had he had his nose to the grindstone or had he been the laid-back guy she knew now? She ran her finger down the list. Bingo.

"He dated Eleanor your junior year. Then Calliope's listed right underneath Eleanor. He left one for the other. We have a why for Drew. Now we just have to hope he has physical evidence to charge her." She took a picture of the Hot and Quits page, then one of just Jackson's relationships, and sent them to Drew. He was going to change his number after this investigation.

"I'm sure there's evidence somewhere." He put the yearbooks back in the box and walked it over to the doorway. "I'm tired of reading about my past. Let's talk about the future. How many kids do you want and are you stuck on owning an Old English sheepdog? I'm thinking about a Great Pyrenees. I'll make tea while you consider your answers. Choosing the correct dog makes the rest of our life together as a couple perfect." Archer returned to the kitchen and filled the teapot with water.

Before she could respond, her phone binged with a text. She read it and laughed. Then she set down her phone. "Drew agrees with you. He told me to put my Nancy Drew personality to bed and have a nice evening. I guess he wants me to stop giving him his suspects on a silver platter."

"It must be hard on a guy to admit that he solves a case because of a book club." Archer's eyes twinkled.

"For the sake of Drew's manhood, I guess it's time to relax and watch a movie. I hope he appreciates my willingness to pause a bit to allow him to keep up." She walked over to the couch and picked up the remote. "Whose turn is it to pick a genre?"

* * * *

The next morning, Rarity kept checking her phone. Was Drew even taking any of the facts they'd found last night seriously? Maybe Archer was right. They needed the smoking gun, or in this case, the fingerprints on the arrow or the bottle of the killing drug. She wondered where she could find a trash collection schedule. Archer could be wrong, and the box could be sitting right there. Waiting to be found.

But if it was, the gallery was on a different schedule than her business. The big truck backed into the alley behind the bookstore every Monday morning. She had settled on unpacking books when Jonathon came in, his leather tote in hand. "How was your group?"

"Insightful as always. Let me get some coffee and I'll tell you about it. Drew was out of the house early this morning and didn't make coffee." He set his tote down and headed to the kitchen. He glanced at her cup. "Do you need a warm up?"

She shook her head. "I just filled up, I'm good."

When Jonathon returned, he started talking about the writers group. Who was writing what, who came to dinner, and what they discussed during the program part of the evening. "One night a month we have a speaker, but usually someone reads their work for critiques. You'd be surprised at how much you learn by critiquing someone's work. I worked until midnight last night just on cleaning up from notes I took during the meeting. That's another reason I come home after these meetings. I'm filled with energy and need to get into the manuscript. I don't want to forget what I wanted to change."

Rarity loved that Jonathon was finding a new vocation in writing. He was caring for it like any other job. Learning how to create, then learning what you didn't know. She set aside the last book that she'd put into her inventory system. She'd done the same thing when she'd moved to Sedona. She knew how to market but hadn't had a clue how to run a bookstore. Now, with a lot of trial and error, she thought she knew some of what it took to work in retail. "It's exciting to hear you talk about your groups this way. Is the Tucson group set up the same way?"

Jonathon talked a little about his home group, then glanced at his watch. "I better get writing. I know you have work to do. According to Drew, I might be heading home soon. He said to tell you that you might have found the secret door."

"What did he mean by that?" Rarity stacked books by genre, then grabbed the first stack to go put on the shelves.

Jonathon shrugged. "He didn't explain. Maybe something we found yesterday in our trip to the time-share office?"

Rarity shrugged. "Maybe. My money's on Eleanor killing Jackson in the meditation area because of a broken heart."

"You sound like it's a game of Clue. I don't think Clue talked about the why of the murder, though." Jonathon chuckled as he booted up his computer. "Although, I probably would proclaim the same conclusion if it was my turn. Everyone in that group seems to be holding on to a secret past. Drew just needs to push the right button."

# Chapter 24

Later that afternoon, Drew came into the bookstore. He paused at the table where his father sat typing away. "When are you going home?"

Jonathon held up a finger and kept typing. When he finished, he looked up at his son. "Sorry, I needed to finish that thought. Are you telling us you have Jackson's killer in custody?"

Rarity took a breath, watching the men chat. This was it. Drew had solved the murder. She set down her pen. She'd been working on marketing ideas for next month, including one with the new art gallery. Maybe she'd have to amend that activity. If she'd been right.

"Eleanor Blanchet admitted this afternoon that she shot Jackson in the back with an arrow dipped in a liquid pentobarbital mixture. She got the drug in the mail. A customer service coordinator at the online pharmacy had told her that the drug would ease Eleanor's terminally ill mother's passing to the other side. She gave the rest of the dose to David after he threatened to go back on his certifications for the vortexes. She thought it might affect walk-in traffic and resulting sales at the gallery."

"She admitted killing him?" Rarity glanced at Jonathon and back to Drew. "Without a lawyer?"

Drew shook his head. "When I asked her to come in for another interview, I guess she called her attorney and had him accompany her. When she started to confess, he asked for time to talk to his client. She refused to talk to him. Then she confessed. She said she loved Jackson but he tortured her with his hot and cold attitude. I guess she thought him asking her to move to Sedona was personal. Not as his gallery manager."

"They dated in college," Rarity told Jonathon, trying to catch him up. "As did Jackson and Calliope. How did you know it wasn't her?"

"Eleanor also admitted that she had lied about the missing paintings. The one you saw, one she'd sold, and a Civil War–era painting that was at the framer's shop getting refurbished. I guess she wanted the stolen paintings to be a reason someone would kill Jackson. However, too many people had seen them after he died." A smile crept onto Drew's mouth. "I figured you might want Calliope to be the killer to keep her away from Archer."

"That's not why, but both Eleanor and Calliope dated Jackson in college. What led you to Eleanor instead of Calliope?" Rarity pressed. "The paintings?"

"Calliope tried to find out who killed Jackson. Although she was sure it was you. The two of you need to talk and stop this silly feud." Drew sat down next to his father. "You haven't answered my question. When are you going home to Mom? She misses you."

"So seriously, why not Calliope?" Rarity tried to bring the subject back to the matter at hand. Jackson's murder.

"She was always dropping by the station house, telling me what she'd found out about Jackson's death. She told me that he and Eleanor had been intimate. After Calliope had been cut out of Archer's life, she saw Jackson as a second chance at love. Then Eleanor kills him and she's alone again. The woman hates being alone." Drew let his gaze meet Rarity's. "She worked almost as hard on this investigation as you did. And she didn't have a club behind her doing the legwork."

Jonathon closed his laptop. "If the culprit is in custody and my favorite bookseller is safe, I'll leave in the morning. Do you have time to have dinner with your old man tonight?"

"I can fit you in. With a confession, the paperwork's a little less overwhelming." Drew glanced at his watch. "Meet me at the Garnet at seven. Rarity? Do you and Archer want to join us?"

Rarity shook her head. "I think you two need some time. Besides, Archer is making finger steaks tonight at the house. I want to watch him with this recipe. He said it's his grandmother's."

"Marilyn Ender was an amazing cook." Jonathon smiled as he tucked his computer away. "I'll head back to the house and start packing. Unless Rarity needs me to walk her home."

"I think I'll be fine. Archer's coming by to get me." She held out a book that she'd kept back from the box she'd unpacked earlier. "Give this to Edith. I know she loves this author. Tell her thanks for the use of her husband."

"You don't have to do that," Jonathon smiled. "But she will love the gift. Thank you, Rarity."

When Jonathon left, Drew moved closer to the registration desk. "Thanks for letting Dad hang out with you. I worry when you and Sam get involved in these investigations."

"Thanks for loaning him to me." Rarity frowned as she thought about the conversation. "I didn't know your parents knew Archer's parents."

"We lived in the same neighborhood when we were kids. That's where I met him and Dana. We were all crazy kids. We'd get on our bikes and take off for the day. I'm sure our moms were worried, but they never stopped us. Dad never forgave himself for the fact that Mrs. Ender's murder was never solved."

"Archer's mom was murdered?" Rarity felt shock as the information settled.

"No, not his mother, his grandmother." Before Drew could continue, his radio went off. He shrugged. "Sorry, I've got to go. Like I said, lots of paperwork and meetings to tie this up."

Rarity got a bottle of water and went over to the fireplace to sit. Killer followed her and curled up on her lap. Archer had never mentioned his grandmother's murder. Rarity thought about their lighthearted conversation about the future last night. Maybe they needed to talk about the past a little more.

The bell went off and Rarity watched Shirley come into the bookstore. She checked her watch. "I didn't expect you today. And it's almost closing time. Did you forget something yesterday?"

Shirley came over and sat down across from her. "No, I just wanted to let you know what happened. I mean, you know both of us, so you should know."

Rarity studied her friend. "Shirley, what's wrong?"

She looked up from the square of tile on the floor she'd been staring at since she sat down. "Terrance and I have decided not to see each other anymore."

"Oh, Shirley, are you okay?" Rarity went over to sit closer to her.

Shirley wiped her eyes. "I feel stupid. I don't know why I'm crying. It's not like we were dating or anything."

"What happened?" Rarity hoped Terrance hadn't tried to take the relationship further than Shirley had expected.

"He told me he was falling in love with me." Shirley stared at her. Her wet eyes were wide open. "Rarity, I'm a married woman. I can't be in love with someone besides George."

Rarity wanted to tell her it would be all right. Maybe George, if he was even here, would understand. But that was the problem. George wasn't here and Shirley was right. She was still married. All she could do was be there for her friend. She didn't have any advice. "I'm so sorry."

Shirley nodded. "Thank you. I'm going to visit my daughter Kathy for a few days on Sunday. Can you handle the Mommy and Me class or should we cancel it? I'll be back for Saturday's preschool group."

Rarity hid her smile. Even in her grief over losing Terrance, Shirley still was taking care of others. "I can do the Mommy and Me class. Although not as well as you do. They'll understand that you deserve a vacation now and then."

Shirley wiped her eyes, then reached down and gave Killer's head a pat. He was sitting in front of her, watching. "Okay, with that settled, I'm heading home for the night. I'm going to run a bath and play some Joni Mitchell and maybe watch some old movies. I know it won't make me forget about my feelings for Terrance, but maybe by putting some distance between us, I can control them better."

Rarity watched her friend leave the shop and sent out a prayer for her comfort. She'd been concerned about what might happen between Shirley and Terrance. Especially when Terrance told Rarity about his feelings for Shirley. This day had been coming from the first time they went to coffee together. They were perfect for each other and both of them needed someone. Shirley just couldn't walk away from George. Neither could she stay married and see Terrance as more than a friend.

Sometimes life was confusing and not fair. She realized that Calliope probably felt the same way after Archer had told her there was nothing between them.

Rarity would just have to take care of both her friends while they were healing. As she thought about ways to do this, the bell over the door rang again. Archer walked in and scanned the room. He had a bouquet of flowers in his hand. When he found her by the fireplace, he frowned and hurried toward her. "What's wrong?"

Rarity stood and fell into his arms. She held him tight as she tried to breathe. Finally, she said, "Nothing, now."

He stepped back and shook his head. "Sometimes you confuse the heck out of me. I brought you flowers because Drew said you helped solve the case. I thought you'd be happy."

She took the flowers. "They're lovely. Let's close up the shop and I'll tell you about my day while we walk home."

Rarity and Archer went through the routine of closing the shop for the day. As she did her normal activities, she thought about how lucky she was, and decided to ask Archer if they were ready for the next step. She knew she was ready.

She'd learned several things about the world and life during her cancer treatments, including the fact that tomorrow wasn't promised to anyone. And if she wanted something, like the bookstore, she needed to grab it now and not wait for someday.

After locking the door to the shop, she turned to Archer, who was holding her flowers and Killer's leash, waiting for her. She smiled and asked, "Do you want to move in with me?"

# Acknowledgments

Writing a book about life after a life-changing illness sometimes can feel overwhelming. I want to honor my own journey and others who have walked this path. Sometimes, during treatment, it felt like I was just doing the work. Going to the appointments, making the decisions, and completing the process. And as a result, and with a lot of luck, I survived.

Writing a book is a lot like that process. You get up each morning and do the work. You deal with the process, good or bad, and just keep going. And sometimes, there are angels there to help you finish your run. Like my editor, Michaela Hamilton. And my agent, Jill Marsal. And the team at Kensington, who believe in the book as well as me. And then there's Quinn, my beloved Keeshound, who spends a lot of time sleeping under my desk, waiting for me to finish my work so I can have fun with her.

# Recipe

I love making quiche, but I'm the only one in the house who eats it. I think the Cowboy thinks it's too fancy for him to enjoy. I guess that's why Archer loves drinking tea and also loves sports. He's a mix of stereotypes. An alpha and a beta male. And Rarity loves him.

And that's all that matters, right?

Lynn

## Easy Quiche

You can use a premade crust for this (or make your own, which is crazy easy, but it needs to rest a bit).

### Pie crust

Mix 1½ cups all-purpose flour and ½ teaspoon salt. Cut in 1 cup chilled butter until the mixture forms small balls. Add ¼ cup cold water and mix until the dough forms a ball. Wrap in plastic and refrigerate for 30 minutes. Then roll out into a 12-inch circle.

Line a pie plate with the uncooked crust. Bake in a 450-degree oven for 15 minutes. Pull it out and let it sit on the counter while you mix up the filling.

### Filling

Fry 6 slices of bacon in a skillet until crispy. I like frying the whole packet and using the leftovers for BLT sandwiches or wedge salads. Or even sprinkled over baked potatoes.

Set aside on a paper towel to cool. Drain the grease from the pan, leaving just enough to sauté the onion (about a tablespoon).

Then add to your skillet:

½ cup chopped onion (1 medium)

Cook on medium heat until translucent. Put in a small bowl to cool.

In a larger bowl, lightly beat 5 eggs. Then add the following:

1¼ cups half-and-half (I've also used whole milk)

¼ teaspoon salt

Dash of ground nutmeg

Mix in 1½ cups shredded cheddar cheese (6 ounces), the crumbled bacon, and the onion.

Pour into the prepared pie shell.

Bake at 325 for 45-55 minutes or until a knife stuck in the middle comes out clean.

You can mix this up by adding mushrooms, replacing the bacon with ham, or even changing out the cheese, based on your tastes. I enjoy adding spinach and mushrooms to make it a little healthier.

Don't miss the next delightful Survivors' Book Club mystery by Lynn Cahoon

**DYING TO READ**

Coming soon from Lyrical Press, an imprint of Kensington Publishing Corp.

Keep reading to enjoy a sample excerpt . . .

# Chapter 1

Rarity Cole sat on the edge of her swimming pool and stretched from side to side. The weather had turned perfect starting last weekend. She'd gone on hikes with her boyfriend, Archer, every day since Friday. Now the normal weekend was over and it was Monday morning. She had the entire day off. Her employees, Shirley Prescott and Katie Dickenson, had started taking turns running the store on Mondays since the first of March. Rarity had a two-day weekend now. She felt like she was back working in corporate marketing. She started making a list of to-dos but then realized nothing else would happen if she didn't get her swim done.

"Workout first," she muttered. It had been her motto since January and one of her resolutions. She felt better when she moved first thing in the morning. She believed in the power of goals. They'd got her through her treatments for breast cancer and the complete overhaul of her life afterward. She'd moved from St. Louis to Sedona. She'd quit her corporate job and bought a bookstore. And broke up with Kevin. The man who was supposed to be her future husband thought she wasn't fun enough when she was fighting for her life.

Okay, truthfully, Kevin had broken up with her, but either way, it had been a big life change.

Now she lived in a three-bedroom cottage in Arizona with a pool she could use year-round. She loved running the bookstore and hadn't worn a suit to work in months. She had a new boyfriend, Archer Enders, who was planning on moving in with her next month. And she had a baby.

Oh, not a human baby. She had Killer, a tiny Yorkie who had a huge attitude. And an even bigger heart.

Killer was sitting next to her watching the water and the yellow ducky float that also served as a way to disperse some of the chemicals in the pool. Rarity leaned down, kissed the pup, and then dove into the water.

When she got out, her phone was ringing. She hurried over to answer the cell phone that she'd left on the deck table. Looking at the display, she smiled. "Hey baby, how are you?"

"Baby, huh?" Archer sounded amused.

"I figured I needed to up my sweet talk since we are moving our relationship to a new level." Rarity wrapped a towel around her and sat at the table. Killer followed her up on the deck and lay near the French door that led to the kitchen.

"Okay, I guess it works. I called to let you know I got a late afternoon hike today, so dinner's out. Sorry."

"Do you just want to move it to later?" Rarity asked.

A pause on the other end of the line made her think she'd lost him.

"Archer? Are you there?"

"I'm here. Sorry, I'm slammed. I can't make it later either. Look, I'll see you Tuesday night after your book club. We'll talk then." Archer ended the call.

Rarity set down the phone and looked at Killer. "Your friend Archer is being weird."

Killer stood and barked at the door.

"Ready to go in?" Rarity asked, standing.

Killer barked again and ran a circle.

"I've got a lot of things to do anyway," Rarity wished she'd said that to Archer, but she wasn't used to playing games with him. If he was too busy to see her, there was a good reason. She just had to believe him. He wasn't Josh.

\* \* \* \*

Later that afternoon, she'd just come back from a run to Flagstaff when a knock sounded at her door. "Come in."

Terrance Oldman, her neighbor, poked his head in the door. "Hey, Rarity. I saw you pull in. Did you get me some of those sausages from the store?"

She held the package up. "Two packages, just like you asked. I could have brought them over."

"I thought I'd come over and see if I could be helpful." He tucked the sausages into an empty bag, then grabbed the milk and juice and put them away in her refrigerator. They worked that way together in silence until all the groceries were put away.

Rarity held up a packet of salmon. "I'm planning on grilling this tonight if you don't have dinner plans."

"I thought Mondays were date nights with your guy." Terrance sat down at the table. He'd pulled out sodas, one for him and one for her.

"Archer's busy." She hoped the snark wouldn't sound in her words. "So I decided to cook. I'm doing a risotto with it."

"Sorry, my dance card's full tonight. The guys down at the Vet Hall have a standing poker game. We do it on Mondays so Drew can come. If you have a police officer sitting down with you, you're less likely to be busted for illegal gambling."

"You're bad." Rarity smiled despite herself. "Hey, can you watch Killer tomorrow? It's book club night."

"Of course. We'll go over to my house and watch a movie. He's partial to Marvel superheroes and you only have channels that show DC superheroes." Terrance leaned down and picked Killer up with one hand. "You can retrieve him anytime your club's over."

"As long as I'm not interrupting your bonding time," Rarity clarified. "So I haven't seen a lot of you these last few weeks. Staying inside?"

"I have a job." Terrance rubbed Killer's neck and the little dog melted into him.

"Really. The neighborhood watch wasn't keeping you busy enough?" Terrance patrolled the neighborhood with a bunch of retirees who called themselves the Grey Patrol. Break-ins had dropped to almost zero in our neighborhood. Drew Anderson was using the group as an example to other neighborhoods on how to lower crime. It didn't hurt that most of the guys in Terrance's patrol team were ex-military members who had come to Sedona for the rest when they'd retired. Then they'd gotten bored.

"I wanted a little more. I'm a handyman over at Sedona Memory Care. They've been having trouble keeping their security system going. Someone keeps turning it off so I'm there to stop it." He didn't look up at her.

"Sedona Memory Care. Where George lives?" George Prescott was Shirley's husband and a patient. He'd forgotten most of their time together now, but Shirley still visited almost daily. "Are you crazy?"

"Rarity, I swear this isn't because of Shirley. Or if it is, it's for her. If George gets out and hurts himself or others, she'll be devastated. I can't turn my back on this. They need me." Now he did look up and met her eyes. "Besides, he's fighting with the assistant director. George seems to respond to me. We're friends."

Rarity stared at Terrance. "You realize that's all kinds of messed up."

Terrance was in love with Shirley. They'd started hanging out last fall, but she'd ended their friendship when Terrance made it clear he wanted more. Being married to George, who was still alive but not really there, Shirley couldn't deal with the feelings she was having for Terrance. It felt like cheating. Even though they hadn't done anything including a good night kiss. To Shirley's mind, she was married. And that was it.

Now, Terrance was not only working at the nursing home where George lived, he'd developed a friendship with the man.

"I know, but I can't step away now. The nursing home needs me to find out why their systems aren't working before someone winds up missing or worse." Terrance sighed. "And when he remembers me, George is kind of a cool guy. I can see why Shirley loves him."

"Oh, Terrance. That's so sad." Rarity squeezed his hand. "Do you want a cup of tea?"

He laughed and stood. "Nope, I've got laundry to finish before I head out to the game. Having a real job again keeps me busy. And I'm going to grill a couple of these bad boys" – he held up the sausages --- "for dinner before I go. Sorry I couldn't fill in for your guy tonight."

"No worries. I haven't finished the book club selection yet anyway. I need to at least skim the rest of it before tomorrow. Shirley's caught me too many times not reading the book." Rarity walked him to the door and watched out the window as he crossed the lawn between the two houses. Terrance Oldman was a good man, but he was playing with fire with his new job. Hopefully, he'd get the security system fixed before Shirley caught him at the home. Otherwise, Rarity thought, he was going to get an earful.

Shirley could be opinionated.

Rarity glanced at the to-do list she'd made this morning. She'd already crossed off shopping and a swim. Her finger stopped at cleaning the house and then looked at the next item, finishing the book. She sighed and went to the bedroom to strip the sheets so she could get them in the laundry. Cleaning needed to be done. She was in a bad mood anyway. She might as well make the best of it.

The next morning, she arrived at the bookstore just a few minutes before nine. Without Killer to walk with her, she was able to leave the house a little later. The dog always had to stop for a smell, or a hundred, as they walked. The two businesses on each side of her, Madam Zelda's fortune-telling and Sam's crystal shop, were still closed. They opened later. Drop-in traffic didn't start until late morning, sometimes after lunch. Especially during the beginning of the week.

Katie Dickenson hurried down the path and followed her into the bookstore. Katie was working on her master's at Northern Arizona in Flagstaff, but a lot of her classes were in the evening, so she had time to work at the bookstore. "Hey, I was hoping to get here first. The store was slammed yesterday. I didn't get all the closing tasks done before I had to leave for class. I hope you're not mad."

"You should have called me." Rarity held the door open for her. "You would have saved me from housecleaning."

"I figured you were out with Archer. I saw his truck go by the shop about three yesterday. Didn't you guys go hiking?"

Rarity started turning on lights. "Friday, Saturday, and Sunday. My calves are still killing me. But I was home on Monday. Next time you get swamped just call. If I can't come in, I'll tell you."

"Sounds reasonable. Anyway, the kids must have been out of school because I had several families who showed up just after lunch. We need to seriously restock the kids' section. I think they might have emptied it out." Katie tucked her bag under the counter and opened an energy drink. "Where do you want me first? Unpacking boxes that came in? Or starting a book order?"

"Let's get everything out and then we can do the book order." Rarity looked around the bookstore. It looked normal, but she knew Katie was a little OCD just like her. She liked things to look perfect. Rarity only stressed about the back door being locked when she left. She'd put the store's temperature gauge on a timer so that was automatic. "How are the bathrooms?"

"Honestly, I didn't check." Katie brought out a box of books. "Do you want me to go clean first?"

"No, I'll do it. Watch the register while you're checking these in. I doubt we get any walk-ins this early, but you never know." Rarity went to the backroom and pulled out the cleaning supplies, including a mop bucket that she filled with hot, soapy water from the sink. She moved to the men's first and quickly got that done. She propped the door open and taped a wet floor sign on the door jamb.

When she went into the women's, she found a book on the wash counter. She grumbled at the long-gone reader. "Clearly you couldn't see the 'please don't bring books into the lavatory' sign."

She walked out to set the book on a table while she finished cleaning. She didn't look at the title. It looked older than what she sold. Maybe someone forgot their personal copy.

Rarity finished cleaning. After she'd taken the trash outside to the dumpster and drained, cleaned, and put away the mop and other cleaners, she went back to the front.

Katie was standing at the counter, reading the book Rarity had found.

"So what is that?" Rarity logged into her system.

"The book? It was on the table. There's an inscription in the front.' To my best friend, I hope you enjoy Alice's adventures as much as I have over the years.'" Katie held the book open and showed it to Rarity. "I think this is a first edition Alice in Wonderland."

"That someone just left in the bathroom at a bookstore? I doubt it." Rarity reached for the book and checked the copyright page. 1865. "If this is right, the book is worth a lot."

"Like thousands?" Katie asked.

Rarity checked the binding and the outside of the book. "Maybe even more. Let's set this aside and see if anyone comes to claim it. They should know the inscription if they own the book."

"This is so exciting. I've never held a rare book before." Katie grabbed a pile of books that needed to be shelved.

Rarity went about the day at hand, but the book kept nagging at her. Maybe she had another mystery for the sleuthing group to solve. And for the first time, this one wouldn't involve a dead body.

That night at the book club, the selection they had read was The Spy Coast by Tess Gerritsen. Holly Harper had suggested it, and the conversation was getting interesting.

"I don't think it portrays old people in a bad light," Holly responded to a statement that Shirley had just made. "The main character is almost in a relationship with her farmer neighbor. Or she would be if she'd get over losing her husband."

"Sometimes, people don't just get over those things," Shirley countered. "But I guess I wondered why a bunch of spies would settle in a small Maine community. It didn't seem realistic."

"Did you read the author's notes in the back? She lived in a town where that happened. I guess if Thanos can have a retirement plan, so can James Bond." Malia Overstreet jumped into the discussion. "I really liked it but it was hard to follow why the one woman was running in the first place."

"I think the author added that character to give you more than one person to focus on." Rarity hadn't liked the opening scene to not be focused on the main character either. "What did you think of the local police chief?"

"I would have solved the murder before I let that jerk from the state police take over." Sam said.

"Sometimes that's not an option." Jonathon Anderson was in town and had called to see what we'd be reading. He was an ex-cop who had started in Sedona, then moved to NYC to work when his kids got out of high school. Now he and his wife, Edith, lived in Tucson near their daughter and only grandchild. His other child was a detective here in Sedona and was dating Rarity's friend Sam. Again. "When a different agency with jurisdiction over a crime come in, you have to step back and let them work. And that character was a jerk."

Sam sweetly smiled at Jonathon. "I'm so glad you agree."

Rarity held up a hand. "Okay, let's take a short break and then we'll finish this up and choose next week's book."

Sam bolted for the ladies' room and Jonathon moved toward Rarity. "Maybe I shouldn't have come. It seems like Sam's still mad at me."

"She'll get over it. She was the one who wasn't sure if she wanted to continue her relationship with Drew. The fact that Edith set him up on a blind date when he visited you guys in Tucson wasn't your fault. I know she just wants the best for him."

Jonathon chuckled. "I have to disagree. Edith wants more grandchildren. If she'd known Sam and Drew had started seeing each other again, she wouldn't have invited Heather to dinner. Drew keeps his relationship status close to his chest. I need to go say hi to Shirley and see how George is doing."

Rarity watched as he made his way over to the treat table, where Shirley was getting more cookies out of her carrier. The woman could bake. She thought about going to talk to Sam, but she decided to stay out of it. Drew and Sam were dating again. She didn't want to jinx it.

After they'd finished the club, everyone but Shirley had left the bookstore by the time Archer arrived. He helped Shirley carry things out to her car, and when he came back inside, Rarity was ready to lock up. She had put the rare book into her safe since no one had come by to claim it. Maybe she'd put a sign up on the community bulletin board.

# About the Author

Photo by Angela Brewer Armstrong at Todd Studios

*New York Times* and *USA Today* best-selling author Lynn Cahoon writes the Tourist Trap, Cat Latimer, Kitchen Witch, Farm-to-Fork, and Survivors' Book Club mystery series. No matter where the mystery is set, readers can expect a fun ride. Sign up for her newsletter at www.lynncahoon.com.

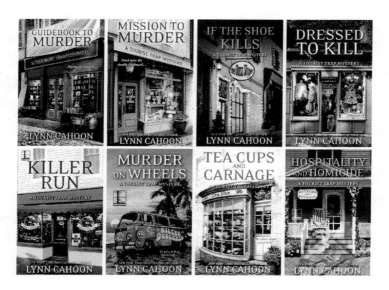

Printed in the United States
by Baker & Taylor Publisher Services